Joe R. Lansdale

LOST ECHOES

Joe R. Lansdale has written more than a dozen novels in the suspense, horror, and Western genres. He has also edited several anthologies. He has received the British Fantasy Award, the American Mystery Award, six Bram Stoker Awards, and the 2001 Edgar Award for best novel from the Mystery Writers of America. He lives in Nacogdoches, Texas, with his family.

Also by Joe R. Lansdale

Sunset and Sawdust
A Fine Dark Line
Captains Outrageous
The Bottoms
Freezer Burn
Rumble Tumble
Bad Chili
Mucho Mojo

LOST ECHOES

LOST ECHOES

A NOVEL

Joe R. Lansdale

VINTAGE CRIME / BLACK LIZARD

Vintage Books

A Division of Random House, Inc.

New York

For Karen, again

Our echoes roll from soul to soul,
And grow for ever and for ever.

—Tennyson

MYSTERY IN EAST TEXAS

———————

Bodies were found in a car at the bottom of a vine and brush-covered hill in the heart of Mud Creek, Texas. The hill, a scenic overlook, was once a popular parking spot for young couples, but is now considered off-limits by most area teenagers, even though the bodies were no more than skeletal remains and the car and remains appear to have been there for several years.

Due to the slope of the hill and a sharp lower drop-off, the car could not be seen from above. It was also stated by one area resident that most people who visited the spot "came there at night, and sightseeing wasn't their purpose."

The car was discovered by hikers who decided to climb down the slope. "We didn't know what it was at first," said one of the hikers, who wishes to remain unnamed. "It looked like a bump of dirt up against a tree, but it was a car, covered up in vines and brush."

Originally, authorities thought it might have been an accident, that the car slipped off the cliff, but the skulls of the victims both revealed gunshots to their foreheads. The couple, a young male and female, have been tentatively identified by the license plate and names in a wallet and a purse, but the names are being withheld by authorities until the next of kin can be notified.

PART ONE

Honky-tonk Rhythms and the Gears of Fate

1

Later, as an adult, Harold Wilkes would remember the childhood events that started it all, and he would think: If only I had slept through the night.

It wasn't much to hang on to. In fact, it was nothing. It was the old "had I but known" cliché from cheap paperback novels. But he thought about it from time to time, and wondered.

Because the way things turned out, hearing what he heard, seeing what he saw, knowing what he knew, it was no way to live.

2

Inside the living room, the way the windows were arranged, it was as if Harry were looking out of the compound eye of a bee. At six years old he didn't know about the compound eye of a bee, but he loved the way the world looked through those windows.

High up there on an East Texas hill, with the blue curtains pulled back, the windows tall and plenty, running all across one side of the room, he could see the road, and down from that a honky-tonk, then the highway and a drive-in theater surrounded by a shiny tin fence.

Wonderland.

If the windows were the eyes of a bee, they were filmy eyes, because they were coated in dust as fine as talcum powder on a baby's ass. At first his parents made an effort to clean them, but with the sandy road out front, the way the cars threw it up when they traveled by, it was an impossible task. They took a whack at it from time to time, and that was it.

Wonderland through dust.

There were the same sort of windows on the west side of the room as well, but they only went halfway across and were less dusty. The remaining room was dirty white, and the windows on the west wall faced a wrecking yard and the woods beyond, and at night Harry thought the cars looked like the bugs that ran across the floor when he turned on the bathroom light. Only they were bigger. Much bigger. Big, rusted, humped-back bugs moving in extreme slow motion toward the concealment of the woods. Or at least he liked to play that way, even though he knew they were cars, frozen in automotive death.

But they didn't look like his daddy's car, and they didn't look like the cars he saw on the road. In the daytime they were red with rust and they sat heavy on their wheels, their tires long worn out or stolen. In the daytime they just looked tired.

Harry had no idea the cars were from the years 1948 through the early fifties. The youngest machine out there was from 1959, and it was banged up worse than the rest and the windshield was starred and cracked from some accident.

He didn't know about those things, the models of cars. They were just part of his wonderland.

The house itself was also a source of awe to Harry.

It was huge and had at one time been fine, but now it was not so fine, and if it had been, he and his family would not have been living there.

As his father said, "If it cost a nickel to shit, we'd have to throw up."

The place still had some class. It was large and there was a broad porch that ran out from the front door and took an L turn and ran alongside the house, then fell off into a set of stairs that matched the set near the front door. Both stairs were askew and you had to walk slightly to starboard to navigate them.

When the wind blew hard the roof shook, sagged a bit, hung low over the porch like an old man's hat. The back end of the house had lost some of its boost, as the stones that held it up had settled into a gopher run. The kitchen didn't have running water, except for a hose that was poked through the window and into the sink. There was an old woodstove that had been converted to gas about the time Eisenhower was learning to wear civvies again.

None of this meant anything to Harry. Not really. He didn't know about being poor. He was six years old and everything was magical and the house to him was home and it was swell.

Especially those windows.

He had been sick that day, the day it began, a Saturday, and that was bad. You got sick, you didn't want it to be a Saturday. He had slept all day in a deep fever, a kind of slow bake in blankets, and suddenly he had awakened, feeling cooled, energized, and bored, and angry that he had missed morning cartoons. Worse yet it was already night.

Tomorrow, he thought, he would play in the apple tree out back of the house, pretend it was a spaceship. He knew about spaceships. His mother had read him a book about a spaceship, and his older cousin had read a book about a spaceship under an apple tree, like the apple tree in his backyard.

The house was quiet. His parents were asleep. He looked out the windows, saw the honky-tonk with its lights and voices, could hear country music floating up from down there, songs about drinking and leaving. Across the highway he could see over the tin fence and watch what was showing on the big white screen of the drive-in.

He didn't know they were having an old-time cartoon festival; he only knew there were cartoons and he had missed them on TV this morning, so he pulled a chair to the window, sat there, and watched the Warner Bros. characters—Bugs Bunny, Daffy Duck, and the like—go through their antics. He couldn't hear them. No speakers. His sound track was from the honky-tonk, an old Loretta Lynn tune at the moment, about blue Kentucky girls, soon to be followed by similar ditties.

Normally, weeknights, when his father had to work on the big trucks, he and his mother sat here in chairs and watched movies. Mostly old movies. Spaghetti Western festivals. Old crime dramas. Sometimes something new. But mostly old. That's what the drive-in was about. It was built new and lit up with the old; the owners were trying to bring back some of that past magic.

He and his mother would watch, and she would tell him what the characters were saying. Which meant she made it up. He thought she had some kind of super mojo going, could read minds, or just knew everything. She was his mother, after all. She would know everything there was to know, including what the tall people on the screen were saying, what the cartoon characters yelled as they fell off cliffs.

Thing was, though, you really didn't need to know what was said. Not when it was cartoons instead of a movie. The story was all in the characters' actions. He didn't need his translator, his mom. As he watched, he thought he could interpret, and he whispered what he thought the characters were saying. Nothing fancy. A *yikes* and a *wow*, this and that.

He watched and laughed, and as the night wore on his burst of energy blew out and he started to feel tired again. He felt hot. His throat hurt, and so did the sides of his neck, but his right ear was the worst. It felt as if a bee were in it. There was a kind of buzz in the depths of it. The bee swelled, filled his ear, and filled his head. The hot beating of its wings was unbearable.

Harry had a hard time sitting in the chair. The cartoons began to swim, and so did the windows. All around him they swam, as if he were being circled by glass demons that spit out honky-tonk light and honky-tonk music, bleeding cartoon colors that danced crazy shadows along the wall. The house whirled. The ceiling dropped and the floor rose up. The bee in his ear went wild.

Wonderland had taken a ride on a Tilt-A-Whirl.

Next morning, his father found him lying unconscious on the floor next to the chair in a pool of urine.

The world was all white and very bright when Harry opened his eyes. He saw a figure move past in white, and something was in his arm; it felt like a toothpick jammed under the skin. It was bright in the room and the whiteness seemed to crawl. He was weak and tired and hot and his arm hurt. He closed his eyes and floated away, down a languid river, into a cartoon-world dream bursting with brightly painted talking rabbits and chattering ducks and big red sticks of dynamite exploding with the words *kaboom* and *blam* outlined in yellow, feathers flying, duck bills floating, coyotes falling off cliffs.

And when the coyote fell, Harry fell with him, and he never knew when he hit bottom.

"It was just the mumps," Harry's mother said. She was a slim, black-haired woman that looked a bit like a Depression-era photo. Pretty, but eternally in need of a dose of vitamin B with iron.

"It's okay, Billie," her husband said. "It's okay."

Jake Wilkes wanted to say more, but there wasn't much he could say. He knew only that his son was sick and his wife was in pain. He was in pain as well. If he could have gotten hold of the pain, the cause of it all, he could have whipped that. He was used to handling things with his hands. His work. His problems, provided that problem needed a strong back and a strong arm, or wanted to tussle.

But this?

He had no idea what to do.

"I can't believe he's this sick," she said. "It was just mumps. Every kid has the mumps. You and me, we were kids, we had mumps."

"You couldn't have known," Jake said.

"I'm his mother," Billie said. "I should have known he'd wake up after sleeping all day. Wake up and overdo. What if—"

"Don't say it," Jake said. "He'll be all right."

They were sitting in the hospital lobby, waiting. Jake had hold of Billie's hand, and they were pressed up close together in the lobby chairs. Billie had on a dark blue nightgown and slippers shaped like bears' heads. Jake had on blue jeans he had pulled over his pajama bottoms. He was wearing a pajama shirt and house slippers. The pajama top had little white clouds floating on a blue background. He thought—or imagined—he could smell sex in the air, a lingering perfume of lust. He and Billie had been making love, perhaps while Harry was roaming about the living room or sitting in a chair watching cartoons through the window. The fact that they had been making love and Harry had been up and they didn't know, or that he might have been lying on the floor while they were doing the joyful deed, somehow made it all seem worse. Billie hadn't said as much, but he knew she was thinking it, because he was thinking it, and after ten years of marriage you knew things like that. At least when the thinking was bad. Any other time it was a long shot, just a guess. But the bad stuff, you kind of developed a radar.

And he knew this from his radar, was certain of it, she blamed herself. And maybe on some level he feared she blamed him.

It would pass if everything turned out all right.

If not, Jesus help him. Jesus help them both.

"I should have brought him to the doctor today," Billie said, not realizing Saturday was long gone and Sunday had sneaked in over the transom. "I should have brought him in for another look. I didn't want to pay for the emergency room. Can you believe that? I thought maybe he was a little too sick, but thought I'd wait until Monday. We could have paid it out if I'd brought him in. We'd have worked it out fine."

"Didn't seem like an emergency," Jake said, patting her hand. "Didn't seem so bad then."

"I'd brought him in, things might have been all right."

"Doctor said it was mumps. We couldn't have known."

Jake said all of this as if saying it would make it true.

Morning light came down the hall at a slow bleed, and shortly, from the other end of the hall, the darker end, came the doctor. They saw him coming, white coated, moving with an even stride. As he walked his dark hair bounced and fell down into his eyes. He was a young man. Jake thought maybe too young. He wasn't their doctor. Their doctor was out of town. Their doctor had diagnosed Harry with the mumps. Then he was gone. Said something about going up north for a while. Some kind of doctor shindig. A meeting of white coats. Probably a golf game.

This doctor was named Smatermine, and he was too young. Jake was sure of it now. Too young.

The doctor came down the hall and looked at them and smiled. "He's going to be all right," he said. "But the ear . . . He has quite an infection. It's a little uncertain how his hearing in that ear will turn out. He could lose a bit of it, or he could retain it all. I know that's not much to hang onto one way or another, except we'll do what we can. For the hearing, I suggest a specialist."

"He's gonna be all right, though?" Jake said.

"Yeah," the doctor said. "He'll be all right."

Billie began to cry.

3

Harry thought it wasn't so bad, except for that pesky not-being-able-to-hear-out-of-his-right-ear part. He got to miss first grade for a couple of weeks, lie up in bed and watch TV. He found a channel that played old movies, and for some reason they appealed to him.

His mother one day, sitting by his bed, talking into his good left ear, said, "There are new shows, you know? These were old when your daddy and I married, baby. These are the dinosaurs of television."

"I like them," Harry said. "I like Tarzan."

"There were a lot of Tarzans. Not just this one. Some of them were even in color."

"I like this one."

"All right," his mother said, standing, moving toward the door. "I'll make you something to eat."

When she was gone, Harry turned his attention back to Johnny Weissmuller swinging through the trees on a vine. He thought he saw a kind of bar that Tarzan was hanging onto, and he wondered about that. Did they have that in the jungle? Vines with bars to hang onto?

He had to sit with his head slightly turned, his left eye and left ear focused on the television. He turned his head too much, the sound was strange. He reached up and tapped his right ear softly. He didn't hear anything, just felt a vibration. The ear itself felt weird. Like someone had shoved an egg inside.

He tapped it again, a little harder. This time there was an explosion. It came from inside and burst out, and along with it came a stream of warm pus that surged out like water from a busted dam. It spurted on his cheek and on the pillow, a green, wet wad.

Harry let out a scream.

Pans dropped in the kitchen and his mother came running.

"Huh," the doctor said.

It was a different doctor from the one in the hospital. An ear-nose-and-throat guy named Mishman. He was about forty and looked every year of it, plus a couple bonus years. His eyebrows were all over the place, like insect antennae. The Wilkeses had been seeing him ever since the day after they took Harold into the emergency room.

Harry was perched on the examining table, his legs hanging over the edge, his tennis shoes swinging back and forth, the doctor probing the inside of his ear gently with the tip of his handheld light.

Billie and Jake were near the table, Billie had her hand on Harry's elbow, holding it gently.

"So," Jake said, "he's all right?"

"Well, there could still be some problems," the doctor said. "You can't say for sure about something like this. But he can hear again. The mumps, they affected his hearing, and he had this pocket of pus in there. Got to say I couldn't see it. I looked plenty, but I didn't see it. That's just being truthful with you. It was behind the wall of the ear. It didn't even make a swelling. Not when I saw him last. But what I think now is the obvious: It swelled while he was at home. And now it's burst. It was tight with infection, and when he touched it, it was ready to go. He's his own doctor."

Mishman went silent, studied the boy for a long moment.

Jake said, "Something wrong, Doc? You're kind of rambling."

Mishman shook his head. "No. It's just . . . Thing like this, something odd about it. Haven't seen anything quite like it. It's nothing big, not fancy in the sense of the medical books, but it's just not playing by the rules."

"The rules?" Jake said.

"It doesn't act like a regular infection. But the important thing is, now he can hear, and I think we're on top of it. Maybe another test or two, but I think he's out of the woods. . . . Listen to him."

Harry had lost interest in what the adults were saying, and as he sat there on the edge of the examination table, he had begun to hum and sing a few lines from "Old McDonald Had a Farm."

He liked singing it because he could hear himself sing with both ears again.

He thought he sounded pretty darn good.

They ran more tests.

Mishman looked for a tumor.

Didn't find one.

The ear looked okay.

But it was odd, way it had worked out. Mishman couldn't say for sure why it was odd, but it didn't feel right. This whole business, it wasn't playing by the rules. It was a medical anomaly.

He would remember the problem as odd for a long time, and then, slowly, he would forget about Harry Wilkes and his ear infection. It was something to consider, all right, but when something other than his Spidey sense started to tingle and he started seeing a long-legged nurse, hiding it from his wife, it took up most of his thinking and his time, and eventually it caved in his practice. The nurse left him, and all he had were memories of how she liked to do it naked except for her nursing shoes.

It was a memory that trumped some kid with an oddball ear infection.

4

Harry noticed little things, but it really wasn't a problem until he was twelve. Age twelve was the year his balls dropped and his hormones rushed, and he really took note of it. Not just the hormones and what they were telling him, but this business with his ear.

First time he experienced it in a memorable way, Harry was playing in one of the old cars out by the house. He wasn't supposed to be there, but he often slipped out and pretended he could drive, sitting behind the squeaky old steering wheel. Sometimes he had his friend Joey Barnhouse with him, but other times it was just him. Most of the time it was just him. He had discovered that he liked to be by himself. A lot. He could make up whatever he wanted and do whatever he wanted. He didn't have to consult with anyone about who was It in a game of tag, or which Ninja Turtle he was, who was Spider-Man, and who was the villain, that kind of thing. He could imagine wheeling about with some girl by his side, Kayla, for example. She had been changing lately, and he liked the change.

Day it happened, day he got a clue of what was to come, he had climbed inside the old fifty-nine Chevy. It had really gone to hell in the last few years. Its paint was all flaked and bubbled off, and someone—a kid most certainly—had thrown a brick into the already starred windshield.

His daddy was always saying if the guy who owned the property next to theirs got rid of all that shit, hauled it off, pressed it up, whatever, just got it out of sight of their house, it would be nice. But nothing ever happened and his dad never pursued it, thinking he ought not tell a fella what he should do with his own land, even if he didn't like what he was doing.

Harry hoped the owner never cleaned it up. It was a great place to play.

When he climbed inside this time, closed the creaking, rusted door, pulled it shut hard, he had a sudden rush of revulsion. Lots of noise, like someone ripping several layers of aluminum foil down the middle, and there was a slamming noise, and in his head a combination of shapes and colors flashed and popped, and he screamed.

Or someone did.

He heard it clear as the proverbial bell, that scream, but he didn't remember doing it. Wasn't sure he had. It filled his head like air filling a balloon.

It was just a flash of color and images and sounds and discomfort. Real quick. A face vibrating and wobbling in his head. A red explosion. A white rip though the mind, followed by . . .

Exhaustion.

A sweat-beaded forehead.

Wet pants.

Nothing much, really.

Over with quick-like.

He got out of the car with his knees a-wobble, slowly closed the door, went in to change his pants and underwear, and never played there again.

5

Here's what happened, down there in the honky-tonk below Harry's house. One night, on a Saturday, after the tonk closed, and all the sights and sounds and parked cars were gone, and everyone at the drive-in theater across the way had long filed out, about three A.M., a half hour after closing, during cleanup time, there was a murder.

No one knew about it until Monday, about two P.M. when the bar was supposed to open.

Guy who discovered the body was a customer named Seymour Smithe, pronounced Smith, but spelled Smithe, and Seymour was always adamant about that. "Name's Smithe, with an e on the end."

Most people just thought of him as a drunk.

He had lost more jobs than a squirrel had eaten acorns.

Thing he did know was how to sell Bibles. He liked selling Bibles. He didn't know dick about the Bible, outside of what he'd seen in *The Ten Commandments*, an old movie, but he could sell the hell out of those damn things, 'cause all the Christians, or would-be Christians, wanted one, liked to pretend they were going to read it.

He appealed to their fear. Fear was always a good way to sell anything.

Insurance.

Politics.

War.

And gilt-edged Bibles.

When Smithe wasn't selling Bibles, he was drinking.

Now that was something he was good at. Drinking.

He was the goddamn Old and New Testament of drunks.

He was thinking about drinking, about how he had to sell some Bibles this day, and he was thinking of that woman he had talked to yesterday on her front porch. What a looker. And he sort of thought she had wanted him to come back, even if she didn't buy a Bible or let him in the door.

But she had smiled. And she had been positive, even if she hadn't bought anything. Something had passed between them; he was almost certain.

Almost.

He wanted to get certain, thought four or five beers would make him certain.

The door was open and the sign read OPEN, so Seymour went right on in. It was cool and dark in there and smelled the way it always smelled, like beer and sweat and sexual anxiety stirred by air-conditioning. But there was something else. It was faint, but he knew that smell immediately.

Once, for a summer, he had worked in a slaughterhouse, and once you smelled that odor, you knew it fresh, you knew it dried, and in each form it smelled different, and yet somehow the same.

It was the smell of blood.

The hair on the back of Seymour's neck poked up, and he thought—or imagined—that above the aroma of the tonk he could smell his own fear, a kind of sour stench of sweat and decay. And in the back of his mouth he could taste copper. He turned slowly, almost crouched, expecting someone to leap from the shadows like a goddamn gazelle.

And he saw someone.

But she wouldn't do much leaping.

It was Evelyn Gibbons.

The formerly attractive, middle-aged Evelyn Gibbons. The owner of the tonk. The breezy little woman with the dark bobbing hair and the bouncy step and the bouncy ass, the latter usually tucked nicely beneath short black dresses, her buns jacked up by thick high heels.

She was sitting down by the jukebox, her head against it, leaning farther than it should have on a neck. That was because her throat was cut from ear to ear, and there was blood all over the jukebox, on her, and the wall behind her. Her hair was matted in blood and stuck to the jukebox like a big spit wad. The floor beneath her had plenty of blood too. Her dress was hiked up over her thighs, and Seymour could see her panties. They were dark, and had probably been white before they soaked up a lot of gore.

Seymour backed toward the door, looking over his shoulder carefully. He figured the blood, dried like it was, meant the murder had happened some time ago. But he looked about just the same, in case some madman armed with a blade should come for him.

He made it out into the blinding sunshine to his car, where he had a cell phone on the passenger's seat. He called 911, and while he waited for the cops to arrive, he wished repeatedly that he had a beer. Maybe some whiskey. A little turpentine. Rubbing alcohol. A shot of piss. Damn near anything.

The cops showed up. They looked around. They took notes and photographs and fingerprints and such. They questioned Seymour until he really needed a drink.

Seymour was the prime suspect for about six months, but that died out. Even those who never gave up on him quit worrying about it when Seymour, full of gin, lost control of his vehicle, slammed on the brakes as he careened off the road, and was struck violently in the back of the neck by a case of gilt-edged Bibles thrown from the backseat. It was a good shot. It snapped his neck and checked him out.

After that, there wasn't much shaking in the Evelyn Gibbons case. There were a few who didn't think it was Seymour at all. They pursued leads, one or two in particular.

But it resulted in nothing.

No idea who.

No idea why.

A year passed.

6

So now Harry, he's thirteen, and he's got the horny on bad. If they rated how horny he was on a one-to-ten scale, he'd been about an eleven, maybe a twelve. So he's got this horny on, and he doesn't know shit from wild honey about such, but he's got it going and he thinks he knows something, and what he doesn't know, Joey Barnhouse tells him. Not that all of Joey's information is right either, but it's interesting, all this info from shithouse walls and the mouth of Joey and the technique of artful guessing.

One day Harry tries to steal a kiss from Kayla Jones, the pretty blond who lives down the road from him, on the other side of Joey, but she whips his ass soundly. After the ass whipping, he likes her even more. Kayla, she's some sack of dynamite. Thin as a reed, hair yellow as the burning sun at high noon, fists like lead. Pissed off because her father yells at her mother a lot, and vice versa, and though Harry doesn't know it at the time, he'd think back later and consider maybe they had, like, some kind of link.

Joey doesn't like her, or says he doesn't, thinks she's too tall and too tough. This because he's about four feet high and one foot wide and growing like dead grass. He's got big feet, though, says that's a sign he's gonna grow, says he's got a hammer like something Thor would carry, provided he could swing it between his legs.

Harry knows better. Joey, like him, darts about in the shower at PE, keeps his back to folks when he can, his hand over his privates, quick to grab a towel.

He ain't showing nothing. Not like William Stewart, who has a goddamn python. Flaps it about like it might strike, maybe grab someone in the locker room, squeeze him dead, drag him up a tree for later consumption.

No, Harry figures Joey isn't any better than him in that department. But it's cold comfort.

He's got that on his mind. Inadequacy. Stuff that his dad at thirteen probably didn't think about at all, or didn't have time to, working most of his kid life away, but there it was. His concerns. The worries of Harry Wilkes in all their glories. Late-night rambles over a girlie magazine Joey had given him and he kept hidden under his mattress.

Yeah, that was him. A magazine in one hand, himself in the other, doing the dirty deed, feeling guilty because of Sunday school and church, a bewhiskered, voyeuristic, smirking, self-righteous God peeking over his shoulder while he brought the juice to freedom.

It made a fella nervous.

No doubt about it, he thought as he lay there in bed. I've got one of them . . . what do they call it . . . ?

Oh, yeah.

A complex.

That's what I got.

A goddamn complex.

On the morning after Harry battled his complex, he awoke with a plan in mind.

Bravery. That was the thing.

Stand up against a ghost, do it in front of a girl. A girl like Kayla. You could show you were tough enough to be the boyfriend of a girl who could beat you like a circus monkey. Going after and seeing a ghost, that had to be worth points.

That said, he wasn't that brave. Decided he would have to go down the road and find Joey first. Might be best to have reinforcements. He figured—hoped—he could make an impression with reinforcements. He liked to think it could be done.

'Cause, you see, there was a ghost, all woo-woo and ectoplasmic. He and Joey and Kayla had heard about it from other kids, older kids in the neighborhood, and he had even heard his mother talking to Joey's mother about it. Down the hill and in the tonk. A specter.

Poor old Evelyn Gibbons's spirit. Trapped in the abandoned honky-tonk, roaming about nights, her head hanging to one side, draped against her shoulder, her neck red as if she were wearing a scarlet scarf.

That was the story. There were those who claimed to have seen her. Some said you could hear her scream from time to time. Joey's older brother, Evan, who beat them all up now and then, even Kayla, though she gave a good fight, said he had heard Evelyn Gibbons scream a couple times, and both times it had pricked the hair on his neck and made him run.

Evan could have been lying.

He liked to jack with them.

But on this matter Harry chose to believe him, because it suited his plans.

He had to believe in the ghost.

Mainly, Kayla had to believe in the ghost. Down there in the tonk, floating and moaning and screaming about.

Down there. Waiting.

The night was oozy-rich with velvet darkness, moonlight and moon shade. Their shadows darted across the ground as they ran, outlined by the silver rays of the moon.

When they got down the hill, near the honky-tonk, they paused to catch their breath.

"My daddy finds out I slipped off," Joey said, "he's gonna give me a worse beating than I got last week."

Joey was talking about his eye. His father had punched him in the eye. Joey often had a black eye or a fat lip or a lump on his jaw or a bump on his head.

Harry had seen Joey's father slap him alongside the head once. For hardly nothing, leaving a drawer open, something like that.

Harry's father said James Barnhouse was a bitter old bastard. Mad because his leg had gone bad in high school. Football injury. Too many big guys on top of his kneecap. Before that he was hot shit, gonna go pro. After that he was lucky he got a caddy job, toting rich dudes' golf clubs, living on a little wage and a few good tips. Reading crime magazines and old sex-and-bondage magazines, beating his boys if they found them and read them. Hitting his wife once in a while just to keep his arm loose and stay in practice.

Coasting. That's what Mr. Barnhouse was doing, Harry's dad said. Coasting. Feeling sorry for himself.

Joey's old man didn't scare Joey enough, though. He was always willing to take a chance and stand a beating. But he was nervous; Harry could tell that.

"I'll get grounded," Kayla said. "No TV. No phone. Nothing."

"It ain't the same as a punch in the eye," Joey said.

"I'd rather get hit than be grounded," Kayla said.

"That's the way it sounds till you get hit," Joey said. "Till my old man hits you; then you'd rather get grounded. You can trust me on that. Harry, here, he'd just get a talking-to, wouldn't you, Harry? No grounding. No punch in the eye."

"My parents aren't much into spanking," Harry said. "And they don't do punching. But I could get grounded."

"Yeah," Joey said, "like when?"

"Grounding or no grounding," Harry said, "I don't want to get caught."

"Your parents don't punish you for anything," Joey said.

This was pretty true. Since he got bad sick as a child, since the ear infection, his mother had been as protective as a hockey goalie. Worrying about asthma, which he didn't have, allergies, which he might have, falling down, which he did a lot—just about everything. He and his dad went outside to play ball, she insisted on knee pads under his pants, wanted him to wear a bicycle helmet.

A bicycle helmet to play ball. Now that beat all. The idea of it— him out there in knee pads and a bicycle helmet to toss the ball around with his dad—well, that just wasn't done.

Bad form, as he heard an English actor say on TV.

He was glad Dad had talked her out of it, 'cause if he did stuff like that, might as well have had a sign painted on his back that said: I'M THE BIGGEST PUSSY THAT EVER LIVED. PLEASE KICK AND HIT ME UNTIL MY BRAINS FALL OUT.

They stood for a while at the base of the hill, looking at the back of the dark, abandoned honky-tonk. Across the way the drive-in screen could be seen. Kung fu personnel were leaping about the big white square, mouths wide open, yelling silence.

"We come to see a ghost or not?" Kayla said.

"Yeah, sure we did," Harry said.

"I don't really think there's any ghost," Kayla said. "My daddy says there aren't any such things, and he's a policeman."

"My brother says there are," Joey said. "A policeman, he might know handcuffs and doughnuts, but he ain't nothin' more than anyone else when it comes to ghosts."

"Since when do you care what your brother says?" Kayla said. "He told us you could get a girl pregnant by putting your little finger in her butt. So what's he know?"

"He was just kidding."

"I don't think so. I think he's that dumb."

"Maybe it was the truth," Joey said. "You want to bend over and let me try it?"

"I do that, it won't be your finger; I know that. Just stay your distance."

"You two are too nasty," Harry said.

"It isn't me," Kayla said. "He's the one's got the stupid brother."

They went on like this for a while, then eased up to the honky-tonk on the dark side. Joey grabbed at the window and pushed. It didn't budge.

"We got to knock it out," Joey said.

"I don't know," Harry said. "That wasn't my idea, breaking nothing."

"You want to see a ghost or not?" Joey said. "That was your idea, man. The ghost. I'm gonna get punched, I think I ought to go all the way, see what's inside."

"Just don't think we should break anything."

And no sooner had Harry finished saying it than he looked at Kayla. She was in shadow, and he couldn't see much of her, but he could see her shape, and in some way that was more exciting than if he could see all of her. He wanted very much for her to think he was brave. He swallowed, said, "Sure, we can do that."

"Maybe we ought not," Kayla said. "It's okay, you don't want to, Harry."

"Nah," Joey said, "it's all right. He's all right. He don't mind. Ain't nobody using this place nohow."

Joey picked up a rock, snapped it against a pane of glass. The glass shattered. Joey reached through the hole, got hold of the window lock, moved it. He pushed the window up easily and climbed inside.

Kayla came next. Harry linked his fingers together so she could step into the web of his hands and mount the window frame.

"Watch for glass," he said.

Kayla smiled at him. She was out of the deep shadow now, and he could see her smile. It made him feel ten feet tall.

She stepped into his hands and through the window. He glanced at the drive-in screen before he clambered after her. It was a bloody death scene. A kung fu master with a sharp sword was beheading a warrior woman.

Inside the shadows were thick, and so was the dust. It choked them, and Harry began to cough. Kayla pulled a small flashlight from her back pocket, clicked it on.

There were tables and a long counter and against the wall a juke-box. The smell was strange. It gathered on them and clung like a cobweb.

"Stinks in here," Harry said.

"Ghosts have a smell," Kayla said. "I read that."

"Do they smell like shit?" Joey said. "Shine the light over there."

They caught a cat in the light, pooled him briefly in yellow. The cat bolted, disappeared behind the bar.

"Must be a hole in the wall somewhere," Harry said.

"Let's get it," Joey said. "Let's get the cat."

"No," Kayla said.

"What for?" Harry said. "Leave the cat alone."

"I don't like cats," Joey said.

"Don't you hurt a cat," Kayla said. "You hurt a cat, I'll never speak to you again."

Joey processed this information for a long moment, studying Kayla, standing defiant behind the small beam of light. He turned away from where the cat had gone, said, "That stink. It's cat shit. Watch where you step."

"That won't be easy," Harry said. "We just got the one light."

"And I have it," Kayla said.

Harry and Joey eased up close to Kayla. Harry could smell Kayla's hair. It smelled like some kind of flowery shampoo. And she had on a heavy dose of perfume. She always wore too much, but he liked it. He felt funny all over. He wanted to put his arm around her, but didn't.

"Shine it on the jukebox," Joey said.

Kayla did. The records were still beneath the glass. In fact, one was cocked up on the spindle, ready to drop.

"I heard she got killed right there," Joey said. "By the jukebox."

"You don't know that," Harry said.

Kayla said, "It was in all the papers, Harry. My daddy told me about it. He talked to the cops were here, down at the station. She was found lying against the jukebox. Everybody knows that."

"Her head was near cut off," Joey said. "Let's see if there's blood."

They went over close and shined the light around. The blood had long since been cleaned off the floor and the jukebox, but there were little spots of something on the wall, and the trio decided to believe it was blood, even if it wasn't.

"It's stuffy in here," Kayla said.

"Yeah," Harry said. "And cold too."

"I thought there was a ghost if it got chilly," Joey said. "You know, they call it cold spots. She'd be in this spot, wouldn't she? This would be the spot, right?"

"I look like an expert on ghosts?" Harry said. "How would I know?"

"There isn't any ghost," Kayla said.

Joey poked at Harry with his finger, making Harry jump.

"Don't need a ghost," Joey said. "Harry's scared enough."

Harry shoved at Joey. Hard. Knocked him back against the wall, stumbling into the jukebox, causing him to lean against it.

"Hey," Joey said. "I didn't mean nothing."

Joey put a hand on the jukebox to right himself, jostling it further. The record on the spindle dropped and there was a clacking sound as it fell against the one beneath it.

The little snapping together of those old-style records was to Harry like the sound of two cymbals being slammed together, and there were bursts of other sounds, unidentified—sounds that seemed to lurk behind some invisible barrier—and there was lots of light, like he had experienced before, but brighter yet, and really hot this time.

And there was Loretta Lynn, singing about Fist City. The words to the song were at first muffled, like some kind of insect beating its wings in a bag, then they became identifiable and loud, as if the words and notes were solid things, invisible creatures hopping about the room, landing on his ears, crawling inside. And inside the darkness of his noggin a paint store exploded. Colors burst in every direction and there was a loud thump, and another sound like someone drawing a line on paper with a ballpoint pen. Then he felt warm, and there was pressure, as if he had been wrapped too tight in fuzzy wool blankets.

Then the images: a room, the very room he was in, lit up bright and very clear. Him standing alone in its center, and yet he was somehow viewing from overhead as well.

There was nothing else in the room in that moment, not Kayla, not Joey. Just the warmth and the light and the tight sensation, and then there was a woman in a short black dress, not a young woman, but someone his mother's age. She was standing against the jukebox. And there was a man. Like the woman, he seemed to come from nowhere; shadows rushed out of some hole, gathered up, and made him. His face was unshaven, and he had a big scar on his upper lip, little ones on his cheeks. When he moved, his thick black hair shook as if it were a mop.

The man had a curved-bladed knife in his hand.

The knife flashed out and the overhead light caught the blade and made it shine like a glimpse of torchlit silver down in a mine. Then it moved out of the light and red beads leaped. The beads froze. In that moment Harry saw that the woman, who had turned and opened her mouth to speak, had a red cord around her neck. Then it came to him that it wasn't a cord at all. It was a cut. A fine line growing wide.

The red beads came unfrozen and flew about, and she stumbled forward, and the man grabbed her, and slung her against the juke-box. She tried to get up, a hand at her wound, but he slashed across her throat again, cutting her hand, severing the tip of one of her fingers. When she jerked her cut hand away, she fell, one hand on the jukebox.

She looked up. Her dark eyes narrowed. Her expression was like the one you had when you found you'd put your hand into something you'd rather not touch.

Loretta continued to sing.

The man leaned forward, hooked the knife under her left ear, and pulled hard and slow under her chin, along the now thick red line he had made, pulled the knife almost all the way to the other ear.

Her head sagged, knocked against the jukebox.

Her eyes went flat and dead as blackened pennies.

Blood was everywhere.

The man stepped back and Harry could see his face, but just for a moment, because the shadows that had made him came apart and fled in all directions and the man was gone. It was the same for the woman, a flutter of darkness, and she was out of there, and the song went with her, as if the words were being sucked down a drain.

Harry was left with the tight warmth and the light. Then the light faded and it got cool and his head exploded all over the place in bursts of color. He ended up finally in grayness, then blackness.

"Harry, you all right?"

It was Kayla. She was holding her arm under his head, and she was leaning over him, her long blond hair dangling around his face

like a curtain, and he could smell that fine shampoo smell, the over-
dose of perfume, and for a moment he thought the ghosts that had
jumped on him, filled his head, sick and ugly as they were, might be
worth it just to have him end up with Kayla's arm behind his head.

"I saw the ghost," he said. "More than one."

"We didn't see dick," Joey said.

"You had to. The woman . . . the knife."

"Dick," Joey said.

"Kayla?" Harry asked.

"Dick," she said.

"I saw it. I tell you, I saw it."

"Dick," Joey said. "There was dick. You fainted, you sissy."

"No, you're not," Kayla said. "You got hot. It's hot in here."

"Sissy," Joey said.

"Tell me about it," Kayla said.

He told them.

"Sometimes some people see ghosts that others don't," Kayla
said.

"We'd have seen it," Joey said. "There was ghosts, we'd have seen
them. What's wrong with our eyes, huh?"

Harry sat up, hating to lose Kayla's arm at the back of his neck.
Hating it a lot, but feeling he had to do it, had to sit up, try and look a
little less wimpy.

"I saw that on TV," Kayla said. "Some people see them, some
don't."

"You seen that on TV, did you?" Joey said. "Where's that? The
Sissy Channel?"

7

"Cut from ear to ear?" Kayla asked.

Harry nodded.

"Wow," she said.

They were sitting on Harry's porch, day after the night of the big event. Joey was not around. Harry was glad of that today. He didn't need reinforcements for this.

"Thanks for pretending to believe me," he said.

"You're welcome. . . . Wait a minute. I'm not pretending."

"Really?"

"I believe you believe it."

"Then you don't believe me? Which is it, Kayla?"

"I don't think you're lying to me, but I think you might have dreamed it, fainted from the heat, hit your head, dreamed it. We didn't see anything."

"I thought you saw on TV how one person could see it and another couldn't. Saw it on the Sissy Channel."

She laughed and punched his arm. Hard. It really hurt. He rubbed it.

"Sorry," she said.

"You never know your own strength. . . . But you don't believe I saw a ghost?"

"It's just hard to accept."

"You went to see a ghost."

"Sure. It was fun. But I didn't really expect to. I just wanted to go because you were going."

"Really?"

"Really. I believe you saw something. Even if you dreamed it. You wouldn't lie to me about something like that. Would you?"

"Nope. You'd beat me up."

"Seriously."

"Seriously, you'd beat me up."

"I would. But seriously. You wouldn't, would you, Harry?"

"Never."

"I didn't think so. Did you tell your parents?"

"No," Harry said, shaking his head. "I couldn't tell them where I was—you know."

"Sure. I wasn't thinking. That wouldn't be smart, would it?"

"You didn't tell your parents where you were, did you?"

"Course not," she said. "Joey's dad found out he was out, like he always does, and Joey got a beating. Both his eyes are blacked. I saw him mowing his yard. He hardly looked at me. He was limping some."

"Wow."

"Yeah. Wow . . . You know what, Harry? I came to see you for another reason. Not just to talk about the ghost."

"What's that?"

"We're moving."

Harry felt as if he had just been hit between the eyes with a mallet.

"Oh. When?"

"Coming weekend."

"Yeah."

She nodded. "I just found out."

"Your dad got another job?"

"No. Mom and I, we're moving."

"Oh."

"Yeah. They had some trouble."

"You don't have to talk about it."

"We've talked about it before."

"He has a temper."

"So does Mama. But this . . . It's different. Dad . . . He was seeing someone else. It's probably best, him staying here. He's not a cop anymore. Gonna open a garage. He likes mechanic work. Mom, she's got a job in Tyler, at a dress shop."

"I'm so sorry, Kayla."

"Yeah. Well, it's how it is, as Mom says. We're leaving pretty soon. Mom has a house rented."

"Oh."

"That's all you can say? Oh?"

"I don't know what to say . . . except I don't want you to go. I want you to stay here, go to school here. We could go to college together. This is a nice town."

"It's all right. But I can go to college in Tyler, maybe come back here and get with the cops, like Daddy was."

"I don't want you to go."

"Me either. You think maybe people are meant for each other? You know, the stars and all that?"

"I don't know about the stars. But maybe some people are. Maybe you get lucky now and then and things are just right. Puzzle pieces fit."

"And now they have to unfit."

"Yeah."

"It doesn't have to be forever."

"Absolutely not."

Kayla took his hand. She pulled it next to her and he could feel the back of his knuckles touching the side of her bare leg, just below her khaki shorts. Her perfume was strong. Harry felt warm all over.

The hairs on the back of his neck prickled. Not like when he had seen the ghost, but in a good way.

They sat silently, their fingers entwined.

"I guess you have to go?" he said.

"Harry?"

"Yeah," And when he said it, he turned his face toward her. She leaned toward him and kissed him lightly on the lips. It wasn't much, just a touch, but he felt a kind of feeling he had never felt before. Not just movement in his tighty whities, but something else. Something strange.

"I got to go," she said. "I've already been here too long. Told Mama I would help pack."

"Sure."

"See you around, maybe?"

"Sure. Of course you will. We're puzzle parts that fit. Remember?"

"I'm gonna miss you."

"You too. Lots."

She got up then and started walking away. When she got to the road she started running, and Harry noted that she could run very fast, and not the way most girls ran, but like an Olympian carrying the torch.

She ran faster yet, and pretty soon he saw her turn the corner and go out of sight around a neighbor's house. He got up and walked quickly along the long porch, followed it around to the other side of the house. Stood on the porch where the sunlight was bright. He squinted, put a hand over his eyes, like the Great Scout surveying the horizon.

He could see her again. She was running where the road had curved, and as she ran she was blocked out by more houses. He watched as she darted between them. It was just a glimpse, but he was glad he saw her. Her long legs leaping out and her blond hair flying.

The road turned away and a house blocked the road and he couldn't see Kayla anymore.

8

Six months later, sitting on the floor in front of the TV, trying to find something to watch, cruising the television airwaves with his trusty channel changer, Harry came upon something unexpected.

A realization.

There really was nothing on.

Nothing he wanted to see.

Nada.

The goose egg.

The family didn't have wide cable access. That was part of it. But they did get a lot of stations with the basic cable. But there wasn't shit on.

He flipped and got the news, but it was all bad and about war and people dying or killing or yelling or fighting. He caught a couple of movies, but the violence was so intense, he sort of lost sight of the stories.

He just sat there flipping through the channels, thinking about Kayla. He had tried to go see her the next day, the day after the kiss, but no one was home, and when he went back the next afternoon, they were gone. The house was as empty as a politician's promise.

But he could still remember the kiss as if it were yesterday, the way she had held his hand, the way her flesh felt when she touched him. That biting smell of perfume in his nostrils.

Puzzle pieces separated. The pattern broken. The puzzle screwed.

"Well, I'll be goddamn," his father said. "Will you look at this?"

Harry turned to look as his mother came in from the kitchen, a towel in her hands. She said, "Don't cuss."

"Look here," Dad said, and slapped a finger against a newspaper on the dining table. "What's this say?"

Harry knew his dad had been able to pick out a few words, but couldn't read well enough to get the whole of the story, all that missed school, something about reversing letters when he tried to read, which was why he had called in Mom.

She read a bit of it from the paper. Harry got up from the floor, strolled over, slid in between them.

It was the front page of the local paper. It had a large headline.

KILLER OF BAR OWNER CONFESSES

There was an article, and Harry's eyes just hit the high spots. *Ex-husband admits to killing his wife, the owner of Rosy's Roadhouse. Had a key. Waited until the place was empty and she was closing. He was upset about their split-up. He wasn't happy she was seeing another man.*

"That's the place down the hill," Harry said.

"That's right," Mom said.

Mom turned the page, went to where the story was continued. There were two photos.

One of the victim.

One of the murderer.

Harry knew them both. Or rather, he had seen them both. Down there in Rosy's. The night he slipped out with Joey and Kayla. The night he fainted.

He leaned over and looked closer at the picture of the man in the newspaper. It was him, all right. The man with the black hair, the scars, and the sharp, curved knife, the guy that cut the woman's throat, knocking her against the jukebox. He could remember the light and the warmth, the record playing. That feeling of tightness. It all came back to him. Just for a moment.

He looked at the woman's photograph. She looked better than when he had seen her, frightened, cut, then dead. But it was her.

His eyes bounced along the paragraphs in the article as his mother read them aloud to his father.

Slit throat.

Up against the jukebox.

Blood on the wall.

Murdered with a knife.

Harry stepped back, and he was no longer remembering the warmth and the light. It was as if his very being were falling backward, down a long cold tunnel. It was a terrible feeling, and it made his stomach churn.

"I saw him do it," Harry said.

"What?" his mom said. "What did you say?"

"I saw him," Harry said.

"You saw this guy?" his dad asked, thumping his finger on the photograph.

"Yeah. I saw him."

"How the hell did you see him?" Dad said.

"In my dreams."

There was a long moment of silence, large enough and empty enough for an elephant to walk through.

"Dreams?" Dad said. "Son, you need some rest. You don't dream people you ain't never met. You seen that on some TV show or something, read about it in one of those crazy stories you're always reading."

"You just think you've dreamed it," Mom said. "You're seeing his face in the paper now, just now, and you're thinking you've seen him before. Maybe he reminds you of someone."

Harry shook his head. "No."

He turned slowly and walked out of the room toward his bedroom. He turned on the little rotating fan and lay down on his bed and looked at the water spot on the ceiling, the one that looked like a bear's head with its mouth open. There was another water spot not far away. It looked like a mouse. The mouse appeared to be running toward the bear's mouth, and the bear, silent and waiting, was going to surprise him. Big-time.

His mother stood in the doorway.

"You okay, baby?"

"Yeah, Mom. Okay."

"We shouldn't have let you see that."

"No. That's all right. I always read the paper."

And he did. He had started last year, because of a school class that was teaching them about current events. And it always depressed him. Someone was always killing or hurting or stealing or lying to someone else.

"It's just someone reminds you of someone else," she said.

"Yeah. Sure. It just sort of got to me."

"You want some water?"

"No."

"Got some Coca-Cola, you want it."

"No. I'm fine."

She reached out and touched his hand. She smiled at him. He tried to smile back.

"Well . . . okay. You call you need something. All right?"

"Sure."

She went out and closed the door.

Night had fallen when his father came into the room. A big slice of darkness lay across the sheets. A bit of wind came through a couple of cracks in the wall, which in the summer was all right. During the winter, though, it was a bitch. Still, it was an all right room. At least he had his own space. Joey, he slept on the couch in a house worse than this, and over there no one even tried to make it a home.

"You sure are upset," Dad said, and stretched out on the bed beside Harry, under the wedge of darkness, causing the old bed to dip. He could feel his father's hand close to his. He didn't look at it and he didn't touch it, but he could feel the heat off of it, and he knew it was short fingered and thick like a catcher's mitt, scarred all over from wrenches that slipped and slammed them into bolts and sharp-edged metal.

"I'm just not feeling well."

Harry said this while looking at the ceiling, studying the bear-head water spot, which was hardly visible now. The mouse he couldn't see at all.

There was some light coming from the hall, but the darkness was stronger. It shoved the light out.

"You sure you seen those people before? Ones in the news-paper?"

"Yes, sir. I guess. I don't know, really."

"Maybe you did. Maybe long ago you did. Then later, see, you dreamed about them, or thought you dreamed about them, when really you were just remembering seeing them. I don't know about that kind of thing, but it could be like that. Down the hill there, you could have seen them, don't you think?"

"Maybe."

"You're letting it get to you, this dream. No use in that."

Harry thought, No, not for you. You handle things when they happen. You just go in and take hold and wrestle them to the floor and beat their ass.

"Well, you listen. After a good night's sleep, you won't be think-ing about all that."

"I know."

"You gonna eat some dinner?"

"I guess."

"Hey, tell you what, this once, what say I have Mom bring it in to you? You can eat in your room, lay back a bit. Just rest."

"Sure, Dad, that would be great."

"You got it," he said, rolling off the bed, causing it to lift Harry up a full two inches.

Daddy turned the little rotating fan on higher. It screeched and pushed some wind Harry's way. His father smiled. It was a lopsided smile, like maybe he didn't really know how to do it.

"You'll be all right," he said, and went out.

It actually was kind of fun, eating in the room, being alone, taking his time, sitting by the window looking out at the night.

They had this thing, his family did, and it was about eating at the table. You always ate at the table, and you talked.

It was never heavy talk. Daddy mostly listened to Mom and him talk, and Harry liked to talk, when it was easy talk. About everyday forgettable stuff.

But there were things he couldn't discuss.

Comics. Books, the writers who wrote them. Neither of his parents were readers of that sort of stuff. In fact, it was his father's shame that he could hardly read at all. Went through school up to the junior year and dropped out. Got that far and couldn't really read. Oh, he could read signs, and a few simple things. Enough to get by, especially if you were doing mechanic work and knew your work and could sign your name. So it wasn't a noticeable problem. But Harry knew it embarrassed him, his inability to really read well. In everything else he was as confident as Superman, but the reading, that bothered him.

And his Mom . . . well, she was smart, appreciated his love of books. But discussing any of the science fiction he read would have been about as much fun as talking to a goat about barbecue sauce. She didn't get it. Same with the handful of video games he played. She couldn't see the point.

His parents watched TV. Sitcoms and news mostly, listened to country-and-western music on old vinyl records. They seldom went out. If they did, it was maybe for a hot dog or hamburger, picking it up at the drive-through window. Visited relatives from time to time. Didn't really have any friends. Not real friends like he had. Joey and Kayla.

Well, Kayla anyway. Joey, he was hard to figure.

But Kayla, she was all right.

He thought about her all the time.

But his parents, they didn't have any real friends, far as he knew. Didn't even have a good friend who moved off. Someone they could remember.

They had each other.

And him.

Daddy had his work, and Mom had him to try and put knee pads and helmets on.

That was pretty much all they had.

But he loved them. Dearly. And they loved him back.

His dad, a real tough guy, but soft when he had to be. He was Harry's hero. Said what he meant, meant what he said. Talked the talk and walked the walk. He wasn't scared of much, that Harry could see.

He wished he could be just like him.

Because he was scared all the time, and here he sat, whining in his room with the leftovers of his dinner. Harry got up, went to the window, and looked out. Dark.

He pushed up the window and took a deep breath. The summer air was as thick as old tire smoke, and just as hard to breathe.

He went to his door and closed it softly. It blotted out the sound of the television and the light from the hallway, left him in darkness.

He turned on the light, got his magazine out from under the bed, the one with the naked women in it, looked at it, but it wasn't doing much for him. He turned off the light, put the magazine back, and lay down on the bed with his hands behind his head.

He thought again about his dad, how he tackled things like this. He wouldn't just lie here. He'd go and investigate. He'd find out.

While Harry was thinking on all this, he fell asleep.

When he awoke it was still dark in the room. He got up, stumbled over, and turned on the light. He looked at the windup clock on the nightstand. It was five A.M.

All right, he thought. I got to do it. Got to be brave, the way my old man is brave.

Harry put on his clothes, turned out the light, pushed up the window, and slipped out the way he had slipped out the night he and Joey and Kayla had gone down to the tonk.

But now it was just him, all by his lonesome, and the sky was so big and the world was so wide and the shadows amongst the old cars and the trees were so dark.

He went softly by his parents' window, trying not to crunch anything underfoot. He traveled across the road and down the hill at a smooth run. He knew the place well, so all he needed was a bit of starlight. He knew all the places around his home; he had played on every inch of that ground. Unless there was a new gopher hole or a snake, he was cool out there in the dark.

He went down and leaned against the honky-tonk, next to the window Joey had broken out.

He started to climb in, but hesitated.

There was nothing but darkness in there, and he didn't even have a flashlight. What the hell had he been thinking?

Just looking inside made him nervous. The dark gave the

impression of crawling, and the place looked even more desolate than when he and Joey and Kayla had been here last. He could feel bumps moving across his back, arms, and neck, like cold-legged beetles. He took a deep breath, took hold of the windowsill. A piece of glass stuck him. He jerked his hand back and bit the glass out and spit it away. He rubbed his bloody palm against his blue jeans.

He leaned over and looked closer at the sill, found some safe spots, put his hands there, and—

He couldn't do it.

Couldn't make himself do it.

He realized he was breathing fast, and it was making him feel dizzy, weak.

He made it as far as his yard, stopped to catch his breath and look over at the old cars next door. They were really ratty now, having been brutally bitch-slapped by weather and time.

He had loved those old cars once; now all he could remember was the last time he was in one of them, long ago, and that he had been scared. He didn't remember exactly what scared him, but he did remember he had been frightened out of his wits and had never played there again.

Scared.

That was his theme song.

Scared with a chorus of Scared Again.

A memory or two unraveled, frayed. And it hit him.

When he was a kid, that's what had happened, out there in the car. Stuff like that night in the honky-tonk. It's why he had quit going to the cars. He had seen faces and heard sounds. He had almost forgotten, or had tried to forget, had tucked it away, but now it was coming back to him.

Harry took a deep breath, went over to the car that was once his favorite. The one that had frightened him those long years ago. He put his hand on the driver's side door, hesitated.

"You got a second chance here, boy," he said out loud. "You don't have to be a pussy twice in one night."

He opened the car door and slid inside, leaving the door open. The seat wobbled and a rat screeched and ran out from under it. Harry let out a little yell. The rat bailed through the open door. Harry watched its starlit shape hump across the ground and into the woods.

Damn.

Maybe that's what had scared him that long time ago.

A rat. A screeching rat. That could explain things. He was young and hadn't seen it. It had startled him and made him run.

Yeah. That explained a lot of things.

"I'm not scared," he said.

He pulled the door shut. Hard.

When the door slammed the sound was like the gate of hell had slammed, and there were other sounds, a whine, and a screech that was near deafening. A scream. Then there were psychedelic lights and flying colors, and the car was new and smelled fresh and clean and the world was bright and full of sunlight and there was a blur of cars out there on the highway and heat waves rippled and he could hear the wind whipping past, and hair, not his own, flicked long and wild in the wind from the open window.

A woman was sitting inside of him.

He didn't know any other way to understand it. She was inside of him, and suddenly something dark appeared. A car, crossing an intersection, and Harry threw up his hands as they collided, and the woman inside of him, she jumped out of him, her head striking the steering wheel, and when it did a red haze filled his vision and splattered against the windshield.

To his right, a doll was thrown forward.

A large doll.

It hit the window hard, shattering it, making glass shards jump: then the doll twisted into a U shape, ricocheted off the inside of the car, passed through him once, striking the woman, bounced back against the glass, came to rest on the floorboard in a wad.

The doll leaked.

Only it wasn't a doll.

It was a little girl.

He couldn't tell much about her looks. She didn't have any. Just a mess of blond hair with runs of scarlet in it, her face a nest of broken glass and a pool of blood. The blood was coming faster now. The car was coated in it.

He thought: Seat belts. Where are the seat belts?

He fell forward and hit his head against the steering wheel and the car went dark and dull and empty and turned old; the door screeched as he jerked it open and let out a yell.

He yelled more than once.

He yelled a lot.

His parents came out of the house and found him lying in the yard on his back, looking up at the stars, still yelling.

9

There were lots of doctors for the next few years. Doctors with charts and tests and even medicine that made him tired and a little loopy. It was supposed to help him focus. It was supposed to help him with his delusions. It made him feel bad.

A little later, he would think, yeah, I felt bad, but I was numb. And numb, that was good.

But back then he didn't know that.

So, he quit taking the medicine, thought: Okay, maybe I'm a fruitcake with extra nuts, and maybe I'm not. And if I am a fruitcake, then I probably don't know it. But I know this: My parents don't have any money, and I'm costing them a ton because I might be nuts.

So I got to quit being nuts.

Or whatever is wrong with me has got to stop.

I'll just stop now.

And he did stop.

Sort of.

He was sixteen and had his license. Had his first chance to go out and see the world from behind a steering wheel, and the truth of the matter was, he was frightened.

There had been other episodes.

One night, while riding in a car with Joey, who got his license first, he had "an experience." It wasn't the same as before. The car door closing was fine. The ride was fine. Then they hit a bump and the glove box snapped open and the lid dropped down with a rever-beration, and it jumped on him.

Different this time. Milder. Just a bumpy ride at midday, a black man yelling as a car came out of nowhere. Just a fender-bender on the right side that knocked the glove box open, that and a high kick start on a rush of adrenaline. The driver even started to smile, happy he hadn't gotten twisted into the metal. Then the man's face fell off like melted black wax and the world Harry knew came back and it was all over.

Joey was sitting behind the wheel looking at him when he came out of it. Joey pulled over, said, "What the fuck is wrong with you? Quit jumping. You're fucking me up, man."

"What?"

"You're hopping and screaming. Ain't even any music on."

"Shit," Harry said.

"That's what I almost did."

"Is this car used?" Harry asked.

"Yeah. It is. What you think, I get an old model and no one's ever driven it? Like it's been sitting on the car lot for a few years till I buy it?"

"Was it ever wrecked?"

"I don't know. How the fuck would I know? Close the glove box. That fucker's always popping open."

"Can we leave it open so it doesn't do that again?"

"You got more pussy ways than anyone I know. Yeah. Leave it

open if it don't make you hop and yell. Most motherfuckers like to listen to the radio, they're gonna do that hoppin' about. But you, you got the silent drummer going on, you know."

There had been other incidents, not in cars. In houses. When he visited Joey, and Joey's father closed the door, there had been images of Joey's mother being shoved up against it, taking a whack. There were places all over that house like that. Memories hidden in the walls where Joey and his mother and siblings had been bounced by Joey's father. That place was a smorgasbord of fear.

It gave Harry a kind of sick stomach to be there. All that angry business hidden in the walls and furniture, the way Joey and his mom and his brother had to glide by without disturbing the air around Mr. Barnhouse. And the way Barnhouse looked at him, as if he were some interloper there to do him harm or take away his television set, which seemed to be Barnhouse's lifeline. Without that, he would have had nothing but silence, the life inside his own head.

Harry figured it wasn't very nice in there, in Mr. Barnhouse's head, and that noise of any kind, beating the wife and children now and then, was welcome. Anything but silence. Anything but being alone with himself inside his head.

He quit going there, waited on the porch until Joey came out. Found ways to be somewhere else, have Joey meet him somewhere, like his own home.

Home was a sanctuary. There were no horrors hidden in that old house, and his parents weren't creating anything that might be recorded.

Oh, there was something by the windows. Where he had fallen when he was six. Once when he stomped the floor there, killing a roach, he discovered a childhood version of himself, and the room went dark and he could see a chair and the windows were full of imagery; the drive-in theater and cartoons across the way, and he could hear loud honky-tonk music. And there had been something just a little different.

He had felt pain.

In his ear.

And then his mother, younger, robed, hair loose and wild, had come rushing from the bedroom, followed by his father. The image began to fade, speed up. He saw them rushing out the door, his father carrying him in his arms. Yeah. Things were recorded—in houses and cars and furniture, and who knew what all?

He just didn't understand why.

Unless it was all in his head, and he was, in fact, crazy.

He was thinking of all this as he sat in a chair with his license in his hand, considering going out. He had use of the family car tonight, the very first time, and he wanted to go, but he was scared, and not of images, but of something more common. The highway. Parallel parking. He had barely passed that part.

"You look nice," his dad said.

"What?" Harry looked up.

His dad grinned at him. He noticed his dad looked tired, and for the first time he realized that he had grayed around the temples and there was a little less hair on top. Saw him every day, and now he noticed. God, when did that happen?

"Said you look good. All cleaned up."

"Ah, you know. Nothing much. A shower."

Dad laughed. "And lots of smell-pretty."

"Got too much?"

"Roll down the window, let the wind blow some of it off, and you'll be fine."

"Yeah, sure."

"You going out, or you just gonna drive that chair?"

"I'm going out. I guess."

"You got the car. You got your license. It's Friday night. What you ought to do is go out. What you gonna sit here for?"

"Just thinking."

"About girls?"

"Not really."

"I suggest you do. Girls are pretty nice to think about. You ain't got the fanciest ride in the world there, but you can go on dates, you know. You got to ask a girl, though. I always found out, you didn't ask them, they didn't show up."

Harry felt himself turning red. "Yeah, I know."

"Listen here, Harry. I know what you're thinking. It's about that stuff."

That's what his dad always called the visions, the bothersome *stuff*.

"Just a little."

"Ain't nothing wrong with you."

"You think, Dad? I mean, the doctors—"

"Hell with them."

Dad pulled over a wooden chair, sat down across from him.

"Let me tell you, you're . . . you know . . . imaginative."

"You mean I make things up?"

"I don't think so."

"You think I believe them, but they aren't true?"

The big man paused, put his hands in his lap. "Son, I don't know. Truly I don't. But it was said there was some in our family had the second sight. Can't say it was true, but it was the story."

"This is sort of like hindsight, Daddy. It's already done. It's like I hear and see ghosts in sounds. It's got something to do with fear, or violence. I've told you all this."

Dad sat and considered for a moment. "Hindsight, second sight, maybe it's all the same."

"Who had second sight in our family?"

"My mother. You never knew her. Dead before you were born, just like your grandpa. All your grandparents, dead before you were born. That's too bad. Least as far as your grandmother—my mother—went. Your mom's parents, good people. My dad, he was a son of a bitch. . . . You know the scars on my back?"

"The barbed wire?"

The old man nodded. "Them ain't barbed wire. Told you I got tangled in barbed wire when I was a kid. That ain't what happened. I didn't want to tell you, not then, that your grandpa beat me with a belt. The buckle. It cut me, made them scars."

"Why are you telling me now, Daddy?"

"I don't know. I think you ought to know. Don't know why, but thought you ought to."

"What did you do?"

"When he hit me?"

"Yeah."

"Wasn't nothing I could do. I was a kid, and he was big and mean and always drunk. . . . You stay away from that liquor, hear me? You might have the tendency. I drank a little when I was young, and I had the tendency. It brought the mean out in me. Your mama, she got me away from that. Told me she'd go out with me, but not if I drank, and if I drank she was through with me. I ain't never taken another drop. . . . Thing is, Harry, there's shit in your life you don't expect. Ain't all of it good. But you got to get around that, got to grab the good, got to get your mind wrapped around that, and let the bad things go. Otherwise you just get caught up in hating or being mad, or being worried all the time. You got what you got, son. But you'll deal with it."

"You think?"

"Hell, boy, I know. . . . Here's the keys. It's got a full tank."

The old man opened his wallet, and Harry could see there was a twenty in there, three or four ones. Daddy took out the twenty, handed it to him.

"No, Dad, that's all right."

"Take it. You might want a Coke or something. Might want to buy a girl a Coke. Take the car out, you ought to try and have a little money. Take it, son."

Harry took the twenty. "Thanks, Dad."

"Hey, that's what dads do."

"Sure."

Harry stood up.

"You be careful out there, son."

"Absolutely."

"She idles kind of heavy at lights, stop signs, but she's okay. I've tuned her up and gone over her good. She'll run like a spotted-ass ape."

Harry laughed. "And how do they run?"

Dad grinned. "I don't really know, son. Just an old saying."

Harry suddenly grabbed his Dad and hugged him. "I love you," he said.

"Yeah, well, you too, son. Hey, you're getting quite a grip there."

Later on, Harry was really glad he did that.

That night, out on the town, doing his thing with Joey riding beside him, Joey drinking a bit, whiskey in Coke, offering him some, but him refusing; out there trying to pick up girls, being awkward and unsuccessful about it; out there on the highways, circling the Dairy Queen, waving at friends passing by in their cars, having the time of his life, his old man, home, sitting at dinner, suddenly stood up from the table, and his mom would tell it like this: "He was just fine: then he stood bolt upright, said, 'I feel kind of off,' grabbed his left arm, and then he dropped."

Heart attack.

Dead and gone.

Things were coming apart.

10

For a few months Harry's life rocked and floundered. He was so rattled that when he read about Kayla's dad in the Tyler paper, he felt for her, but there just wasn't enough left in him to respond.

And there was the fact he hadn't seen her in years. Thought about her from time to time, but that was Kayla then, not Kayla now. There were times when he thought about her and felt as if a piece of him were missing. That puzzle part. But it was probably just wishful thinking. Kid memories.

Maybe a good word would make her feel better, maybe not. He didn't know if he had a good word left, or that she would really remember him, not the way he remembered her.

Still, it was surprising, way it had gone down, her dad's death.

He zeroed in on parts of the article:

Jerome Jones was found dead in his part-time garage on High Street, hanging by a lamp cord from a door inside the building. He was discovered by his daughter about eight P.M. Thursday after he failed to return from work. Suicide is suspected, but not confirmed.

Poor Kayla, he thought. What was she doing back here? Had she moved back? Was she nearby?

Goddamn. To hell with Kayla.

He tossed the paper aside.

And the beat goes on.

11

The ceiling had shadows on it that looked like the blades of a fan, and this was because the light fixture on the ceiling had little slats inside.

The big man lay on the bed looking at this, considering something or another about it, but he was uncertain what. A spider crawled out of the light fixture and dangled out to the side of it, and he thought, if it falls, it will fall on her.

He turned and looked over at the woman beside him, then at his partner, who was on the other side of the female sandwich, grinning. His partner was up on one elbow looking at him, so he rose up too, and grinned. They were just a couple of Cheshire cats tossing grins across the room.

The big man swung his feet to the side of the bed and sat there and looked toward the open door of the bathroom, thought about the car. They had to get rid of the car, and they needed to do it soon. It was good to stretch out for the moment—all the activity, the adrenline, had made him tired—but you could stretch your time too far, and if you kept stretching, the whole thing was going to snap. You had to think about that. Had to.

They had found her at the motel. It was one of the places they liked to look, and mostly they weren't lucky, but this night they were. They cruised in, and out back of the place, getting out of her car, heading toward the row of rooms, was the girl.

Quick was their middle name. They were out of the car and had her before you could blink an eye, hand over her mouth, pulling her into her own ride, hitting her with a tire iron, dropping her down onto the floorboard, taking her keys, him driving her car, his partner following in theirs. On out to the woods to leave their car and take her car back to the motel room. She had a key. Number seven. There could be a man in there. A family. That was all part of the game.

They took her back to the motel and into number seven and there was no one else. It was easy, and they did to her what they wanted to do. Had fun.

He looked at the young woman lying in the center of the bed. Her dead eyes looked at the ceiling in the way his live eyes had, but she saw nothing. He had seen shadow slats and a spider. It was all shadow to her and no awareness of shadow.

He liked to think about that, try and understand it. What was it like to be nothing, to know nothing? How was it to be dead? He didn't want to experience it himself, but in her eyes, in that last moment when he fastened his hands around her throat, after she had come awake from the blow to the head, after they had finished with her, he thought, for just an instant, in her face, in her eyes, he could see the shadow of death move into her head behind the windows of her soul.

It was quite a feeling.

The big man got up and started for the bathroom, scratching his naked ass as he went. Behind him he heard his partner get up, and when he looked, he saw he was getting dressed.

That didn't surprise him. They had used protection, condoms, and they had disposed of the condoms down the toilet, but his partner wasn't even going to wash his dick. He ought to wash it just because he ought to. Had to be some real nasty on that dude.

He turned his attention to the woman again.

Still dead.

She hadn't miraculously come back to life.

They had had that happen once. Thought a gal was dead, had her at a drive-through eatery, covered in a blanket, down on the backseat floorboard, and while they were waiting on their burgers and fries, looking at the kid on the other side of the window hustling around at the register, they heard a sudden gulp of breath.

The woman they thought dead was not dead.

He remembered it as if it were yesterday, though it was . . . two, three years ago. She had gulped air, and with his partner at the wheel, he had reached back between the seats as she rose up like a zombie from the dead, the blanket over her head and body, and he grabbed her throat. Grabbed it right through the blanket and squeezed, cutting off the hose, not letting the fuel get into her system. Held her tight.

She thrashed. Her arms came out from under the blanket.

He looked at his partner, who saw what was going down, then he glanced at the kid behind the register, gathering up a sack now, turning his pimple-painted face toward them, reaching for the sliding window, and with all his might, he pushed down with his hand, squeezed with his fingers, and the woman—girl, really—kicked a couple of times. But the kid, he didn't notice shit. There was music inside, and you could really hear it now that the window was slid back, some canned shit that ran all day long at the place, and he was saying, "Two burgers, all the way. Fries. Two Diet Cokes."

"Yeah. Yeah," his partner said, and gave him a bill.

A big bill.

Damn.

Now they had to wait for change, and there he was, trying to hold that bitch down, and she was goddamn strong, and it was work, doing it with one hand stuck back between the seats, trying to look casual, hoping the burger doodle guy didn't see her feet moving around back there, didn't hear them against the seat. All that, and his partner gives the guy a big bill and waits.

Later, his partner would say, "Shit, man. It's what I had. Don't want him to remember I gave him a twenty, some such thing, said keep the change, something like that, 'cause he sure would remember that, don't you think? So I had to wait on the change. Had to."

And of course he was right. But there was the kid, passing sacks and drinks along, taking the money, and there he was, his hand tight on the woman's throat, doing what he thought he had already done, and then, as her arms, way out from under the blanket, thrashed and she dug her nails into the back of his hand and he gritted his teeth to keep from yelping, the kid closed the window and his partner juiced the car.

He looked back through the rear window, saw a car behind them, some kids. But they weren't paying lots of attention. And when they drove off, the kids pulled to the window and stopped. He let out his breath. When they turned the corner and went back on the road, he turned and slipped between the seats, catching his shoe and pulling it off on something or another. He dropped down onto the floorboard, bringing his knee into the middle of her, jerking off the blanket, letting go of her throat, hitting her three, four times with his fists.

And when she was out, slowly, carefully, he went back to squeezing, feeling her neck bones crackle beneath his strong fingers. He strangled her, finished her. And then when they were out in the woods, he cut off her fingers and they shoved her out and he took the fingers with him. Later he dug his skin out from under the nails on the fingers and trimmed them down, and put the fingers in an ant bed; after a while, a week or so, he went back and dug them up and put them in a bag and carried them out with him fishing, left them in the water out by the dam, each one with a fistful of sinkers tied to them.

But this one, lying on the bed, she wasn't coming back from

nowhere, and she hadn't scratched anyone. She had gone over. She was dead, dead, dead. 'Cause he knew how to do it now, how to be certain.

"You gonna run the water?" his partner asked.

The big man snapped back to the job at hand.

"Sure. Give me a minute; then bring her."

His partner, completely dressed now, walked to the curtains and stood in front of them. The bright yellow sign with the red light that blinked MOTEL throbbed through the curtains and made the room pulse like a heat blister.

"I get worried," his partner said. "I have fun, and I'm okay, but afterward I get worried. Always think there's DNA all over the god-damn place. Some skin cell off my ass or something."

The big man paused, put a hand on the bathroom door as he looked at his partner. "See my hand on this door? Think I'm fucking scared? Think I'm worried about prints?"

"You ought to be. You know we ought to be."

"All right. There's some fear. Wasn't any fear, would you do it?"

"I don't know. Maybe."

"I wouldn't. I don't think you would either. Thing is, I'm gonna wipe the place clean. I'm gonna run a tub full of water, and we're gonna clean her, and then we're gonna let her soak in the water. Where guys who do this fuck up is, they take souvenirs. We aren't going to take any. I mention that, 'cause I saw you eyeing her ankle bracelet."

"I thought about it. She's got a ring through her pussy too. I seen you look at that."

"It's there to look at, but I don't want it. That's like asking for it. Guys do this, take that stuff, they're just asking for it. And they kill in the same place, same way, dispose of the body the same way—"

"We've done some of that—"

"Yeah. But we change up too. And we don't do it all the goddamn time. You got to hold back some. Have some self-control. It's more fun when it's built up some steam, and then you still got to be careful. That's the thing matters, self-control."

"I don't know. We had self-control, we wouldn't do it."

"It doesn't take any self-control not to do it. It's the self-control to do it that matters. To know you're taking a chance, and still keep your head."

His partner turned back to the curtain and the lights.

"I suppose."

Sometimes he worried about his partner, thought maybe he was just a little flaky, out there on the rim, wobbling.

"I'm gonna wipe the place down," he said, "do the cleaning. Then we're gonna go. Got some DNA here . . . well, they got to connect it to us. Isn't any reason to connect it to us, is there?"

"I suppose not."

"Most little burgs like this, you know they don't even have fucking DNA tests. Costs to get that done. Costs too much for little towns. You know that. So it ain't like a fucking television show where they find one nut hair and know some fucker in Cleveland did it. Not if we're careful. Shit, man. Risk is part of it, isn't it?"

"Yeah. Sure."

"Then, we do what we're supposed to do, any DNA they got, we don't worry too much about, 'cause they got to match it to us. And why would they? It's the more practical shit ought to worry you. Like leaving your fucking wallet or some such thing."

"Yeah. You're right."

His partner was back at the bed now, looking down at the nude woman's body.

"She was sure easy. I didn't get, you know, what I was looking for. I sort of feel sorry for her. For me, she was kind of a waste. I don't like to waste. Get what you want, it ain't a waste, but she died and I didn't get what I wanted."

"Sometimes it's a thrill. Sometimes it ain't much. It's like dinner in a strange restaurant. You can't count on anything. But sometimes it's pretty special. You got to take a run at it, see how it turns out."

The big man went into the bathroom to run the tub full of water.

Later they drove away in her green Dodge, leaving her in the motel, at the bottom of the tub, covered in soapy water, this after cleansing and rinsing her a few times. They drove the Dodge to the woods, both of them wearing gloves now.

They got out and paused to light cigarettes and lean against a tree and look up through the branches at the moon, careful not to toss their cigarettes, so as not to leave anything of themselves behind.

Finally they loaded up in their car and drove back to where they lived, some hour or so away. When they got to the big man's house, first thing they did was remove the shoes they had bought at Goodwill, wiped them down and put them in a bag and took them to the Dumpster.

The big man thought it all over. By the time anyone found the car, maybe found their tracks, even if they came to them, checked out their shoes, looked for them in the dump, if they could find them, those shoes would be plowed way under, could be anyone's shoes, mixed in with coffee grounds and used Tampax and rotten tomato slices.

Living this kind of life, even taking precautions, keeping the kills down to different towns and wide apart, you still had to be careful. DNA could really be a problem. His partner was right about that. But it could be beaten, this DNA. Wasn't magic. Was beaten all the time. Otherwise nobody would get away with anything.

Besides, what was the game without the thrill of discovery? Fear of prison and the hot needle full of drop-you-down-dead? Fear of getting caught, that was the hullabaloo that kept it all exciting. Gave life the juice. 'Cause without death, without fear of it, without having it hanging over your head like a slow-tipping bottle full of acid, the whole of existence was merely about floating from one moment to another, like a frog on a lily pad, and he didn't like to think of himself as a frog.

No. Had to compare himself to some other kind of critter, something that had to do with water . . . well, he'd go for big water. The ocean. And he would be a great white shark.

Yep. He was a shark. And his partner . . . well, he was a sucker fish clinging to his belly. No. His balls. Sucked up tight on his balls. That's how he liked to think of him.

A sucker fish.

And him, the shark, dragging his partner through the water, clinging to the old shark nuts.

PART TWO

The Ghosts in the Noise

12

When he and Joey came into the bar it was cool and dark, and Harry wanted a beer. He wasn't supposed to drink, remembered the talk with his dad, but lately he had been tying them on. Thing he found out, just by accident on New Year's, was that when he drank he didn't hear the sounds and see the images, no flashes of color. The alcohol numbed something inside of him. You could beat on a spot where a sound had leaped at him before, and it would lie dormant.

He knew this for a fact because of Joey's apartment, and something that had happened there, but he didn't want to think about that. Not now. Not ever.

He hadn't told Joey about it. It was the same as how he didn't like to go over to Joey's house when he lived at home, didn't want to go there because of Mr. Barnhouse, who could be all right one moment, then find offense at most anything the next, fly off the handle, go into a cuss-a-thon, snatch Joey up and beat him like a bongo drum. And now that Joey had moved out, he didn't want to go to Joey's new place.

Mr. Barnhouse wasn't there, but . . . now there were new problems.

He told himself he wouldn't think about that and now he was. But he wasn't going to keep it up. He was going to let it go. Now if he went to Joey's he always went snookered, and it worked, but he had the memories too, and they were with him all the time, and when he was at Joey's, well, they were there, like those flickering movie images seen so long ago through the windows overlooking the drive-in show. Alcohol helped with some things, but it didn't really help all that well with the memories.

He wanted a beer. Several.

He hoped, as he always hoped, that no dark sounds, as he had come to think of them, lurked somewhere within the bar. Sheehan's Place it was called.

Place like this, where the alcohol seeped up out of the floor with a spoiled-ham kind of smell, would be where some past violent event might be contained inside a stool used to bean someone, a table where a face got slammed, the walls where someone might have been thrown against them.

That violent stuff, that past business, it could skulk about almost anywhere. And at the right moment, the right sound could reinvigorate the event. At least for him.

A scratch, a wham, a slam, a thud, and his head would be a bag full of noise, colors, and bad mojo.

Yeah. He wanted to get numb quick.

He thought maybe he had to quit going out altogether, except maybe to the store down the block. Buy his medicine in the liquor section, keep himself in a stunned condition. Sober up just enough to make it to the liquor store, get his stuff, start all over again.

He and Joey ordered a pitcher of beer at the bar, carried it and the glasses to a table in the corner, where it was rich in shadow.

There was country music playing, and there was dancing, and there were a lot of great-looking women on the floor, guys with their hands on the women's asses and such, and Harry found himself jealous. Or lonesome. Or both. He wasn't sure.

"That one right there, the one in them jeans and the red shirt," Joey said, "she ought not to wear pants so tight. She either looks like she's got a tallywhacker or she's on the rag. See there up front, it's pushing out the zipper."

"Oh, shut up. She looks all right."

"If you like 'em with a dick, or on the rag. Think she'd use a feminine-protection plug or something, not that old rag deal. Something stuck up there, out of sight, like a gopher in a hole, that's the way to go, not a rug over a manhole. That's just nasty. Hell, maybe it is a dick. I think she could be a man. I think she's got a bit of a mustache, now that I look."

"Joey, no wonder you don't do well with women."

"Like you do?"

"You got a point there."

They sat and watched and listened and drank. The music was loud but good, came from a sound system, all recorded stuff. The lights became dimmer and the dark profiles of the dancers moved and the lights behind the bar fuzzed. The shapes danced this way and that, and after a while it seemed to Harry they all danced at a tilt, and that the table was on a boat, and the boat was on a nasty sea.

Harry was downing one cold glass after another, ordering pitcher after pitcher, thinking it all tasted like rubbing alcohol. Hell, he didn't even enjoy it. But it treated him right when it came to the sounds.

He thought about his mom in that old house. He hadn't been to see her in a month. Had to drive back over there. Had to go. But it was no longer a sanctuary. There was a trauma there, where the kitchen table was. What if he moved the chair his dad had moved when he stood up, right before keeling over?

Would it—that bad moment—be there, hidden in a scraping chair leg?

After his dad died, for the three years he continued to live at home, he never ate at the table. Never moved that chair.

To please him, his mother didn't move it either. She must have thought him nuts, but she didn't move it. She listened to him. She let him have his way, like she always did. She sat the chair out on the porch, laid it on its side, way he asked, and it stayed there while he lived at home.

But, the times he had been back, he saw the chair had been replaced. That she had been sitting in it. Her husband's chair. The last place the old man had sat before his heart exploded.

Harry felt as if it were lurking there, waiting for him: the bad memory of it all, trapped in a scrape or a thump.

Still, he had to go home. His mother hadn't been looking well. Pale. Scrawnier than usual. Walking kind of funny. Bit of a limp. Too much work at the dollar store, ringing up purchases. She had worked there three years now so he could get out on his own, go to college. And he had worked too. Bit jobs. Part-time at a bookstore. Had a scholarship and a college loan.

He liked being out of the house, because of that one sound he knew was there. Maybe two. Daddy had to have hit the floor after he pushed back the chair. Did the sounds register if you were dead, or was it all in the dying?

He wasn't sure.

He poured another beer and sudsed his lips with it. Drank quickly. Thought: Got to go home. Have to check on Mom. Have to. Soon. Real soon.

"Look over there," Joey said. "Those guys are giving that old fucker some shit."

Harry looked where Joey was nodding, toward a table that could be seen through a split in the dancers. One moment you couldn't see the guy, then, when the dancers moved a certain way, you could.

The man was sitting alone. He wasn't really that old, Harry thought. Fifties, maybe. Kind of stocky-looking. Bit of belly, thinning gray hair. Lined face. But Joey was right about one thing: Guy was taking some smack. And he was shit-faced. Harry could tell that because he was shit-faced too. You could recognize a fellow traveler on the alcohol river, and like him, this guy was navigating without a sail. Might even be a hole in his boat.

The guys bothering him, there were three of them. One was standing on either side of him, the one on the left was rubbing the old guy's bald spot, saying something and laughing. The third guy was at the front of the table, drinking directly out of the man's beer pitcher.

"Assholes," Harry said.

"They're just having some fun," Joey said. "Ain't hurtin' nothin'."

"It's not their beer."

"You gonna set it right for him?"

Harry shook his head. "Not me against three, no. But somebody ought to do something."

"Yeah, well, maybe somebody will show up. Me, I don't see it's so bad. They're just having some fun."

"Why do I hang with you?" Harry said.

"My charm."

"Yeah. That's it."

The dancers closed, and for a moment Harry forgot about the man at the table.

When the dancers parted the man was gone, and so were the guys.

Then he saw them heading toward the back door. One of the guys had his arm around the man's shoulders, and the man was wobbling.

"They're gonna mug that guy," Harry said.

"What?"

"They're gonna mug him. See there?"

Joey looked. "You don't know that."

"I got a damn good idea."

Harry got up and the floor tilted way left. He put one leg out, trying to find his drunk legs, and the floor tilted the other way. The music was loud and it wrapped around him like a hot gel. He put his head in his hands and closed his eyes and took a deep breath.

When he opened his eyes he saw the guys taking the old man out the back door. He stood up straight and started after them, making big drunk steps, like he was stepping over something on the floor.

Joey stood up, grabbed him by the elbow, stopped him, said, "Man, don't go out there. You might be right, and they're gonna mug him. And your ass might be next. I ain't going, man. You're on your own, hero."

Harry didn't listen. He kept stepping. Big and serious, trying to focus.

When he got to the back door and pushed it open, the cool air hit him, sobered him a mite. That along with the stench from the alley, the smell of urine and rotting food and waste from the Dumpster. It was like a bracer.

But what he saw, it made him think he was major-blowout drunk. Maybe even hallucinating.

Joey was there with him, came up beside him after all. Was he hallucinating him too? Was he having some sort of sound flash? What the hell was going on, because, you see . . .

The man with the thinning hair, the older guy, the slightly thick one, he was pretty drunk, or seemed to be, but one of the guys, the biggest one, one who had drunk from the old man's pitcher, he hit the old man in the side of the head with his fist, real quick-like, and the old man, he moved.

Man, did he move.

He wasn't drunk anymore. That one shot to the side of the head kicked the drunk out of him, and what Harry saw next amazed him.

The guy who hit him, he was the first.

The old guy jerked out a leg. Sloppy-like, or so it seemed, but it caught the guy's knee, took it out with a sound like someone snapping a garden-fresh green bean.

One of the other guys started for the man, and the man grabbed him by the crotch with his right hand and shoved his left palm into the attacker's face, took his feet out from under him, let his head drop like a cantaloupe on the cement.

Third guy was coming in now, and he was big, and he was gonna fix the old man's clock big-time, you could see it on his face, but the old man ducked, and the punch the guy swung went over the man's head and the man snapped out with a right and a left, two loose shots to the solar plexus that made the assailant straighten up, then bend over in pain, trying to puke. The old man made with a kind of quick drunk step toward the guy, and standing sideways to him, brought his forearm up under the puker's throat, drove his head back. Then the old guy slid in and snapped a sideways elbow to the dude's chin, just under it; then that loose kick flew out again, this time a little higher, right in the old chicken neck and two potatoes.

Down the guy went.

The one who had his head bonked on the concrete got up at a wobble, came at the old man, really mad now, and the old man stepped sideways and the guy went past, and the old man stuck out a foot and caught the guy's ankle, and it was asphalt rash all over that dude's nose and chin, and he didn't get up this time. Harry thought maybe he could get up, but didn't want to, was trying to play dead, maybe even imagine he was buried six feet under, out of this old guy's way.

The guy with the ruined knee lay on the ground, screaming. The old man grabbed him by one arm and the hair and rolled him on his belly. He got the guy's wallet out of his back pocket and took the money. He went to the other two, did the same.

He saw Harry and Joey, standing in the doorway, their mouths wide-open.

"How's it hanging?" he said.

He grinned, shoved the money in his pocket, turned, and fell over on his back, stiff as a board.

"Well, I'll be fucked in the butt," Joey said.

The guy with the screwed knee was still making sounds, writhing.

Harry and Joey eased past him, over to the older guy, looked down at him, amazed.

He was snoring.

13

"I'm a goddamn drunk," the old guy said.

"No shit," Harry said. "I thought I was ripped, but you were torn, mister. You may still be messed up. Me, after what I saw, I'm dead sober now."

"I come in, and I go out," the man said.

"Do what?"

"Sober, then not so sober. Never what I would call completely sober, but on the edge of it. Just enough to know I need to not go there. It's an ugly place, this sobriety. Therein lies worry and evil. Have I talked much while I've been here?"

"Mostly you been out," Harry said.

"That's probably best for you. I like to talk. Weren't there two of you? Or was I just seeing two of you? Though usually, I do that, one of you doesn't look different."

"There were two of us."

"Good. I'm just drunk. Not crazy. Though I got to wonder sometimes."

"You and me both."

A spear of moonlight cut through a gap in the curtain and stuck in the linoleum floor like a spear. The man sat up and looked around. "I'm on the floor."

Harry turned on a lamp, pulled up a chair, sat, and looked down at the man on the pallet he'd made. The pillow had a faded Batman pillowcase. Batman had come to look more like an inkblot than the Caped Crusader.

"I made you a pallet, right after you puked in the bushes outside."

"Outside where?"

"My apartment. It was hell getting you upstairs."

The man studied Harry.

"You know, if I sucked your dick, I got to apologize. I like women, but when I drink, who knows what I do. Maybe I thought it was a tit."

"Nothing like that."

The man blinked, adjusting his sight. He looked about some more. What he saw was one small room, a couch with a sheet and pillow on it, a chair, a table, a cheap bookcase stuffed with books, a lamp on top of it. On the table was a hot plate, some paper plates, cups, plastic utensils. There was no sink or kitchen. There was only a little mini refrigerator in one corner. It hummed like a tone-deaf moron.

All over the walls were flattened cardboard boxes and egg cartons. They had been taped to the walls from top to bottom. There was a pile of flattened cardboard boxes in the corner of the room.

"You slept on the couch?" the man said.

"Always do. That's my bed."

"This place sucks."

"Thanks. Three-fifty a month, plus bills. You can't imagine how proud I am."

"You got a shitter?"

"There's this room and the shitter. You might have to suck it in some to get in there, and the toilet wobbles. Try not to go all over the place. You did before, pissed on the wall. I had to clean it up. Don't want to do it again. By the way, it smells like Lysol in there."

The man started to get up, couldn't quite make it. Harry helped him toward the bathroom.

"I don't get it," Harry said. "You were drunk as a skunk back at the bar, and you whipped three guys tried to roll you."

"I did?"

"Yeah."

"That's why my face hurts?"

"One of them hit you."

"That's what did it. I got hit; instinct took over. I think sometimes it's stronger than drink."

The man pushed through the door into the bathroom. Harry returned to his chair. A few minutes later the man came out. He looked fresher. His face was moist from washing, and his thin hair had been dampened and was combed back. He was walking better. He leaned his ass against the wall and, with his legs slightly out in front of him, crossed his arms.

"You been lurking over me all night?" he asked.

"We've only been here about an hour or so."

"Why'd you help me, kid?"

"I don't know. It wasn't just me. Friend of mine, Joey. He helped me get you to the car. I dropped him off; then it was just me and you, out there dancing on the curb, then you throwing up in the bushes."

"You could have let them have me."

"I didn't do anything about that, keeping them off of you. I might have thought about it, but I never had the chance. You whipped their asses. It was funny to see it. It was like you were stumbling, but everything you did was right. I think you broke one of 'em's knee."

"No shit?"

"No shit. How'd you do it, drunk like that?"

"Lucky."

"I don't think so. Was it some kind of martial arts?"

"Something like that. You want to know something? I don't remember doing it."

"Do you remember taking their money?"

"Money?"

"You went through their wallets, took their money, stuck it in your front pocket."

The man reached in his front pocket, pulled out a wad of bills. "I'll be damned. . . . Hell, I made forty-two dollars."

"And you don't remember doing it?"

"Nope. Guess it was a sense of fair play. Tit for tat. You said they were going to take my money, didn't you?"

"Looked that way."

"Guess I wasn't as drunk as I thought. . . . But I was drunk enough I don't remember much." The man moved away from the wall and stuck out his hand. "My name is Tad. Tad Peters. Thanks for not leaving me in the alley. Drunk luck only goes so far."

They shook and Harry told him his name.

"Drunk as I was, you're lucky I wasn't one more beer ahead," Harry said. "I might not have left the table. And you'd be lying out there in the alley, passed out. You did, you know? Pass out, I mean. Right after you took them down and took their money."

"You drank and you drove?"

"Guess so."

"You don't look like a stupid kid. If you knew you were gonna drink, you don't drive there. You get someone that isn't going to drink to drive you. Or you walk. Sobers some folks up. That's what I do. I walk home."

"For someone who robbed three fellas, I don't know if you should be giving advice."

"I'm hell on advice, just not too good at following it. This Joey, this friend of yours, guess I owe him too."

"Naw. Not really. I mean, he helped get you to the car. But he wanted to leave you. Figured it was your problem."

"He's not all wrong, kid. I'm a drunk, plain and simple."

Tad lay down on the pallet, doubled the pillow over, stuck it under his head, crossed his hands over his chest. "I don't go a night I'm not ripped."

"That must be tough on your career."

"I don't have a career. I have what you might call a trust fund, or something like that. I don't know. Stock market, never understood it. They send me a little check each month. I made some investments before I was a drunk. They've panned out, though it isn't much. Pays the bills, keeps me in beer and whiskey."

"What did you used to do?"

"I taught martial arts."

"No shit?"

"No shit, kid, and I was a thing of beauty. Not like now."

"What I saw was pretty amazing. Never seen anything like it. It wasn't a bunch of jumping around and yelling. It was quick, to the point, and it looked like it hurt like hell."

"Sure it did. Thing is, if I wasn't a drunk, I wouldn't have been in that position. So you see, it's all my fault. Let me give you some of that advice I'm free about giving. Quit drinking. You might have some sort of chemical reaction makes you hooked, or DNA, or genetics. Whatever that shit is. Some people, they got the tendency, you see."

"You?"

"Nope. I can quit anytime I want. I just don't want to. It ain't genetics with me, kid. Not at all. Me, I'm a self-made man."

Harry didn't have classes that day, and no work schedule at the store, so he slept in. When he awoke, sat up on the couch, and rubbed his face, Tad was at the hot plate, making coffee.

"Couldn't find any coffee filters," he said, "so I used one of your socks."

"What?"

"Just fucking with you. I used some napkins. Coffee might be a bit strong for you. Wasn't sure how you liked it. I ate one of your snack bars, which, by the way, taste like solidified chicken shit, and I left you one on the table there. No wonder you're so skinny, eating that crap. I bet you don't have a steady girlfriend either."

Harry shook his head. "No. I don't have time. I work part-time in the school bookstore, and go to school."

"Tell me you're out of high school."

"Of course, I'm twenty. I go to the university."

"Shit, I can't tell age anymore. Unless you're my age, you're a kid. What I like seeing is people older than me. I practically live for it. You gettin' any pussy?"

This question startled Harry. It was like an ambush.

"Now and again."

"Naw you ain't."

"Just said I was."

"Naw, you ain't gettin' any. Way you said it, I can tell, already told me you don't have a girlfriend."

"You can't tell shit."

"Let's try it again, kid. Are you gettin' any pussy?"

"No."

"There you are. Guy your age, you ought to be out there banging hole like there's no tomorrow. Later on you'll wish you had."

"Hole?"

"Pretty nasty, huh?"

"I'll say."

"Hell, boy, when you're my age it isn't nasty, it's just colorful."

"Well, what about you? You asked me, so now I'm asking you. You getting any?"

"No. I don't think about it much anymore. Just when they have a swimsuit special on TV. Most of the time I think about other things."

"What do you think about?"

"Actually, I wish a lot."

"About what?"

"I wish my wife wasn't dead, that's what I wish. I wish my son wasn't dead. That's what I wish."

Harry let that go, said, "I had a girlfriend, but she got religion. She was a lot more fun when she didn't have it. Though, I guess the truth was, I didn't really care all that much for her, and she wasn't all that enraptured with me either."

"Religion sure can fuck you up."

"She let me feel her up good, but anything other than that, she wasn't into. God didn't mind titty rubbing, I guess. But the other stuff, that wasn't on his okay list."

"He's quite the stickler. But it matters who it's with and what it means. Before I married Dorothy, I had girlfriends, and I had one that got religion now and then. Mostly between fucks, but then she'd get the remorse, you know. Jesus this, Jesus that. But after a time, Jesus, he'd take a nap or somethin', and I'd get a trip to the cavern."

"You sound very romantic."

"I can fool you, kid."

"You're not thinking you're gonna move in or nothing, are you?"

"This shithole? You got to be yankin' me. Might as well take up nesting in a buffalo's butt. . . . How long has that roach in the corner been dead?"

"I think he's just patient."

"He's dead. Been that way for a while. Ants have been at him. They're at him now. You'll be covered in them, you don't get some spray or somethin'."

Harry got up. He was wearing the clothes of the night before. Tad said, "You need to get you some pajamas, sleep in your underwear or something. Sweat on your clothes ain't good for you. Makes you stink."

"It's not a habit. I even take showers."

Harry took the snack bar off the table and dragged up the chair he had placed by the pallet. Tad sat down on the couch.

"About that pussy," Tad said. "You got to be careful these days, you can get the disease. That's what rubbers are for. They ought to pass those things out free."

"Some places do."

"Unless the place has got Jesus. Then it's a crime to keep your dick from falling off. You ain't supposed to do it, you're some big high-muckety-muck Christian, but hey, people fuck. It's what we do. Ever notice how Christians quote the Old Testament more than the New Testament? That's so they can say mean things, talk bad about the queers and such. New Testament, that's the Christian book. The stuff in red, that's the Jesus talk. That's what they're supposed to live their life by, but, no, they like the God of the Old Testament, the mean, judgmental one, before he was on Zoloft. Noticed that?"

"You're quite the intellectual."

"You're seeing my sober side. Look quick. I don't stay this way long."

14

Harry was surprised, because the neighborhood he drove Tad to was pretty nice.

Correction.

It was damn nice.

Fact was, the place was ritzy.

Harry thought Tad must have bought his place before it all got built up. Must have some little house tucked away amongst all the expensive stuff. A yard with a tree and a run-down house and a car on blocks. Maybe some beer cans tossed about. A dead cat under a bush.

Tad said, "Pull over to the curb."

"You got to puke?"

"No. This is home."

"Here?"

"Yeah."

Home was large, adobe style, and around the house was a high brick fence. There was a gate drive. The gate was open, and oak and sweet gum trees grew high and shady around the house, which covered a lot of ground.

"You have an apartment in the back?"

"They let me sleep in the yard, under a tree."

"What?"

"It's mine. Even the fence."

"Damn."

"You haven't seen my housekeeping yet. Hey, you want to come in, have a Coke, some more coffee, somethin'?"

"I guess."

"Well, I won't get out here then. Take a right, go up the drive."

"There never were any murders in this house, were there?"

"What?"

"Murders? Any violence?"

Tad studied Harry. "You're serious?"

"Yeah. Kind of am."

"I don't know of any. Wife's family property, got the place when we were twenty-five. Her folks lived here before, but I never heard of such. They may have had some vicious games of Go Fish, however."

Harry drove through the open gate onto the estate. Inside they had a Coke. They sat at a long table in a large room. On one end of the table was a pile of books; the other end held a collection of crumpled beer cans. There were beautiful carpets hanging on the wall, some pretty snazzy paintings that appeared to be of . . . well, they were of colors. If they were supposed to be of anything in particular, Harry couldn't make them out.

One wall had a shelf of knickknacks, little ceramic animals: elephants, tigers, lions, bears. They ranged from pink to green to blue.

The place was dusty, and there were clothes thrown about the floor.

"You are a shitty housekeeper," Harry said.

"My wife was great. She called in the maid. Me, I had to let her go. The maid, I mean. About ten years back. I take out the trash and toss out paper plates and such. Live kind of like you do. Mostly I stay in this room. It was the family room. There's a television behind that wall. Sliding panel and all. I think it still works. Fact is, except for the toilet and a room or two, I'm not sure I remember what all the other rooms are like."

"Except, you have a lot of rooms."

"Twenty rooms, to be exact, not counting kitchens and bathrooms. And the dojo."

"Dojo?"

"Japanese word. Gym. Workout room for martial arts. I used to teach it. An art called Shen Chuan."

"What happened?"

"Life happened. About that murder business—why'd you ask?"

"You wouldn't want to know, and if I told you, you'd think I was nuts."

"Maybe I would, but what else you got to do? What do you care if some drunk you don't even know thinks you're nuts? And it would be entertaining to me. Nuts tell good stories."

"You tell me about you, and I'll tell you about me."

"I didn't want to play fair," Tad said. "Just wanted to hear about you."

"Then no deal."

Tad nodded.

"All right, kid. I'm not sure why I'm telling you, but, okay. Maybe I owe you one. . . . Naw, bullshit. I need to talk about it. I talk to the fucking wall, no one's here. And, except for you, no one has been here in years. Except an old parrot named Chester. Belonged to my wife. I was one happy motherfucker when that feathered bastard died. Was always cleaning out shitty newspapers from his cage and such. There's lots of things I miss, but that parrot ain't one of 'em."

"Your life story is about taking care of a parrot?"

"Let me put it this way, kid. Back when I was a little older than you, I was a drunk."

"You're a drunk now."

"True, but let me tell my story, all right? So I was a drunk. And then I met my wife. This woman, she was so beautiful she made my back teeth ache. Oh, there were probably more beautiful women, but for me, she was it. Before her I was just banging tail. Wasn't lying to anyone to get it. Just dating, doin' the thing, you know. It was the seventies. There was so much free pussy it was like money from home. Then I met Dorothy. I loved that woman deeply, my friend. I don't know how often that happens, that kind of love, but when it does, it's an amazing thing."

"My mom and dad. They were that way."

"They're lucky. . . . Were?"

"Dad died of a heart attack."

"Well, me and your mom, we got similar tragedies. But me and Dorothy got married, I quit drinking, and we had a boy. A fine boy. Dorothy had an inheritance, and she worked as an interior decorator. She was good. She made big dough doing that. Me, I had a martial arts school, and though it wasn't the sort of thing that would make you wealthy, it was a good living. Believe it or not, boy, I was once considered one of the best."

"I believe it. I seen you do it, remember?"

"That was some drunk shit, but back then I was deep in the martial arts. Not just the ass-whipping part. I found my center."

"Your center?"

"The center of my being. That sounds all metaphysical and shit, but it isn't. It's about finding the core of who you are, living with it, learning to accept it, and becoming calm. Like you're the eye of the hurricane, and all around you the world is a-spin, but you're focused. Nothing fazes you. That's how I was. Nothing fazed me. I didn't think anything or anyone could disrupt my center."

"But something always can," Harry said.

Tad nodded. "Way I worked is I had small classes, some private lessons. People who wanted to be here and were willing to pay me what I was worth. Then there was the accident. Day it happened, I had a private lesson, a beautiful young woman. There was nothing between us. No monkey business, outside of that feeling any man gets when he's around a woman that amazing. I mean, it was just great to be with her. Nothing like my wife, that was a whole 'nother thing. But teaching that woman . . . well, one day her hour is up, her private lesson is over, and she's got a few questions, and so I say to myself, 'All right, I'll stick.'

"Now, you see, I'm supposed to, right after that lesson, go and pick up my wife and son. He was ten then. It was a Saturday, and they went to the movies, some cartoon thing, and the deal was, soon as my lesson was over, I was supposed to go get them.

"They had about a fifteen-minute wait between the time of the movie being over and my lesson ending up here. Wife's car, it was in the shop. No big deal. Fifteen-minute wait, fifteen minutes for me to drive over; they got thirty minutes to kill.

"But me, I'm talking to this woman like I'm trying to pick her up, and I'm not, you see. My wife was it, but I wanted to see if I still had the old charm. You know, if I had some appeal, 'cause then I was in my mid-thirties, starting to lose a bit of hair, and no matter how hard I worked, no matter how good I was at Shen Chuan, I was getting a bit of a pouch, you know."

Tad patted his belly as if to prove it.

"So, I'm chatting up the young thing, and I realize suddenly, Damn, I've forgotten about Dorothy and John. But you know what? I think, well, another five minutes isn't going to hurt. Because I'm explaining some special moves to this gal, nothing she's ready to do, really, but it's fun to show my stuff, you know. Show what I got. And finally I think: Shit, I got to go, so I do.

"Dorothy called the house. I didn't know this until later, 'cause there's no phone in the dojo. Later, I see the phone light blinking, turn it on, and it's Dorothy. 'Honey, are you okay? We're waiting, and I'm a little worried.' Worried. She was worried. About me. I should have been there, and she's worried something happened to me. And me, I'm chattin' up poontang like I'm on the hustle, just to keep the old ego polished.

"So later I learn they went to the little café next to the theater, had a Coke, something like that. They came outside to see if I'd made it yet, and a truck—this is like something out of a bad fucking movie— but a truck, a fucking dump truck full of gravel, going down the main drag, not where it should have been hauling that shit, makes a corner too fast and turns over. It doesn't hit my family. But the gravel does. Like thousands of little bullets.

"When I got there, they were under it, kid. Under all that god- damn gravel. Someone says, 'There's a woman and a kid under that shit,' and I knew . . . knew it was them. Started trying to dig them out with my bare hands. On top of that fucking pile digging like a goddamn dog. People all around helping."

"I'm sorry."

Tad held up a hand. "Let me get to the bottom of it, kid. They were dead. My fault. Had I been on time, they wouldn't have been there when that truck came around. They'd have been fine. Just gravel on the sidewalk. They were the only ones standing in that spot. Can you believe that? Just the wrong place at the wrong time. Standing there. Waiting on it.

"You want some fucking schmaltz, now. You want the shit they put in the cheap fucking movies? John, my boy, he had a card in his pocket. Wasn't Father's Day, wasn't Christmas, wasn't my fucking birthday. But at school he made a card with his own hands. I still have it. It says, 'World's best dad.' Cops gave it to me later. All crum- pled and shit, but it's my most prized possession. Is that schmaltz, kid? Is that the shit?

"I began to lose my center. I thought it was just the pain at first, and a year later I'm trying to pull it all together, reestablish my classes. The young woman I was talking to, one I was trying to impress, she wanted to come back, but I couldn't do it. Couldn't look at that woman again. It's not that she did anything. I did something. Let my ego loose. That's about the first thing you learn in martial arts. Put your ego in a sack and take a stick to it. I just couldn't do it, couldn't see her again, or anyone else I knew.

"Got all new people. Started being too rough. Hurting people. If they fought back hard, I hurt them more. I quit teaching. I didn't need the money. My wife had money, and now it was mine. I was all alone. No wife. No son. No students. The in-laws hated me, as they should have.

"I took to the bottle. So here I am. Sober for the moment. Thinking about a drink. Seeing you, all drunk like me when I was young, I got to think, is it just fun with you, or is it something else? I think it's something else."

Harry didn't know what to say, so he said what he had said before. "I'm really sorry."

"Yeah. Me too. But what about you? What about that drinking? What's your story?"

"You wouldn't believe me if I told you."

"We had a deal."

"Okay." And Harry told him about the honky-tonk, about the old car when he was a kid. When he finished, he said, "Now what do you think?"

Tad studied him, scratched behind his ear. "Sounds, huh?" Tad said.

"Yeah."

"That's some weird shit."

"You think I'm nuts?"

"I've heard some say we've lost abilities over the centuries, since we crawled out of the primordial soup. Things like extrasensory perception, the ability to smell a female in heat from a mile away, a prehensile tail, an inordinate love of bananas. Maybe you rediscovered some of it. Or maybe you're just fucking nuts. Ever been dropped on your head? I'm serious now. You been dropped, you know of?"

"No."

"Hit with something?"

Harry shook his head. "The mumps, like I told you. That's it."

"Do they cause brain damage, the mumps?"

Harry sighed.

"You got to let go of that booze," Tad said. "Trust me on that, kid. Follow my advice, even if I don't take it."

"You don't believe me, do you?"

"What happened to me, happened. This shit about the sounds, I don't know. I'd ask your mother about being dropped, that's what I'd do. Get some specialist. Somebody knows about the brain, can get in there with a cutter, the pliers, fucking tire tool and a truck jack. Whatever it takes. Maybe you're schizo. It's no crime. It's a condition. You got it, you didn't ask for it. Just showed up, and now you got to deal with it, and the way you do that, you see a doctor."

"I've seen them. They can't help me. I live with this every day, and it's not schizophrenia, and I wasn't dropped on my goddamn head."

"Don't shit yourself. Just said it could be something like that."

"Let me tell you something. When I first found my apartment, I went over every inch, stomping, slamming doors, whacking the walls, scraping the chairs, seeing if there was, so to speak, a ghost in the machine. None. That's why I live in that shithole. Not just to save money, but because I'm certain there's nothing lurking inside it.

"Just to make sure I didn't miss some spot, I taped cardboard and egg cartons all over the walls. Didn't want to drive tacks—afraid I might find a spot, you see. A spot holding some disaster. Hear what I'm saying, Tad?"

"Loud and clear."

"I don't even go to my friend's Joey's bathroom. You want to know why?"

"Sure, kid. Lay it out."

"I was in his shitter, doing my business, stood up after the wiping, and my pants, which were still around my knees, caught the toilet lid, popped it up and down, and there was this guy in the sound, and I could see him sitting on that toilet long before Joey was renting the place. He had a sawed-off shotgun under his chin. I just clicked the goddamn toilet cover, the one with the hole in it, one you sit on—"

"Yeah, I got you."

"Clicked that with the back of my pants, and I see him, the sawed-off under his chin, and he pulls the trigger. Blood and brains and skull everywhere. The sound of that gun going off in that small space . . . it was deafening.

"Why did I see him? Why? Because he's getting ready to do it, his pants around his ankles, and he rose up a bit and clicked that fucking lid. When he did, he pulled the trigger and the lid snapped down again, holding the sounds. Can you believe that?"

"I'm working on it."

"It's enough to drive you crazy."

"You may already have taken the trip, kid. Relax."

"I looked it up. This suicide. I'm a bear on research because of this stuff. But I looked it up in newspapers, on the Internet, and sure enough, a guy killed himself there. Despondent over a breakup with his wife, something like that. I never told Joey. Just don't use his bathroom. I'm over there, and I got to go, I hold it. Fact is, I try not to even visit unless I'm drunk.

"This research I do—because of it, I know every spot on campus, around campus, where there has been a major car accident, where anyone was killed or even badly injured. I got a notebook in my back pocket, got it all written there, if I ever need to be sure."

Harry pulled the notebook from his pocket, tossed it on the table. Tad picked it up, flicked it open, glanced at it. There was writing and little crude maps drawn inside.

"Pretty detailed," Tad said.

"I wear soft-soled shoes, rubber tipped. That way, I hit some stone wall with my shoe where there was a car wreck, step hard on some spot where someone was thrown clear of a wreck, I don't activate it. Trapped memories can be anywhere. You wouldn't believe how many rapes there have been on campus. People don't report them all."

"So," Tad said, "it's like someone gets hurt, they touch something, the sounds, the whole event is in what they touch?"

"No. Woman gets slammed violently against a jukebox, that records. Guy kills himself in a toilet, and the lid clicks as the gun goes off, that records. Not only the sound. Not only the event. The emotions. Sometimes I get echoes from the original sounds. Reverberations. Old images . . . only I'm not so sure they're images. It's like . . . there are ghosts. Spirits. Not religious bullshit, but some bit of something left over from when they were alive. Their emotions. I feel it, and I can hardly shake it."

"I want to believe you, but—"

"It's amazing how much violence there is in the world. Sometimes it's just a kind of mind bump, a push, a sound and color flash, and it's gone. Not always something big-time serious. But it's there, and I can hardly go anywhere without coming up against it."

"You got a point, kid."

"The world is full of it, stuffed with it. And it's not just the hidden stuff. I got to deal with that, then I got to deal with what everyone else hears as well. All the anger and meanness. It's in the music. Fuck this, motherfucker that, kill this one, fuck that one. Death to cops and queers and women. If it's not the music, it's the way people talk to one another. It's the goddamn talk shows, the political shows, all that arguing. Never stops. And you want to know why I drink? Why I won't stop?"

When Harry finished talking, he slid down in the chair and took a deep breath. He had almost worn himself out.

Tad studied him for a moment, said, "Kid, you ever go to a real city, not some burg like here, some big place like Houston, someplace like that, and this sound shit is real, or you even think it's real, you're gonna have the top of your head blow off."

15

Harry drove home, wondering why he had told Tad about it, this problem he had. It wasn't something he talked about anymore, not since Joey and the doctors thought he was crazy. His mom too, though she would never say such a thing. And now he had told this guy.

But it was different. He didn't know Tad, really, so it didn't matter what he thought. This way he got to rant, get it off his chest. Tad would just write him off as a nutter, go back to the bottle.

They would be drunk nutters together in different places.

Something like that.

Harry had a full day to kill, and he killed it studying, when he could concentrate. But he spent a lot of time thinking, thinking about Tad and his family, the way the old man had whipped the shit out of those thugs out back of the bar, whipped them while drunk, took their money and didn't even know it.

He believed Tad didn't remember taking the money. Believed it wasn't so much robbery as irony. An object lesson for assholes.

He tried to concentrate on his psychology book, but a shadow fell over him and the page went dim. He looked up to see night come early. Or so it seemed. It was a rain cloud, and it filled the room until it was black as a wedge of chocolate on chocolate.

Harry sat back, didn't bother with the lights. The dark was pleasant. He could feel and taste the ozone in the air, could hear the wind picking up, the rain pounding lightly on the roof, then he heard it grow heavy, as if the drops were full of lead.

He got up, pulled back the curtain, and looked out. There was a bit of light in the shadow, and he could see big balls of hail. Lightning tore at the darkness like an angry child ripping at paper.

He thought about his car as he listened to the hail hit. There wasn't any kind of garage; place didn't have one. But he thought maybe the big oaks on either side of the drive would protect it some. Not that it was anything special, anything to be proud of, any kind of chick wagon. It was a brown car of nondescript nothingness.

He hoped at least the hail wouldn't crack the windshield.

The ice came down hard and beat on the roof, and some of it clattered against the glass. Harry tried to figure if there was any way some horror could be trapped in the sound made by the hunks of ice; if in their impact on the roof there was an event, colorful and loud and terrible, just waiting to leap out. What if there was a guy drowned in a lake, thrashed and screamed and slapped the water a lot before he went under; say later some water evaporated, became rain, or hail—could that hold the memory?

No, that was too much. The water would have been transformed; wouldn't happen. He hoped.

Harry moved back a bit, and it was a good thing. A ball of hail struck the glass near the windowsill, broke through, came bouncing into the room, rolling across the floor, sprinkling glass, shedding ice slivers. It came to a stop between his feet.

He picked it up. It was cold and firm. Felt like a small baseball found in morning-dew grass. He took it into the bathroom, dropped it into the sink to let it melt. That cold touch made him think about a cold beer. He had a few in the little refrigerator. But he decided against it.

A thing the old man had said, about the drinking. It stuck with him. How did it go exactly? Something about being a self-made man.

Yeah. That was it. A self-made man. Tad said he was a self-made man, a self-made drunk.

Tad told him he was driving the same road.

Harry tore off the edge of a cardboard box and got some tape and taped the cardboard over the hole in the window. Maybe the landlord would fix it.

He got a broom out of the bathroom, where it leaned against the edge of the shower frame, swept the glass onto a piece of firm paper, picked it up, and tossed it in the garbage can.

Harry moved his chair to the center of the room and sat listening to the summer hail. It slammed against the house for about fifteen minutes, subsided. Then there was a slice of light in the darkness, and it slipped through the curtains and filled the room.

Harry didn't move.

He sat and listened, and the last of the hail, smaller now, passed, followed by a smattering of rain, then it too was gone, and the light outside grew brighter yet and he could see clearly in the room.

He sat in the chair and listened.

There was nothing now, not even cars out on the road in front of the house.

There was only silence and sunlight, and he sat in the warmth of the light and listened to the nothingness of silence for as long as it lasted.

16

"The Beast in Me" sung by Johnny Cash was playing on the FM station as Harry drove to campus. He thought, the beast is not in me. It's out there, and I let it in from time to time. A beast belonging to others. That's the rub. It's not even my beast.

As Harry drove he navigated according to his knowledge of "bad places." He felt he was safe in the car if he stayed out on the road. He had never had one of his experiences just driving on the road, but he thought it could happen. Maybe hit a pothole where some tire had hit and blown and the car had gone off the road. If driving into a pothole frightened someone enough, it might be recorded, because things were like sponges when it came to fear; they soaked it up and held it.

And he squeezed it out.

God, was there anyone else in the world with this problem?

He couldn't be the only one.

He drove onto campus and found a spot. When he got out of the car he slung his backpack over his shoulder, locked the car door, and started walking, keeping himself aware of where "things" had happened, at least the ones he knew about.

He had a path he always took, and he knew it was a safe path.

He'd worked it out, followed it for weeks, and nothing had leaped out of the architecture at him, off of the sidewalk.

He avoided touching anything as he walked.

This way he knew he was safe.

Which was why, on this Wednesday morning, he was so upset. The path he usually took was blocked.

Construction. The sidewalk was torn up and there were barriers all about, big, burly men working at banging up the concrete with jackhammers and the like.

For a moment Harry just stood and stared.

Blocked.

Can't go my route.

Shit.

He thought all manner of things, but none of them were any good.

Like trying to go under the wooden barriers and weave his way through the workmen.

He figured that wouldn't work out. It would only cause him to possibly be part of a violent moment himself, though, in his own estimation, that was easier to handle. You couldn't see what was happening to yourself, only feel it. It was seeing their faces, feeling their terror that made him crazy.

He slipped his backpack off his shoulder, laid it on the ground, got his notepad out of his back pocket, studied it.

All right. He could go left, then skirt around all this business, but he didn't know that territory. Most likely, as was the case with much territory, it would be safe. Nothing hidden.

But you never knew. It was always a struggle.

Shit, he told himself, you go to bars. You do that, and they're worse places to go than a college campus.

But they've got the beer. Enough of that, I'm okay.

It would be easier to blow it all off, buy a twelve-pack, take it home, sit in the dark inside the tested room with the cardboard and egg cartons on the wall.

There had been a rape in the bushes on the right. He had found that out by shaking the shrubs, just passing through, grabbing at them idly, shaking them, going from sunlight to late night and seeing it all, her hand clutching at the shrubs. Some girl coming back from the library most likely. Some guy she knew thought she owed him a piece, and decided to take it.

He had never found any record of it being reported.

The guy got away with it.

Son of a bitch.

From the way they were dressed, or almost dressed, it looked to have happened way back. The seventies, perhaps. Maybe she never told anyone. Maybe the guy bragged about it. Did it again.

Don't think about that now.

Not now.

You can't undo the past. It's not even your past.

He studied the notepad awhile, mapped out some safe spots. Problem was, he had to go over uncharted territory to get to those known safe spots. Anything could happen.

He put up the notebook, grabbed his backpack, and went left.

17

Harry sat down and wrote:

Tad, I'm not drinking.

Right now.

I didn't drink last night either.

And already good things have come to me.

For one thing, when I woke up this morning I didn't have a headache and feel like forty miles of bad road.

I know you haven't been sitting up nights, between drunks, thinking about me, worrying if I was drinking, but there was no one else I could tell but you.

No one else I could turn to.

Well, there are others. I could tell Joey, but he's a dick and wouldn't get it. And my mom, but she's got enough worries. And there's a special reason I'm writing you.

I want to stop drinking.

No, that's not true. I like drinking. I need to stop drinking. That's different.

You see, I don't really think I drink to forget, like you. I drink to numb, so I won't have, you know, the experiences.

Okay. I drink to forget as well. I've seen some bad business, stuff to do with the ghosts in the noise.

But I've told you that.

Let me put it like this: You haven't always been as fucked-up as you are now. Me, I've been pretty much like I am always: insecure, worried, and confused since I was a kid.

My parents didn't do it.

The sounds did.

I'm not going to tell you what I already told you, and I'm not going to try to convince you I'm not a fruitcake (I'm not, by the way), but I am going to say it again.

You haven't always been so fucked-up.

Me, I have. For a long time.

You once had a center.

Before the mumps, as a little kid, maybe I was centered. I don't know for sure.

Maybe when my mom and I used to watch cartoons out the windows, watch them at the drive-in theater across the way. I might have had a center then.

Shit. I don't remember if I told you about all that. The drive-in and stuff. But it's unimportant. It's not the point.

What I'm saying is this.

I want to find my center.

You know how to do that.

Maybe we can help each other. You can relocate yours, and I can find mine.

And there's a real special reason I want to do this. Something wonderful happened to me today, Tad. Something fucking extraordinary. I haven't felt this way since I was a teenager and Kayla, my neighbor, gave me a kiss, and I thought, at least for a moment, I was Emperor of the Universe.

With a gearshift.

Think on that one.

But this feeling, I'm crazy with it. I'm consumed with it. I'm on fire with it. I'm covered up in it and eaten up by it.

I'm talking about love here, Tad.

The arrow through the heart, my man. Cupid's straight shot.

It's what I've always wanted.

And you know what? She might even like me.

Here's what happened.

Dig this. Because of construction, I have to walk around my usual path. For me, this is a BIG FUCKING DEAL. No shit. A big deal. I'm like Superman doing this, taking a different route, because the world—again, for me—is full of all kinds of uncomfortable surprises.

It's like a world filled with dog doo and I've got to thread my way around it blindfolded. Only the dog doo, it's not just messy, it explodes, and I see—

Again, been over all that.

But this construction thing, this holdup, this snag, this snafu . . . Guess what? I gird my loins, and—

I do it.

I go around the construction that's messing up my path, and nothing happens. I didn't really expect anything, but you never know. Stuff is out there lurking.

So I'm moving along, you know, preoccupied, and as I go, guess what happens?

I get knocked down.

That's right. I'm going into the building, to my class, running up the steps, almost to the top, head down, and the door blows open, and bam, I'm knocked on my ass.

Fortunately, no one has taken a beating there before, so my rolling over the steps doesn't excite anything in the stone, and I wonder if, in that sudden moment of surprise, or fear of falling, if my own thoughts are registering there, and would I be able to read them, wondering all that while

I'm falling, see, and I'm pissed too, because all I was trying to do was go to class, and someone has thoughtlessly and carelessly knocked me on my ass, and then—

You know what, Tad? All of a sudden, I'm not wondering about any of that stuff at all.

Because, what they say about there being angels, and how they show up in times of need, at least for some people, it's all true.

An angel was looking down at me.

I'm at the bottom of the steps, on my back, legs almost over my head, my pack has slipped off, and the books have come out, and there's a paper of mine twisting in the wind over my face, and as it floats down past me, it's replaced with the face of that angel I was telling you about.

A really good-looking angel, but with features that are, well, a little devilish. A really fine mouth, thick lips, and you know what some anthropologists say—the reason women with full lips are attractive is that the lips, they remind us of those other lips, down there; and man, maybe that's true. And her hair, it was black, black, black, and long, long, long, the eyes, big doe eyes, and she's leaning over me, and she's just absolutely fucking gorgeous. And I'm trying not to look down her shirt, which is hard, because she's right there bending over me, and she looks so frightened, and those breasts are banging together like two wrecking balls.

She says, "Oh, shit. Are you all right?"

"Sure," I say, and I'm witty, Tad, get this, I really said this, said: "The concrete broke my fall."

She grinned.

Let me tell you. She has the most beautiful teeth you have ever seen. A brand-new piano doesn't have ivory like that.

Nice teeth.

She puts out a hand, and I take it, and she helps pull me up (strong girl), and I grin at her, and she says, "Really, you okay?"

I tell her, "Yeah, I'm fine. You ought to see how I look when I jump out of a plane without a parachute."

Okay, I was reaching. But it wasn't bad, and she laughed a little, and she started helping me pick up my books and recover my papers, put them in my backpack.

Then she sees the papers.

She says, "You got old man Timpson for Psychology."

"Oh, yeah," I say.

"Well, I'll tell you a little something: He talks stuff in class, but if you take notes, it doesn't do you that much good."

"I'm finding that out."

"Yeah, he gives tests on the book. You can forget his lectures. Read the book from cover to cover, and that's the test."

"Really?"

"Oh, yeah."

Now I'm really looking at her, Tad, and she's got on some really tight jeans, and there are no bulges. She looks like a model. A movie star. A goddess.

"Well," she says, and she's really smiling at me all the time she's saying this, "I'd take you out for coffee, to make up for the fall, but I don't want to keep you from class."

And you know what, Tad? I'm thinking, she kind of likes me. Maybe I'm not too ugly after all. You know, maybe I'm all right. And I think, what the hell, and say, "I've been known to miss a class now and then. Especially since I know now the tests come from the book."

So now get this. I go over with her to the student lounge, not even thinking about places that might hide bad memories, bad moments, and she buys me coffee. Two creams, no sugar, Sweet'n Low. We take our coffee just alike.

I know. It's a little thing. But it's a start. I'm beginning to get a sense of things here. I'm feeling comfortable.

And we talk.

We've got a lot in common, Tad.

The coffee business. It was a good sign.

We talked until I missed all of that class, and then the next, and she looks up, glances at her watch, shrieks. She's missed a class too. She had one during the next hour. So I've missed two and she's missed one, and she says, "Well, we're screwed now. Why don't we just go to lunch?"

I'm thinking, you know, we'd go there, on campus, but we walk out to her car—and here's a big flash: I'm not even thinking about the bad places. Not even once. I'm thinking about her. Hanging on her every word.

And she's smart, Tad. Did I say that? Smart. I can tell by the way she talks. She's not some airhead.

But we get in her car, which is some cool ride, by the way, brand-new, and we go to lunch at Cecil's. You know the place. Kind of nice. Nothing fancy, but the food's good, and when we finish I'm worried about the money, see, but I've got just enough to pay for us both, but she says, "No. I still owe you for that fall. You get the next."

And she pays, Tad.

Well, there's not much to tell after that.

She dropped me off at my car, said, "See you," but it wasn't a dismissive kind of "see you," 'cause I got her name and phone number, and let me tell you her name. It's Talia McGuire. Isn't that just the coolest name?

Talia.

I like saying it and I like writing it. Talia.

So I don't want to be a drunk like you.

I don't want you to be a drunk anymore like me.

I want us both to quit. I want you to teach me how to find my center while you find yours.

P.S. I hope this letter doesn't embarrass you too much. I know looking it over, I feel a little queasy.

Help.

18

That evening Harry drove over to Tad's, parked at the curb, went to the front door. There was a letter slot there. He took a folded envelope out of his back pocket, looked at it.

On the front he had written in big block letters: *TAD*.

He slipped the letter through the slot and turned away.

Inside the house, Tad, drinking a beer from the can, heard the letter slide in.

He went to the door, looked out the peephole.

Nothing.

He went to the window.

He watched Harry's back as he walked away briskly.

Tad started to go to the door, call out to him.

But didn't.

He feared it might interrupt his drinking.

He put the envelope on the table, sat in a chair at the dining room table, and kept sipping at his beer, considered when he should break out the whiskey, maybe get some Kleenex, shell the old corncob.

Nah. All that drinking. It would be too limp.

He might just watch some TV.

Course, he had already gotten up once to go to the door, see who was out there. Getting up twice, he had to give that some consideration.

You didn't want to overdo it, this getting up business. Not when you had drinking to do.

Besides, the channel changer was far. He had left it in the kitchen. Why he had been carrying the channel changer around was beyond him, but from the dining room table, he could see it lying on the counter. Waiting for him.

"Come get me, Tad," it called.

Course, he got it, then he had to find the TV.

He looked at the envelope on the table.

If he opened it, he might get a paper cut. Might be best just to let it lie, call in the paper cut squad, have them open it for him.

Was there such a thing?

Really ought to be.

A whole team, glove wearing, so they could open letters and not get cut, a bunch who would do it for someone didn't want to take the chance.

A paper cut, it could be downright annoying.

Under certain circumstances it could even get infected and you could die.

He patted the letter and let it lie.

Tad took a long drag on his beer, held the can up, said, "Yee-haw. Ain't life grand."

19

Harry went over to Joey's that night. He was surprised at himself for doing it, but the girl, the fine girl, Talia, had emboldened him. Still, he thought he'd stay out of the toilet, make sure he was drained good before he went over. Didn't want to go there and have his new confidence shaken by the rattling of a toilet lid.

Joey's place wasn't much worse than his own, actually. It was down a back alley behind some buildings that looked like a place where Death might go to die. The alley smelled of urine and vomit, and there was a drunk or a bum or a drunk bum always laid out against the wall on a piece of cardboard. It was his home, that stretch of concrete, that piece of cardboard, or one like it. When it rained he was somewhere else, but most nights, when it was warm, he was here.

How'd a guy end up that way, sleeping in an alley on cardboard? How could something like that happen?

Harry went past the bum, carefully up the rickety stairs that led to the second floor where Joey's apartment was. There was a porch of sorts up there, and a bug-swarmed dim light by the entrance. The bulb was on and there was a knife-thin slit of light sliding out from under the door. Harry knocked.

"Who is it?" Joey said. The walls were so thin it sounded as if Joey were out on the landing with him.

Harry answered, and Joey let him in. There wasn't much to the place, and like his joint, there wasn't even a bed. Joey had a foldout couch he had quit folding out months ago. Now he just slept on the couch, same way Harry did. The air smelled funny. A mixture of boiled soup, alcohol, and jack-off juice. There was a kind of stink from the bathroom as well. Which was all the better reason not to go in there.

The lightbulb, a single job in the center of the room in a dusty glass cover, had a greasy quality to it, and it gave the room the feel of a cell.

Joey was in his skivvies. His short, skinny body looked even more emaciated than usual. His ribs poked at his skin as if they really belonged on the outside. His black hair was twisted up on top of his head in what looked like a midnight rooster's comb.

Joey dropped down on the couch, scratched his balls, said, "What's up?"

"Nothing, just thought I'd drop by."

"Midnight?"

"Shit. Is it that late? I had no idea. Believe it or not, I thought it was, like, eight, nine maybe."

"No, it's fucking midnight."

"Hey, I'll go."

"Naw. Couldn't sleep anyway. Was trying to jack off, but I couldn't imagine a pretty sheep. Sit down."

There were two chairs and a table with sugar packets under one leg to balance it. Harry took one of the chairs and sat, cautiously.

"You didn't come over here this time of night just to hang out, did you? Shit, you ain't come here in a coon's age. We're always at your place, or the bar. Which reminds me, weren't we supposed to meet there?"

"We didn't say that."

"You always get drunk on the night after school, sleep in the free day, work in the afternoon. . . . Hey, how's the job?"

"For ten hours a week, it's okay. I like bookstores. But I'd like more hours."

"Well, I got more hours than you do, times four, and I don't like it much. You build enough mobile homes, you sort of get so you see one parked somewhere, you want to get out and rub dog shit on it. I hate them sons a' bitches. You saw how cheap they was made, you would too."

"Yeah, well, I could use some hours."

"You, you'll get through college and make something of yourself. Me and the rest of the winos will keep making mobile homes. I'm looking to fucking retire there, and I'm only twenty-two years old. You know what kind of future that is?"

"You could take some college courses."

"I'm about as good for school as you are for the women."

"Things change."

"You coming over here this time of night, looking like you look, kind of moony, I'm starting to think you might have got lucky and got you a piece," Joey said. "Am I in the box on that one, or were you in the box?"

"Nothing like that . . . It's not like that."

"It's always like that. You meet a girl, it's always about the business, you know? There's always the talk of love and romance and how we're gonna plan our life, but you get down to it, it's about the ol' dunkin' stick."

"It's not that way."

"Is it a girl?"

"Yes."

"Then it's that way."

Harry felt himself getting hot under the collar. "I just met her, and it is about romance. I think. I don't know, really. It's not like we're going steady."

"You stalkin' someone?"

"No. Hell, no."

"Lighten up, Harry. I'm kiddin'."

Harry began to think: This is a mistake. Joey, he's not the guy you open your heart to. Should know that by now.

"Who is it?" Joey asked.

"Her name is Talia. Talia McGuire."

"No shit. That gal?"

"You know her?"

"Seen her. Know who she is . . . Do you know who she is?"

"I've had coffee with her."

"You have, have you? Well, her old man, John McGuire, he's, like, a big dog in the oil business. He's got more money than a wild dog has fleas. Everybody wants to hump his leg. He owns the golf course where my old man works. He owns a mansion just back of the golf course, through the woods there. It's huge."

"No shit?"

"No shit. Man, Talia McGuire. You must have been fuckin' drunk when you met her, to think she's got anything going for you. She's a goddamn babe. I seen her wear a pair of pants tighter to her skin than a tattoo. When she walked, it looked like her thing was peelin' a peach. There ain't an ounce of fat on her, and all the meat that's there, it's sweet, dude. I'd give my left testicle to get a piece of that. So would you, but I wouldn't be cuttin' it off, buddy, 'cause you ain't gettin' none of that. That stuff, it's for the fraternity dudes, guys with money and fast cars, not that turd-brown piece of shit you drive."

"I'm not so bad."

"Hey, you're all right. I like you. You'll go to college, get a job, do okay. Buy a fuckin' Volvo. Do better than me. But Talia McGuire. Man, she's outta your fuckin' league, that's what I'm tryin' to tell you.

Me and her, I might as well be on Mars, but even if you and her are on the same planet, you're like, you know, Antarctica, and she's here. Hear what I'm sayin'? No use jerkin' you, and you endin' up all disappointed and shit. She's like some kind of goddess, and you're like a fuckin' goatherd. Hell, compared to her, you're the Elephant Man. And she's noted for fucking with people. It's what she does."

"You don't know that."

"Telling you what I've heard . . . She really had coffee with you?"

"Yes."

"What were the circumstances? You were in the cafeteria, you were both drinking coffee at the same time, at different tables?"

Harry told him all about it. When he finished, Joey said, "There you are. She felt sorry for you. She was being nice. She knocked you down. Probably didn't want you to sue. That would mean her daddy might have to shut down one of his about, oh, I don't know, ten zillion-million oil wells."

"Fuck you, Joey."

"Hey, man."

"It wasn't like that."

"Sure. Whatever you say. Doll like that, and you. Think about it. See what you come up with."

Harry got up so quick the chair fell over.

"Don't fuck the furniture up," Joey said.

"Yeah, it's so fine. Fuck you."

"Well, fuck you. Get out of my shithole, be it ever so humble. Get the fuck out."

Harry stomped out, and when he slammed the door the landing shook and the whole damn apartment vibrated and the light went out, and—

—there were all manner of flashes in his head, sounds, pictures, jump cuts of violence. Joey's place was full of it, and the place was so flimsy, the slamming of the door activated it all, and it came rushing into his noggin like a flood.

The shotgun under the chin, the guy on the toilet, an explosion, brains and blood and a yellow light, a glimpse of that overlapped with a woman being slapped, a man with a young woman bent over a couch—a different couch than Joey's—throwing the meat to her anus while she screamed—

A yell at a table, a man standing, grabbing up a plate of food, throwing it—

And the lights flicked inside his head like little atomic explosions, and the sounds grated and scratched and the screams all blended and the colors of violence ran together into a mural of darkness.

And as fast as it came to him, it went away.

Harry was less energetic going down, as the whole porch was starting to shake, and he felt as awkward as a man on wooden legs.

He went to the bar straightaway and started drinking. Some of what he was spending was for the water bill, but right then that seemed a long way off. He needed another kind of liquid refreshment right then.

The scrawny bastard was right, telling it like it was. A girl like Talia, a vision like that. She was taking pity on him. What would she want with him? Maybe she thought it was funny. Her sitting there slumming, and this guy drooling over her, trying to be cool, and her thinking: What a chump, and, isn't this fun, and, maybe I'll get close to him, let him smell—

What was it, the way she smelled, what was it?

Vanilla. That was it. She put vanilla behind her ears. He was sure of it. It was nice. It wasn't overdone like Kayla, and it didn't smell as good as Kayla, but it was good.

She had to be thinking: He leans toward me, that little hint of vanilla behind my ears, maybe I can get him to wet his pants. Wouldn't that be funny?

Poor country mouse with about three dollars and fifty cents in his pocket, give or take a nickel, wetting his pants over a girl who never even had to buy groceries, a beautiful girl, a magnificent girl, sitting there inside her fine clothes, laughing inside, thinking, what a loser. . . .

And she didn't know the half of it.

Didn't know about his superhearing, his constant blasts from the past, or that he had a bit of a drinking problem, and that right now he was dealing with his drinking problem by drinking, and pretty soon, he thought, I'll not only be numb to the sounds, I'll be numb to life.

And so he sat in the bar, all manner of talk going on around him, about this and that, how good a lay so-and-so is, and she's extra good because she swallows, and what about them damn Cowboys, couldn't they put together a good team, like the old days, and someone said, "You know, they're going to reinstate the draft," and someone said, "Yeah, we ought to just kill them all. We go all the way over there, give them freedom, sons a' bitches don't want it, ought to kill them all, just drop the big one," and someone else says, "Wouldn't Jesus be against that," and Harry kind of thinks he hears this guy being hit, puts his head on the table and thinks right before he passes out that it was him who said it.

20

Tad woke up certain that during the night a cat had shit in his mouth, but not owning any cats, he decided that, unless he left a window open somewhere, this wasn't likely.

He sat up in his bed, only to discover he wasn't in his bed.

He was under the dining room table, him and some empty glass and aluminum soldiers lying this way and that.

He managed to bump his head on the table bottom, as well as rattle his noggin by disturbing the cans and bottles around him. The sound of them being touched, moved, was loud in his head, and in that moment he thought:

What if that kid is telling the truth?

Maybe he does hear sounds.

And maybe, like me, he's just a drunk.

Either way, he's fucked-up. And if the sounds are real, he's double-screwed.

Tad crawled out from under the table, got to his feet, which only seemed to take about a week, made a quick wobble to the bathroom, got down on his knees, dunked his head over the toilet bowl and let it fly.

It was like his insides were going to come up with it, not to mention his balls.

Goddamn, he thought. I been drinking quite professionally for a long time, but I must have tied a good one on last night.

He vomited repeatedly.

When he finished, he noted there were drops of blood in the vomit.

Rawness from his throat.

That was it.

God, he hoped that was it.

He reached up, flushed, then fell back against the wall.

He sat that way until his brain came back down from outer space, bringing along with it an anvil that dropped right on top of his head. Using the toilet bowl as an aid, he got to his feet, wandered into the kitchen, got a beer out of the fridge, and sipped it.

Hair of the dog that bit him.

He stood by the refrigerator for a while, stumbled into the dining room, sat at the table.

In front of him was the note Harry had dropped off.

He read it.

"Shit," he said.

21

As Tad got out of his car, a light rain was falling, pushed about by a chill, brisk wind.

He stood a moment by the car and lifted his face into it. The air smelled fresh, and he knew when the rain passed the world would smell like a crisp starched shirt. Somewhere a police car made with a *whoop-whoop* sound.

Tad looked at the stairs to Harry's apartment, noticed that since he had been here last the railing on the right side of the stairway had been broken, a couple of slats knocked asunder.

He went up the stairs and knocked on the door, lightly at first, then, when no one answered, harder.

Still nothing.

He took a notepad from his shirt pocket, a pen, wrote: *Got your note. Come see me. Tad*

As he started down the stairs, through the gap in the railing, in the shrubs that surrounded the stairs on that side, lying there like a big bird that had fallen, he saw Harry, his shirt ripped, one shoe missing. His pants were torn and there were blood spots on his face.

Tad went down quickly and pushed into the shrubs, squatted, and held Harry's head up.

"Kid, you all right?"

Harry made a strained noise that sounded a bit like someone trying to pass a stubborn fart.

"Hey, kid. It's me, Tad."

Harry opened one sticky, bloodshot eye; the other eyelid quivered, but the curtain did not go up. It was black under the bloodshot eye. Harry had taken quite a lick there.

Tad tried again. "It's Tad. You know, the drunk you helped?"

Harry smacked his lips, said, "I had some beer."

"Yeah, I can smell it. Think you had something besides beer, maybe some whiskey, some hair tonic, maybe an ass whippin'. You're lookin' rough, Harry."

"I fell."

"Figured as much, part of the reason you look rough."

Harry contemplated this, finally got his other eye open.

"Think it's rough out there on the surface, ought to see inside my head."

"I'm only a few hours and two pots of coffee ahead of you, kid."

"Coffee. My kingdom for a pot."

"Come on, kid, let me help you up."

"You got a car?" Harry said. "Told me you walked everywhere."

Tad leaned over and fastened Harry's seat belt for him.

"Said I walked when I drank. Tonight I'm coffee'd up after a drunk, and I'm your designated driver."

"Cool. What kind of car is this?"

"Mercedes," Tad said, buckling himself in.

"No shit?"

"No shit."

"I'll be damned."

"If there actually was a hell, we all would be."

"That's the goddamn truth. Hey. Karate guy. Ain't you supposed to be monklike or something? Got this car, that house. That ain't no fuckin' monk stuff."

"Actually, what I do is not, strictly speaking, karate. Or jujitsu. It's a cousin. And, to make another fine point that will most likely go in one drunk ear and out the other, I'm a capitalist who is too often too drunk to work. Thank goodness for all my money. If the Republicans knew I broke ranks and voted Democrat, they'd probably take away my tax cuts. But if it makes you feel any better, the car is not new, the house is inherited, and me, I'm too lazy to work."

"Damn right it makes me feel better. That's more monkish."

Harry laid his head against the door as Tad pulled away from the curb, and was asleep and snoring before they had gone twenty feet.

When they were almost to Tad's place, Harry suddenly awoke, sat up straight in his seat, said as if in midconversation, "I ran me a tab. Problem was, I didn't have enough to cover it. Offered an IOU, signed and everything. Bartender offered me a fist in the eye, then took a hammer handle to my head. I got more bumps on it than bubble wrap. Tried to do what you did, you know, that loose fighting. Just made me fall down."

"It'll happen, kid."

"And some guy, he poked me for saying something about Jesus. I don't remember if it was good or bad, what I said. Tell you this though, that fucking place isn't getting any more of my business."

"Just lean back and be quiet, kid."

Harry leaned back and closed his eyes. "Where we going?"

"My place."

"What for?"

"To start over."

22

He sat in the dark and smoked and drank and thought about things, came to a solid and firm conclusion. It wasn't that he had to really consider it. He knew it. Though he did think about it from time to time, and it was this: He wasn't a serial killer. He was Code Name: William. That's who he was when he killed, and he did it because he wanted to. But he didn't have to. He had the power and the control and he could stop at any time, and because of that, he wasn't a serial killer.

Murderer. Not serial killer. That was a horrible thing. Someone driven by some inner demon, and he wasn't that way. Not in the least. He didn't mind murder, but he loathed any kind of loss of control.

He often went months without killing. Sometimes years.

He had been more active in the last two years than before, but it wasn't a frenzy, as serial killers often ended up doing. He wasn't driven, and he was being careful. Real careful. And he was making sure Code Name James was being careful as well.

He'd have to watch James, but so far, no big deal.

There hadn't even been anything much in the news. And over the years not one of the crimes had been connected. He'd have thought there would at least be that. Someone saying, "Maybe these are linked, because . . ." Well, not because he and James—and he liked to think of his partner as James and himself as William when he considered the murders—had done anything to give them that lead, but because the authorities might just put together the fact that in the East Texas area there had been a half dozen unexplained murders in the last eight years.

Of course, there were a few others the authorities didn't know about.

He remembered the first time. Couldn't believe he did it. A young girl, and he was twelve. She was in the park, and he came there, and there were just the two of them. She must have been nine, maybe ten. He was sporting a black eye from where his old man had corrected him.

It really pissed him, that black eye. He hadn't done anything. Not really. Nothing for his old man to get mad like that. Had put his hand down on his cigarette pack, crushing some smokes. That was it, and his old man had beaten him like a tambourine.

And there he was, banged up, and there was the little girl, looking clean in her dress and smiling, her hair back in a bow, and she looked so goddamn happy out there on the merry-go-round, pushing it with her foot, going around and around, laughing, not thinking about any kind of punch in the eye, just maybe birthday parties and hugs and presents and a fine future.

He watched her for a while.

No one else was in the park. He walked down there and grabbed at the merry-go-round, and ended up on it, dragging a foot, slowing it down.

"Don't do that," she said. "I'm playing."

Playtime was over pretty quick after that. He stopped the merry-go-round and dragged her off of it and down to the creek, her screaming like a wildcat, and there he hit her with a rock, tried to do some things to her, but wasn't sure how. He got her panties off and left her, and when they found her the same day, just before nightfall, he saw her father on the television, blank eyed and lost, and it made him feel . . . odd. Not sad. Kind of good inside. He had managed to kill someone and wound someone else, as if by ricochet.

A week later he read the mother hanged herself.

Two for him. None for the other guys, and there was still one wounded as well. Out of commission for the human race team.

So he was actually at two and half.

No one ever suspected him.

He went for years not killing again.

Thought about it, but didn't do it. Even then, as a kid, he was cautious. When he was sixteen he caught his old man not looking, out in the carport, bent over a dismantled motor he had on some greasy cardboad. He picked up a wrench, said, "Hey, Pops."

When his father turned, he hit him across the mouth with the wrench, making blood and teeth fly. The old man went down and tried to get up, and he hit him again. When he ran away, the old man was holding the back of his head with one hand, cursing at him, spitting blood and teeth. And the curses were like the joyful song the sirens sang.

It made him happy. He laughed as he ran. Never looked back.

He got out of his chair, went to the bedroom, opened the bottom drawer, and pulled back his socks and underwear. There was a little box back there. It was a watchcase. He opened the case. The watch, which had been given to him long ago by a girlfriend he dumped shortly thereafter, was still in the case. It was fastened to a cardboard slide, and he slipped that out. Behind it was a single pearl earring.

He had taken it when James wasn't looking. He told James not to take souvenirs, and that was right. You shouldn't. James shouldn't because he might get sloppy. But this one pearl earring from long ago, what could it matter now? Who would look here and find it? He had taken it off a young woman whose body had yet to be found, her and her boyfriend. Out there in the wild, eaten by ants and the like. Sometimes he thought about going out there to see what might remain. But it had been so long ago and he had been so strong, not going out there, it was best to hold to the plan.

Don't get sloppy.

He took the earring out of the box and ran his thumb and fore-finger over it. He thought about the ear it had been fastened to. Small, with the aroma of cheap perfume.

He sniffed the pearl. The perfume was long gone, of course. He put it in his mouth and rolled his tongue around it, then took it out and let it lie in the palm of his hand so that he could stare at it, think of her ear. A small, delicate thing.

After a moment he replaced the earring in the box, returned the cardboard and the watch, closed the box, put it in the drawer, and closed it up.

He leaned on the dresser and took a deep breath.

For some, this would be too much. They couldn't control them-selves. It would make them want to kill again.

And he would.

But he would not be a slave to passion.

He would wait until he was ready.

He wasn't going to be pushed around by anything. People. Fate. Urges.

Not him.

He was a rock.

A goddamn mountain.

He could kill again if he decided to, but if he thought he should stop, he would stop.

That's just the kind of guy he was.

PART THREE

Get Me Naked,
Show Me the Moon

23

When Harry awoke, he was in his underwear in a big bed in a big room that was really nice, except for spiderwebs in the corners. He sat up slowly, felt as if an elephant were sitting on his head. A thin gush of light was slipping through the dusty beige curtains over the windows.

He propped a couple pillows under his head and tried to go back to sleep, but the body wasn't having any more of that. He lay there for a while trying to remember where he was.

He was only slightly certain *who* he was.

He remembered Tad leaning over him and him lying on the wet ground.

Slowly he swung out of bed and put his feet on the floor. It was covered in nice carpet. He wiggled his toes in it.

He put last night together. Joey. The bar. An ass whipping from the bartender. Going upstairs to his place, awakening on the ground, Tad leaning over him.

Shit.

It was morning.

He was supposed to be at the bookstore.

He started to move more quickly, found he didn't have the energy. But he didn't want to lie back down. In fact, awake or lying down, his head spun, and so did the world. Sitting up like this, he felt only marginally miserable.

After a time he stood up, noticed his clothes folded on a chair, his shoes under it, a note taped to the bedroom door:

Shower. Please. And use lots of soap. Your clothes have been washed. Fresh towels in the bathroom. Coffee's made. Tad.

24

Feeling better after a shower, dressed again, but barefoot, Harry shuffled down a hallway and into a kitchen dining area. Tad, looking clean, thinning hair combed tight against his head, dressed in loose white shirt and pants and tennis shoes, was at the counter, sitting on a stool, reading a book.

There was a sliding glass door on the far side of the room, and it was filled with daylight.

Tad glanced up.

"Dead man walking," he said.

"Oh, yeah."

"Come. Sit down. Have a cup."

"How about a bucket's worth?"

"I'll keep making it long as you want to drink it. Got enough for a lot of cups. Italian coffee. Kona coffee from Hawaii. Plain old American coffee, and instant coffee. Much as I liquor up, I keep plenty of coffee. Got enough so you could fill a tub and bathe in it."

"Think I'm supposed to be at work. Know I am."

"Where do you work? You told me, I've forgot."

"Bookstore. Downtown. University bookstore. I work in the

stockroom a few hours a week, do the shelves now and then. Keeps me in beer and my fine abode. Or did. I've missed before and they didn't like it. Way I remember, one more fuckup and I'm out in the snow."

"It's not snowing."

"You know what I mean."

Tad took his thumb out of the book and slipped a piece of paper into it, closed it, laid it on the counter, said, "You wrote me a note."

"That was when I thought I was hot shit. That I was in love. And I am. But now that I know who I am and where I stand, it don't matter anymore."

"Sure it does."

"Think so, huh?"

"That note, it got me to thinking. You and me, we *have* lost our center. You still want to get it back?"

"The girl I wrote about, I think it's over before it got started. I don't know if it was going to start. Not now. I think it was wishful thinking."

"She tell you that?"

"She didn't tell me anything. Joey made me see the light. I didn't like how bright it was, but he made me look at it."

"So this guy tells you she's not for you."

"Said she's too good for me. And she is."

"You believe that?"

"Oh, yeah."

"You wouldn't if you had your center. Things between you and her might not work out, but you'd feel different about it. You'd know how to deal with pain."

"And you're the master of dealing?"

Tad shook his head. "No. But we can master it together. Once I did master it—to some extent. You're always gonna have things that make you wobble, but the trick is to not let yourself wobble so far the balance tips so much you can't bring it back in line. That's what mastering it means. It doesn't mean life doesn't come at you, and that it doesn't try and shove you around, but it means you can negotiate the storm."

"What if your balance is really fucked? Like I've gotten tipped bad, see, and I've fallen over and I can't get up."

"You can get up. You can always get up. Maybe not physically, sometimes, but mentally, emotionally, you can always get up."

"No offense. But maybe you're not the best example."

"Point taken. But things have changed. For me. Or I'm trying to change them. You can be part of that change—for me, and for you. Interested?"

"I don't know."

"Remember, you're the one who asked me."

"Yeah, but it was during a period of euphoria."

"People think being happy is an all-the-time thing. It's a series of balancing acts. If you were standing—which I'd rather you not do too much of right now—but if you were standing there, you wouldn't be balanced."

"Because I don't know how to stand?"

"No. All that karate-front stance, locked-horse stance, all that stuff, it's bullshit. You were standing there, you'd be constantly trying to find your balance. I'm talking standing there without thinking, you know, just hanging out. What a person does is they constantly shift to find balance. We all do it. Gradually. You're standing one way, you get tired, you got to shift—reason being, you got to renegotiate your balance. Same thing when it comes to life. Happiness is about renegotiating balance."

"That one of those Zen things?"

"No. That's a Tad thing. It's what my teacher taught me. My instructor of martial arts and life. He was a balanced kind of guy. He knew some shit. Once, I thought I was balanced and knew some shit, then I realized I didn't know half the shit he did. But, still, there was a time when I knew *some* shit."

"You can teach me?"

"I can teach you what you want to learn. While I reteach myself. Interested?"

Harry sipped his coffee.

"Will it hurt?"

"Sometimes. Pain is an indicator of life, you know."

"Yeah, but I don't know how alive I'm wanting to feel."

"How good do you feel now?"

"Not so good."

"You just answered your own question."

"So this wanting to teach me, does that mean you believe the stuff I told you?"

"I don't know. But I looked some things up. Right here in my own library. Got a lot of books, Harry. Used to read all the time. I got medical books—I used to study the body for martial arts. I got all manner of books. I went to the library for one—one I was reading when you came in. Hold on."

Tad went away, came back with a big, thick book.

"Medical volume," Tad said. "I want you to listen to something."

He began to read:

" 'There have been numerous cases where, either by accident or birth, or due to catastrophic injury, or even childhood disease, the brain has been affected, or altered, in such a way that it can perceive color as smell, or even sound. Meaning, to some, seeing the color red could activate sensors that would cause the observer to smell cinnamon, or rose, or even fecal matter. In reverse, smell can sometimes be perceived as color. There are cases of images being activated by the audio as well, resulting in the ability to interpret sounds as visuals. And there is some questionable evidence of sounds containing images of past events that have been recorded in the surroundings.

Rocks, dwellings and the like, even the designs on pottery. Trapped in the manner of sound trapped in the grooves of old-style records. Sometimes, these "recordings," like the remembered voices and sounds of songs sung, come back in flashes of sound, appearance, and, most destructively, emotion.

" 'Some people believe this is the source for the belief in ghosts, and since not everyone has this innate, or acquired, ability, this is why some people hear or see "ghosts" and others do not.'

"That's from the *Texas Medical Journal* volume *The Mystery of Senses, Perceptions, and the Brain*, by James Long-Williams, Ph.D."

Tad closed the book, put it down, picked up the book already on the counter, flipped to the marked page, said, "Now this:

" 'Audiochronology: akin to second sight, but instead of the ability to see the future or the past, it is the ability to determine past events through the transference of sound and its transformation to visuals of past events contained within the sounds hidden within objects or structures. Often a sound will activate images, wherein the audiochronaut can travel back in time, at least in the sense of seeing past events as they happened and were recorded in inanimate objects. Often these images are retained in the objects due to a violent discharge of bioelectrical energy being absorbed by the surroundings and, in turn, being reactivated by sound, therefore discharging the bioelectrical energy, which in turn now acts as an audio, visual, and emotional recorder. The slamming of a door, the scraping of furniture, provided the door and furniture were a part of the violent past event, can easily stimulate this action in an individual prone to this ability. The person experiencing these events not only hears what happened in the past, sees what happened in the past, he receives the emotional energy in such a way that he or she may be affected to the point of nausea, illness, or disgust.

" 'The facility is often inherited, or is sometimes brought on by injury to the brain, or even disease, or perhaps a combination of all three.'"

"Damn," Harry said. "That sounds right. That a medical journal too?"

"No. This is a book on supernatural and preternatural abilities. *Latrell's Encyclopedia of the Strange and Unnatural*."

"Swell."

"But the thing is, Harry, my man, they—the medical and the preternatural businesses—agree, even if they give slightly different reasoning . . . really not that different. That's the interesting part. So, could be something to that shit you're talking."

"Thanks."

"Really doesn't matter. That's not the point. I think we can help each other. You can give me impetus, and I can give you the knowledge you need to at least control, to some extent, your ability to deal with this sound business."

"If you don't know for a fact you believe it, then how can you know if you can give me control over anything?"

"Anything and everything is about self-control, Harry. Discipline. Organization. Even creativity. It's not about wild abandon. It's about control of yourself to the point where you can feel what you need to feel and reject what is unnecessary. Interested or not?"

Harry sat for a moment, looking at the counter, at the book Tad had laid there on top of the other. He lifted his head slowly.

"When do we start?"

"Today."

"Tad? You doing this for me?"

"Kid, wish I was so unselfish. I'm doing it for me."

25

They were outside, in the backyard, if you could call about three brick-walled acres covered in well-spaced walnut and oak trees a yard.

Harry knew people who would call this a farm. Maybe a plantation.

Light was slanting through the trees and there were leaves coasting down from the branches, twisting in the rain-flavored wind. The smell was good and cool and hinted at the beginnings of fall.

Tad looked at Harry, said, "First thing, before you start trying to control things, is you got to learn you can't control shit."

"Guess that about does it for me today," Harry said. "I'll go home and think that one over."

"Just listen."

"I'm already fucked, Tad. That sounds like what we in the university environment call a big fucking contradiction. I don't know I'm up for all this kung-fuey shit, this Zen double-talk."

"Just pay attention. Those leaves blowing there. They are flowing with the wind. Not fighting it—"

"Leaves don't have a choice, Tad. They don't have a brain."

"Who's the instructor. Me? Or you?"

"All right, I'm cool."

"Let the leaves be your guides."

"My guides?"

"Yeah. They don't fight the wind, they go with it. They are part of the universe. You and me, at this point in time, are not part of it at all. You following me? What are you thinking?"

"That maybe you're a nut shy a peanut patty."

Tad sighed. "Listen, man. I spent the morning reading my former martial arts instructor's books. One of which I helped him write. I'm trying to regear a lot of old stuff. You got to trust me. It makes sense, all of it. Not at first, maybe, but just try to stay with me. Okay? We try it for a couple of weeks, we don't get some improvement, feel a few things snap in place, sense the wobble stopping, you and me, we'll go out and buy a case of whiskey and see just how drunk we can get. Deal?"

"Deal."

"Good. Now, listen. You got to be like the leaves. You have to find your connection with the universe, not your separation. You've got to not fight the wind, you got to go with it. Look there, see those leaves blowing close to the ground, touching the ground? They flow, they skim the earth, they go back up and float back down—"

"The wind's doing it."

"I know that, moron. Just pay attention, okay? So now close your eyes. Do it."

Harry closed his eyes.

"Listen to me. Put one foot forward. . . . Not like that. Not some kind of stance. Forget all that shit you've seen in the movies. You want mobility. Relax. Try again. . . . Good. Very natural. Now, I'm going to stop talking for a moment, but before I do, I want you to listen very carefully. I don't know that ear of yours gives you better hearing in general or not, but let's find out if you can hear at all. I want you to hear the universe. The wind. The leaves, the sounds they make. I want you to really listen. And I don't want you thinking about pussy or beer or whatever. I want you to think only about what you hear. What you sense. You got that?"

"I'll try."

"I'll tell you when to stop. Just breathe deep like you're lying in bed, about to go to sleep. Relax. Listen."

The wind was cool and Harry could feel it, heavy at first and then, as he relaxed, lighter, and he could hear leaves blowing across the ground, and he thought he could even hear them snapping in the air as the wind twisted them, and finally the wind was light and full of rain smell and he became less aware of the world and the ground and it was all good, but then he started thinking about Talia and how she looked, how she smelled, how her body looked in the tight clothes and about what Joey had said—

"Stop it," Tad said.

Harry opened his eyes. "What?"

"You're not blending, Harry. First I thought you were, but you're somewhere else. I can tell from the way your body is reacting. You were light starting out, arms even came down by your sides, you were so relaxed. Then they came up again, hands and fingers tense. You got to work with me here."

"I'm trying."

"I know. And it ain't easy. It'll take some time. This time we're going to try again, and when I feel you're relaxed, I'll say step, and you just take a step forward. Not a conscious step that pulls you out of connection with things, but a step that is like a leaf blowing in the wind. Let the elements control you; it's not about you controlling them."

"If I lift my foot, aren't I controlling that?"

"At first. You'll be dealing with your conscious mind. But think about this: When you go somewhere, walking, it may well be your muscles doing it, but they're responding in a way that is unconscious. Learn to drive a car, at first you think, Hands on the wheel, eyes forward, need to press the gas, and so on. But in time you get in the car and drive, and you're not aware you're doing it. That's what we want here. We're going to get past the conscious mind and into the subconscious. The one that is most tapped into the universal connection between man and nature."

"No shit?"

"No shit. Once again, Harry. Relax. Close your eyes. Listen."

26

Harry practiced with Tad in the yard for a week, when he wasn't in school or at his job, which it turned out he had not lost. They wanted to fire him—he was sure of that—but workers were hard to come by, and for the most part he was pretty dependable.

He stayed with Tad at his place, so he wouldn't be tempted in the middle of the night to take a stroll to the liquor store, and he could make sure Tad didn't take a stroll or a ride to the store himself.

Harry discovered he wasn't so fond of liquor that he thought about it all the time, but he did miss it some. Tad, on the other hand, paced at night and cussed and rubbed his mouth and went out into the yard and moved slowly across it, with loose steps, just doing his thing, working hard to reconnect to the universe. "It's the way we all are right before we're born, in the womb," Tad told him. "Natural. Then we lose it."

Harry would find himself watching Tad, decked out in an old T-shirt, sweatpants, and tennis shoes, admiring the simple, loose sort of steps he made across the yard and the way the moonlight painted him and the way the leaves turned and sailed about him. Sometimes they spun as if in a little tornado, Tad at their center, the calm, smooth eye of the storm, moving across the yard, his entourage of dry, crackling leaves in swirling pursuit, he and the earth, the moonlight, and the air, all the same.

And finally there were more than steps across the yard.

Tad would move in other ways. His arms would flash out, loose like a monkey moves, then the legs would move, never high and never in some kind of cocked kicking motion, just quick and easy, his hips moving with it, his body flowing across the ground, and even when Tad did this, these moves with arms, legs, and hips, he never seemed to disconnect from the fabric of the night, the fabric of time. He was all and the same, him and the big ol' universe.

It was just too cool to see.

And there was another thing.

A very nice thing.

Harry slowly discovered, in that week, he wasn't as afraid as before. He was still up there in the scared-as-shit department, but not quite into the scared-shitless range. This, though minor, was an improvement.

Oh, he wasn't throwing away his well-worn paths. He stayed on those. But he wasn't thinking about it all the time, the hidden sounds.

Even found he was moving better. Felt better as he walked to class or moved around the bookstore. Maybe, he thought, it was all in his head, but even if it was bullshit, it was better than the other thing.

The sounds, with their deep wells of memories.

27

"I didn't mean to get your panties in a bunch," Joey said.

"Sorry I got so mad," Harry said. "Mostly."

"Just didn't want to see you hurt."

"I'm not so sure, Joey."

"Look. I brought a peace offering."

Joey was standing on the little porch, lit up by the porch light. Bugs swarmed above him and around the light and made a little chitinous halo over his head. The peace offering was a sack squeezed around a bottle, the neck of which poked out of the top of the bag. Joey looked sweaty, even though the weather was cold. Harry knew he had walked a great distance—first from his place to the liquor store, then here. It's the way he always got around—by foot. More so lately since his car had been squashed at the wrecking yard and made into a toolbox or some such thing.

Maybe that's why he wants to be friends again, Harry thought. So he can get a ride. Be just like the cocksucker.

Joey moved toward the doorway, but there was no passage. Harry was filling it, and for just that reason, so Joey couldn't slide by. Joey had a way of doing that. It was like when you trapped a rat against a refrigerator, only to discover it could go thin on you, slide through the grille work down there, disappear into it and come out the back way. That's the way Joey was. He was like a rat that could go thin on you. Didn't watch yourself, he'd be around you and inside before you knew it.

Harry figured if he had known Joey was out there, he wouldn't have answered. Should have peeked through the window. Checked it out before opening the door.

Course, if he had, Joey would have seen him. Like a rat, he was observant. Ever ready to take advantage or scuttle for safety.

Son of a bitch surprised him, just knocked, was standing there with his sack and his lopsided grin, and now Harry didn't know what to do. He had been caught at home. The rat was already starting to go thin on him; he could sense it.

"Look," Joey said. "I'm an asshole. I've always been an asshole. But I'm your friend."

"That's the unfortunate part."

"Come on."

Shit. I'm being outratted, Harry told himself. I know it. He knows it. But I'm a creature of habit. A fucking lab rat myself. A response machine. I always forgive him. I always let him by.

Harry stepped aside.

"All right, asshole," Harry said. "Come in."

"That's more like it," Joey said.

Joey scooted in, removed the bottle, dropped the sack on the floor, clanked the bottle onto the bookshelf. He took off his coat and tossed it on a chair.

"I'll get some glasses," Joey said.

"Just get one. I'm not drinking."

Joey paused, looked at Harry. "What kind of celebration is that?"

"It's not a celebration. Shit, Joey. What are we celebrating?"

"Us still being friends."

"I don't know that's such a cause for celebration." Harry sat on the couch and studied Joey. "I've known you, what? How many years?"

"I don't know. Since we were kids."

"And what I got to ask myself is, with friends like you, why would I need enemies?"

"That's cold. Clichéd, but cold. Anyone else from your life still with you, my man? Is it like I'm on the bottom of a long fucking list of good, caring friends?"

"You aren't on any kind of list. Not made by me."

Harry watched as Joey got a jelly jar and opened the wine and slowly poured some in the jar. No. Not some. A lot. He poured the jar nearly full. That took half the wine bottle.

Harry could smell the wine from where he sat. He wasn't really a wine guy. He liked beer, whiskey, some gin. But the wine smelled like flowers and honey and clean women when they took their pants off. The alcohol made his nose hairs twitch. It was very red wine, dark as the strawberry jelly that had originally been in the jar. Harry licked his lips.

"Sure you don't want some?" Joey asked. "You look like a man would love a drink."

Harry shook his head.

"Just a sip, Harry?"

Harry considered. That wouldn't be so bad. Just a sip.

No. One sip. One glass. One bottle. One case. It was all the same. He shook his head again.

Joey found a chair, sat there with his jelly jar of wine, and sipped. "Ah. That's good. Cheap. But good. You don't know what you're missing."

"Yeah, I do. Sickness in about three hours. A bathroom that smells like vomit. If I make it that far."

"Oh, come on. It isn't that bad, is it? It's not like it's a crock of wine. It's one bottle."

Harry watched as Joey took another long sip, wondered if when

Joey finished that glass, he would pour another. If he did, there wouldn't be any left.

Joey watched Harry watch him sip from the jelly jar, said, "Oh, for Pete's sake. You talk like you're an alcoholic."

"I may be."

"Don't be silly. You can lay it down anytime."

"That's what I'm trying to do."

"What could one drink hurt? It's a toast to our friendship."

"Which isn't going that well."

"Sure it is. You always forgive me, don't you?"

There was a knock on the door.

When Harry answered, Tad was standing there. He wasn't dressed up, but he had on a sports coat and his hair was combed and his bald spot was shiny under the porch light. Coat he wore was one of those writer-style jackets—blue corduroy with black leather elbow patches.

"Tad?"

"Yep. Thought I'd take you to dinner."

"Dinner?"

"Sometimes called supper."

"Sure . . . Why?"

"I'm bored."

"Come in."

When Tad came in he sniffed slightly, eyeballed the wine. He looked at Harry, then at Joey.

"I'm not drinking," Harry said.

"I wasn't going to ask."

"Hey," Joey said. "You're the drunk."

"What?"

"The other night at the bar."

"Oh, you must be Joey."

"That's right. I helped haul your ass out to Harry's car."

"Thanks. Lucky you didn't help haul me up these stairs. You might have gotten a hernia. Harry managed that by himself."

"You did some funny stuff that night. Drunk luck?"

"Sure," Harry said. "Not that I really remember."

"What's your name?"

"Tad."

"How about a drink, Tad?"

Tad paused, took a deep breath. "No thanks. Smells cheap."

"It is, but it still does the deed."

"So does hair tonic."

Joey raised his glass to Tad. "You sound like a man of experience."

Harry cut in quick. "I don't know about dinner, Tad. I mean, I got Joey over."

Tad studied Joey. "Any friend of yours is a friend of mine. Aren't we ex-drunks together, you and I?"

"Ah, so this is the guy's got you on the wagon," Joey said.

"I got myself on the wagon," Harry said.

"We're both on it," Tad said. "I'm just the guy drives the wagon a little."

"That's thoughtful of you, Tad. That's good of you," Joey said.

"Kind of guy I am."

Joey grinned and licked some wine off his lips, said, "You and me, 'cause Harry's your friend, we're friends?"

"Friendly enough. Sure, I'll enjoy your company."

"Damn nice of you, Tad. Damn nice."

"Very well then," Harry said, pulling his coat off the back of the couch. "I could eat something. Where to?"

"Steak place. New. I don't know the name of it. Something like Attila's."

"Khan's," Harry said. "I drove by it."

"I love a good steak," Joey said. "But alas, I seem to be temporarily short on funds."

"Come to think of it," Harry said, "how ritzy is this place?"

"It's on me," Tad said. "The both of you."

"Can't beat that," Joey said. "Let me get myself a little refresher, and I'll be ready."

"Going with me, leave the wine," Tad said.

Joey paused. "Leave it?"

"Yeah."

"Why?"

"Because I don't want it in my car. We go in my car, no wine."

"We can meet you there in Harry's car," Joey said.

"Not if I'm buying."

"Leave it, Joey," Harry said.

Joey sloshed the wine in the jar, then turned it up and chugged it down. He walked over to the bottle, poured the jar full, tipped it to his mouth, gulped. Some of the wine came out alongside his mouth and ran down his chin. He chugged it all. He picked up the empty wine bottle and dropped it in the trash can, wiped his face with the back of his sleeve.

"Ready," Joey said.

Harry felt nervous. Here he was with his oldest friend, a big old asshole, and his newest friend, who was kind of an asshole. He wondered what this said for him, riding around with two assholes.

Thing was, he was scared. It was a new route, and that meant new sounds. He tried to concentrate on the things Tad had taught him. Tried to draw his focus in, let everything that was unimportant remain outside. Way outside.

So far, in the car, it was working swell.

28

For a little town the steak place was pretty swank. They had a valet that took the car, guy that walked you to the door, and a gal he handed you off to inside. She walked you to your table, menus under her arm, left those with you, told you your waitress would come soon.

Actually, it wasn't a table. It was a booth, and it was one of the few spots in the place that wasn't so well lit you felt like you ought to do a dance number. Fact was, it was a little shadowy over in that corner because there was a kind of canopy over a series of booths there.

Rest of the place was bright and loud, with music playing, some guy at a piano in a suit, and Harry thought it was all kind of silly in a town like this, people dressed up like they were going to church.

"They didn't ask for reservations," Harry said.

"Already had one," Tad said.

"They didn't know how many," Joey said.

"I made a reservation for a booth."

"You some kind of big shot?" Joey asked.

"No. I just have money."

The waitress came. She was cute and so happy and sweet, and her name was Sandy, and there wasn't anything she wanted to do more than serve them, and she told them so, and gave them smiles. Harry had the taste of saccharin on the back of his tongue when she left.

He sat there and hoped there were no sounds outside of the loud music, guy at the piano. Nothing hidden in anything he might bump. It was a new joint, so maybe it was safe.

Joey was not loopy, but the wine had made him happy, and something of a loudmouth. Or a louder mouth. He was talking about the waitress and how he'd like to give her an exploratory plumb, or some such thing, so Harry decided to go to the bathroom.

Tad and Joey watched Harry thread his way through a new batch of patrons, and Joey said, "You a queen, Tad?"

Tad turned to him, said, "Now say that again."

"I said are you a queen? You got a thing going for Harry?"

"How do you like your steak?"

"I asked you a question. I didn't mean anything by it, asking you if you was queer."

Tad gently placed his menu on the table, shifted his position, and laid an arm across the back of the booth.

"All right. Let's you and me get down to it," Tad said.

"Suits me."

"Thing is, other night, that stuff happened with those thugs. I don't remember it. Harry told me about it. But none of it was an accident. Just take that note."

"Trying to scare me, Tad?"

"Just make that note, like I told you."

"Tad—"

"Shut up, Joey. What I got is a major drinking problem. I don't happen to be gay. If I were, though, I want you to know that I would be the best goddamn dick sucker ever fumbled with a zipper. I tell you this to let you know when I decide to be good at something I am. I tell you this to let you know that I am very good at whipping people's asses. I tell you this because I don't think you're any kind of friend to Harry. I think you're a fucking little parasite that would suck the blood out of the withered balls of a dead hyena."

"You don't have to get nasty."

"You opened the door, shit-dick. You wanted to know about me, and now that I'm in touch with my true feelings, let me stay in touch. I think you are one rotten piece of stringy, sun-whitened dog shit lying windswept on an ant-infested hill. And you want to make everything and everyone around you turn dead and white too. Can't stand the fact Harry's got something going and has a chance and could quit drinking. 'Cause where would that leave you? Folks that didn't grow up with you, they wouldn't give you fifteen minutes in an outdoor shithouse unless it was on fire and you tied to the toilet.

"You are the biggest goddamn loser since losers were invented, and you're like a fucking disease. You spread your loser, withered-white-dog-turd sensibilities wherever you go, just hoping you'll drag everyone else down into the sewer with you, you piss-and-turd-gulping piece of glorified dog shit that almost walks like a man. Now, I've got that off my chest. I got one more thing to say, a question really. Would you like your steak to go, you fucking odoriferous weasel ass?"

Joey started to open his mouth.

"Oh. One last thing. You speak loudly, cuss me, act nasty in any way, you will wake up with a fucking tube in your nose and one in your dick. You'll think you're a spaceman, so many tubes will be running out of your body. I will beat you and slam you and toss you and kick you and stomp you and just about anything I can think of, up to hitting you with some of these chairs, and possibly some of the patrons. So don't. Don't say anything. Not a goddamn word, even if it's in Greek."

Joey closed his menu, slid out of the booth, and walked briskly toward the door.

The waitress, Sandy, appeared.

"Hi," Tad said. "Uh, there will just be two of us after all. Our friend remembered he left the stove on."

In the bathroom Harry washed his hands carefully and looked around and felt nervous, but there were no sounds that had sounds beneath them, light and shadow, images and pain.

No. He was cool.

So far.

He dried his hands under the blower, took a deep breath, went back out into the restaurant.

When Harry came back to the booth, Tad was reading the menu. Harry said, "Where's Joey?"

"He left."

"On foot?"

"Sure looked that way."

"Where to?"

"I'm not certain. Liquor store would be my guess."

Harry picked up his menu, said, "He coming back?"

"I don't think so. . . . I would say no."

"You two get into it?"

"Heavens, no. We just talked."

Later, back at home, in the dark, Harry took off his clothes and sat naked on the couch. He sat there for a long time. Slowly he got up and went to the trash can and took out the wine bottle and held it near the window so the outside light could shine through it. There wasn't even a drop left. He set it on the bookshelf and looked at it for a while, then he put it in the trash can again.

He sat on the couch and looked at the trash can.

He sat that way for about five minutes, then got up and got the bottle out of the trash and held it against his nose and smelled it. It smelled like strawberries and a back rub. He ran his tongue just inside the bottle neck. He began to work his tongue savagely along the outside of the bottle. There was just the faintest taste of wine.

He noted he had an erection.

Holy shit. I'm so fucking horny for liquor, I've got a hard-on.

That old dog won't hunt.

Harry broke the bottle in the bathroom sink and picked out the glass and put it in the bathroom trash. He cut himself in the process. He sucked his finger and looked at his face in the mirror. The light was off, so he could not see himself well. He could see enough to notice a man with his hand in his mouth, sucking. All of this over a goddamn wine bottle.

He washed his hands and his face and put on a fresh pair of shorts and got his pillow and blankets out of the closet and lay on the couch and covered up.

He thought about how the wine had looked in the jelly jar, and how Joey had acted as he drank it. How he had smacked his lips and how the wine had beaded on his lips, how he had licked at it when it splashed onto the sides of his mouth.

Harry got up and found the jelly jar Joey had drunk out of. There was just the faintest bit of wine in the bottom.

This is silly, Harry told himself. I want a drink, I can have a drink. Hell, one drink, that isn't anything. Maybe I could go to the store, get a beer. Just one.

In *Rio Bravo*, the drunk in the movie had quit drinking the hard stuff, just had a beer now and then. That worked for him. He could drink a beer. It was the hard liquor he couldn't have. A beer. That would be cool. Just one. A cold one.

Shit, Harry thought. Dean Martin was an actor. He didn't have to get over being a drunk. He was playing drunk. In my case, Harry thought, I am not playing.

He washed out the jelly jar, in case he should start trying to drink the dregs, and went to bed. After a long while of thinking about drink and thinking about the sounds that made him drink, the faces he had seen, the pain he had felt, he drifted off to sleep.

29

So Harry, he's doing his center-of-the-universe thing with Tad, and he's got a lot of spare hours (drinking took up more time than he realized), and he's spending the rest of the time going to school, studying, working, not drinking, not missing Joey, trying to find that damn center, and then, surprise, he finds the center of the universe. Easy. It's right in front of him.

And its name is Talia.

She's looking just two beats above movie starrish. Hot mama on a cool fall day. A dream a-loose in the world of mortals. All in white, and the light loves her. Her skirt is not that short, but looks short because her perfect legs are so long, and the white top is frilly, and her breasts, dark as if touched with cool shadow, are plenty full and plenty showing, and her face is alight with a smile, teeth so white and full an orthodontist would bow to them as if to a shrine.

It was then that Harry noticed the pack of folks with her.

Four boys, dressed to the nines, bodies by health club, clothes by designer wear, hair by stylists, combed perfect and not subject to the wind.

Harry wore faded jeans—and not fashionably faded—a loose shirt, and his hair was a twist and wisp that crawled all over his head.

He was whiter than typing paper seen in a bright light. It got that way when you hid from the world.

There were a couple of nice-looking girls with Talia as well—one of them may have been with one of the boys, the other solo—but that left three guys to be with Talia. If the other girl only appeared to be solo, and was in fact with one of the other guys, that still left two.

Harry thought: Unless all the unfettered guys are gay, odds are bad for our hero.

And then Talia looked at one of the boys and smiled, and then, the universe be praised, she looked directly at him.

He felt a movement in his pants that wasn't shifting pocket change.

"I didn't mean to separate you from your friends," Harry said, taking a sip of his coffee, watching her over the top of his cup.

"That's all right," Talia said. "I've wondered about you."

"Me?"

"Sure. I've been looking for you."

"You have?"

"Yes, I have. . . . This could be called our spot, couldn't it?"

They were sitting and having coffee in the same place as before. "Yes," Harry said, "I suppose it could. I've thought about you a lot too."

Talia looked pouty. "If you have, where have you been?"

"Busy."

"You haven't been coming to class. I waited. I went by where you were supposed to be. I thought you dropped out."

"I missed a couple classes. Been helping a friend."

Talia smiled, and Harry thought: Wow. She left her pack to be with me. That's pretty damn cool.

Now it was just him and her.

And, of course, everyone else in the place.

Still, it meant something, way she acted. She had to really like him, leaving her friends like that. She had looked back at the guys when she came over, before he asked her to coffee, and he wondered about that, her looking back, but, shit, you could read something into everything, and that was his problem.

Take it as it is, he told himself. Take it as it is.

He said, "You know, I don't know if you like movies much, me, I'm a movie buff."

"I love them."

"But I was thinking, you know, this weekend we could catch a movie. Together."

"Of course together." She laughed. "We could even go at the same time."

"Well, yeah. That was silly. Sure. Together. Could be there's nothing good on, I haven't checked, but we can see. Maybe what we can do is I can pick you up, or meet you on campus, and we can walk over to Dineros for something to eat, then go to the movie. Oh, and there's this new steakhouse. Khan's. It's good. I ate there when it first opened. But Dineros is close, and that might be best."

Shut the fuck up, he told himself. You're babbling.

"That sounds good. I'm in. But I've got to go right now. Can we do it tomorrow afternoon? You can pick me up here."

She took out a pen and paper, wrote down her number. She had already given it to him before, but he said nothing. He wouldn't have minded having a collection of the number, as long as it was written with her hand.

"Call me before then. Okay? We can iron out times and when and where to meet."

"Absolutely."

He didn't realize it until he had walked to his car and driven home, but he hadn't bothered with his planned route, hadn't even thought about it.

Just walked to his car and drove home in a stupor.

The world was spinning better, had to be. The sun was brighter and the air was sweeter. Every dog, even one with acute audio-choronological hearing, had his day.

Bark. Bark.

Harry went home and began taking the cardboard and egg cartons off the walls.

30

It was late afternoon and the sun had fallen earlier than the day before and the shadows were longer and the wind was cooler and full of smells. Tad and Harry, side by side, moved across the yard in the dim light and the windy swirl of leaves, and Harry could feel it now, the thing Tad had told him about.

A sensation of being one with it all.

And he could feel it even thinking about Talia.

It was different, thinking about her this time. It wasn't distracting. It was part of his focus. Part of a whole. He was the world. The universe. He and Talia, all part and parcel.

Fact was, he felt as if he were king of it all.

One with nature and—

When he fell it hurt.

"Watch them roots," Tad said. "Bunch of old roots over here near this end."

31

Saturday, day of his date with Talia, he saw something in the paper that surprised and delighted and somehow disturbed him.

It was a photograph of Kayla.

She was no longer a kid. She was full-grown. Looked good. She was wearing a police uniform. A uniform for the town's force. She was back.

She was in a photograph with a bunch of other cops, her eyes shining out from under her cap. Her hair was tied back. She had a big gun on her hip.

She was part of a recently graduated class. She was tops in her class, in fact. Said so in the article. Said, too, she had finished most of college while in high school. Some kind of smart-kid deal. Then she finished the cop training program.

Kayla had fulfilled her dream.

She had become a cop.

He thought of how it felt when he touched her that day so long ago, and how it had felt when she had leaned over and kissed him.

Branded him with her lips.

How she had smelled. So wonderful. Two pieces of a bigger puzzle. Missing hunks of the universal pattern.

Kids, he thought.

We were kids.

By now she had most certainly found love. May even have a kid. She was piecing someone else's puzzle.

And there is another thing.

There's Talia.

Lovely, Talia. Goddess on earth.

I have a date with her.

Woo-hoo.

32

It couldn't have gone any better, that date. Talia, she looked ravishing in just blue jeans, a simple shirt, and sandals. Way her body filled those clothes, it was if she were liquid that had been poured into them and solidified. She was tall, dark, lean, but not skinny like so many women these days, and she was sensual in a kind of I-would-fuck-you-to-death-then-suck-the-marrow-from-your-bones kind of way.

Harry stopped to pick her up on campus, where they agreed to meet. She looked at his car, which he had detailed. Eighty-five bucks at Downtown Auto Shine and Repair, so the Cheetos under the seat, Snickers wrappers would be gotten rid of, all the dirt on the floor mats. And when he got out, opened the door, invited her into his chariot, she asked if he kept the car because it was some kind of classic or because of sentimentality, and he said, "Oh, no, not that. It's all I got. I'm the classic, and I'm not that sentimental."

She laughed at that and they went to dinner. It was a good dinner at Dineros, though he ate nervously, hoping they wouldn't surpass the money he had in his pocket, though Tad, good old Tad, had given him another twenty, just to help.

They ate and went to the movie. In the movie they held hands, and afterward, at the Java Palace, they talked and drank too much coffee.

Talia had been all over the world, shopped in some pretty fancy places, spent a lot of Daddy's money, and yet she seemed really interested when he told her about his life, about coming from a good but poor family, about his mom, and how he was going to visit her soon, and needed to.

Not once, not even in a passing thought, did he worry about his curse.

He didn't mention it either. Didn't tell her. Wasn't any reason to.

What would it matter?

He was getting it under control.

No more worries.

Things were cool.

Life was full.

33

Each day he trained with Tad, and each day was a door to something new. He felt wonderful, and he could see that Tad felt good too. As Tad rediscovered what he had known, he began to stand taller, drop pounds, and his sense of humor was sharper and he laughed a lot.

They both did.

Tad showed him not only how to move, how to concentrate—meditate, actually—but how to blend with movement, and pretty soon Tad was having him attack, and it always ended up badly for Harry, thrown hard, thrown effortlessly. Grabbing at Tad was like trying to grab the wind. And if you did luck out and grab him, it was like holding an empty sweatshirt.

When he wanted to strike you, he always found you. He didn't do anything with his fists, just moved his hands, or his arms, maybe a leg, never in a kicking motion; just seemed to move it, and it would connect. Somewhere.

And boy, did it hurt.

And he wasn't trying to hurt.

Finally it was Harry's turn to try and take on Tad. Tad was going to grab him, and the thing was . . . thing was, he was going to move in the way Tad was teaching him, and Tad was going to fly.

Except it didn't work that way. Tad grabbed him and Harry twisted, and Tad stood right where he was.

"Try to drop your hips; don't think about the fact that I got you by the shirt and, if I wanted to, I could kill you. Don't think about that. Just drop your hips and think of emptiness beneath your feet. But you . . . you can stand on air. It's me that has to go into the abyss. Got it?"

"Yeah."

Tad grabbed him. Harry sank his hips and imagined the gap beneath him. But there was a problem. He fell into the pit, pulling Tad on top of him.

They tried a dozen different scenarios, and they were all about as successful as the proverbial rubber crutch.

Harry stood up, brushed himself off.

"Not doing so good, am I?"

"No, you're not."

"I suck."

"You do."

"I'll never get it."

"Could be."

"Toss me a bone, Tad. Something."

"You fall good."

"Thanks."

"Welcome."

"For goodness' sake, Tad. Do you always have to tell it like it is?"

"You're doing great, kid."

"But now I don't believe you."

"Look. Your self-defense—it sucks. You're not a fighter at heart. But you got to not think of this like fighting. That's what you're thinking. The exercises. The concentration. Stuff that's helping you not worry so much about the sounds, or control them, whatever, that's the same stuff. You're trying to separate them. Look here. Reach for me, real quick. Quick as you can—"

Harry did it soon as Tad finished his sentence, thinking he'd surprise him. But Tad just raised his arm. And it didn't seem that fast, yet he intercepted Harry's hand, and the moment Tad touched him Harry felt his balance shift. He was on the wobble. His center was knocked off.

"It didn't look like you moved that fast," Harry said.

"Didn't. Listen. It's not necessarily who's the quickest. It's who's the smartest. To deflect what you do, I only have to move your arm a little bit. You have to reach for me, the full length of your arm, but all I got to do is reach up my body, a shorter distance than where you're standing, and bump your hand, and when I do, when I touch you, I shift me into you, and now you're weighted off balance, and not only with your weight, but, as I shift my hips, some of my weight.

"Once you're off balance, then, if I chose, I could push you down, throw you, or just bring my arm out, catching you in the void, and it would be like getting hit by a truck. That's the trick, Harry. There isn't any other. But doing it, that's a whole 'nother sack of worms. Balance out here and balance in life are the same. Lose your balance, you get knocked over easier.

"Thing is, you're getting the meditation part. You're starting to walk smoothly, and with confidence. You don't need to think so much about or worry about this other part. Don't imagine how you could beat the shit out of somebody, just imagine what I tell you to imagine until it's real. The rest is a piece of the whole kit and caboodle. You got to be like a monkey. Monkey is a selfish little shit. He wants something, just reaches for it, takes it. He doesn't worry about if his other arm is held, or if it's not a perfect line from him to the fruit; he goes for what he wants. He doesn't even think about his opponent, just what he wants, or wants to do, where he wants to go, and he goes there, loose as a . . . well, as a fucking monkey. It's hard to hold on to a monkey. And he wants what he wants. In that way, you have to be selfish, like the monkey—"

"And still be one with the universe?"

"Exactly."

"Don't monkeys sometimes get eaten by lions or something?"

"They do. And that's the other lesson. It doesn't matter what you know or who you are, there's always the certified, gold-plated fuckup waiting in the wings. You avoid it better if you train and prepare. But it can happen to anyone at any time. Martial arts isn't magic. It's a piece of magic. But sometimes somebody—due to their own training, accident, your lack of awareness that day, just plain old fucking luck, that shit—it becomes your lion or tiger, Harry. Sometimes the monkey gets eaten."

"Maybe I should be the lion?"

"You could. But he's not perfect either. Other lions get him. Monkeys or apes gang up on him, run him off. Throw shit at him, literally, toss limbs and rocks and fruit. Disease gets him, accident, hunters. There is no free lunch, and no perfect armor, and you got to watch when you zip up, least you hang the meat. Rules to live by. Got me, kid?"

"Yeah. I got you."

"One last thing. You listenin', now?"

"Yeah."

"That shit you called a friend. The turd. What was his name? You know who I'm talking about."

"Joey."

"That's him. I'm going to be honest. Me and him had words. Well, I said all the words. But he decided he wasn't hungry when I finished and he left."

"I figured as much."

"Letting him fall out of your life, that's probably best. He's like one of those not-so-brave monkeys that tosses his own shit. It's his only ammunition. Get what I'm trying to tell you here?"

"I think so."

"Let me put it so even you can understand it. Here it is, on a platter. The bastard is a loser and he wants you to be one too. That girl you're seeing, he said you couldn't do that. You are. And, you know what? If it should come to you not seeing her, it doesn't change a thing. You are what you decide to be. Your worth is of your choosing. Here's some more business. What I like to call a goddamn tidbit. Get out your net and grab this one."

"I'm hunkered down and ready."

"Sometimes, my erstwhile friend, you shake a bad thing, and you think it's gone. But it never is. Not really. You got to always be ready to deal. 'Cause bad things, they come back. And sometimes they bring friends."

34

At work Harry felt he was pretty safe from sound, and he was safe from drink, but he thought about both. He liked to get into something like book filing. It was the kind of work that allowed the mind to drift away, and sometimes he would peek inside a book and read a bit of this, a bit of that. It was akin to what Tad taught him, about how to become one with his surroundings. To find joy in the moment, in the now.

Place like this, the bookstore, was great. No shoot-outs or wrecks or robberies, or anything hidden in the clang of the registers, the hiss of the automatic doors. And he wasn't getting so many of those flashes. Those emotion barbs that had been given to him by past audio experiences.

Sanctuary.

Drink was another matter. He really missed it. There was nothing like a good, bracing drink after work. And then a trip to the coolness of the bar, where he could sit at a table and watch little beads of condensation on the outside of a big pitcher of beer. He liked the way it looked, golden, like nectar, when it was poured from the pitcher into a tall, thick, mug.

And that first taste.

Oh, Jesus, that first taste when the cold beer hit the back of your throat and the alcohol bit and there was a sweet bitterness to it all, because then you knew you were on the path, and after the first beer there was no taste, just the coldness of it. And pretty soon there wasn't that. It was just the beer, and it was a motion, lifting the mug and pouring it down. Yeah. He thought about it. He wanted it. It went through his mind. A lot.

But now it was easier not to think about the beer—all the time, anyway. Because there was Tad and the one-with-the-universe business, and there was Talia, and she was the center of that big old universe into which he wanted to be absorbed.

"It's been a long time."

Harry jumped. He had been bent over, pushing some books into place, and when the voice came from behind, he jerked up, clipped his head ever so lightly on a shelf.

He turned and looked.

Kayla.

"Oh, shit. I'm sorry. I didn't mean to startle you," she said. She looked concerned, like a big kid who had only wanted to surprise.

Harry looked at her while he massaged his head. She had on a lot of perfume. It was so strong it made him step back, ending up with the backs of his legs against the bookshelf.

Perfume aside, she looked healthy. Blond. Coltish. Those beautiful eyes of hers. She was the same kid he had known those many years ago; now the kid moved beneath the fine mature bones of her face and in the sparkle of her eyes. Pretty, but not like Talia, who was a lust bomb enveloped in flesh. Kayla was more like the girl next door. Talia . . . Well, she was Talia.

"Damn. You're going to have a bruise," she said.

"I'll say."

"Not quite the way I wanted our first meeting after all these years to turn out."

"Oh. It's all right. It's good to see you."

"You too."

"You signing up for courses?" Harry tried not to rub his head, but couldn't help himself. It hurt.

"No."

"Come to look at books?"

"No."

"Can I help you with something?"

"I came to see you."

"Me?"

"Yeah. You know. Just to say hello."

"How'd you know I work here?"

"I'm a cop, Harry. I find things out. . . . I called your mother."

"Oh."

"She sounded well."

"She's all right."

"You look good," she said.

"Thanks. You too. Yeah. I'm fine. You're fine?"

"Yeah. Still have . . . the sounds?"

"Oh, that. No. Nothing like that anymore. A phase with me. You know, kid stuff. Imagining."

"Imagining?"

"Sure."

"You imagined the ghost in the honky-tonk? You remember that?"

"I remember . . . I don't know. Not really."

"Not really what?"

"I mean, I don't know."

Kayla nodded. "Well, it's good to see you."

"You too."

She laughed. "Didn't we just do this?"

"Some."

"I was thinking, Harry. It's been a while, but maybe—"

"Friend of yours, Harry?" It was Talia. She had appeared as if she were an apparition. She came and stood close to him and put an arm around his waist. She looked as if she had just been pulled off the front of a fashion magazine, all hipped up in tight pants and a top, thick-heeled shoes that made her ass stand up as if it were peeking over a fence.

"What happened to your head?" Talia asked.

"I bumped it."

What Harry noted, however, was Talia was not spending that much time looking at his injury. She was looking at Kayla.

"Oh," Harry said. "This is Kayla. She used to live near me. We went to school together. Grade school. She moved away."

"That right?" Talia said. "Just moved back, I suppose?"

"A little while now," Kayla said.

"Catching up on old times?" Talia asked.

"Some," Kayla said. "Nothing big. Just a word or two."

"It's great Harry can reconnect with his little friends," Talia said.

"Little friends?" Kayla said.

"It's nice to look back at your past," Talia said. "You know. See where you've been, think about where you're going."

Kayla scratched the side of her head a little. Harry noted that she still had those long, lean muscles that she had used in youth to beat the shit out of him.

"Or to consider that maybe you've gone too far," Kayla said. "Sometimes, you know, you can be in a good place, and then, before you know it, you can make some wrong choices. End up in a cesspool."

Talia smiled, but it seemed to hurt her to do so. She said, "So you're not someone who believes a person like, say, Harry should think about moving on. Learning from his past mistakes."

"I think you have to be careful you don't, how shall I put this, fuck up any future plans."

"You're so thoughtful." Talia sniffed the air. "That perfume. Nice. Strong stuff. But very nice. Dime store?"

Before Kayla could respond, Harry said, "Kayla's a cop."

"No shit?" Talia said.

Kayla's grin widened. "Yeah. No shit."

"You could arrest us, you wanted," Talia said.

"You'd have to do something."

"Like insult an officer?"

"That would work. Or, if you did that, and we're just talking here, I could just forget I'm a cop and beat the living shit out of you."

Talia was silent for a time. Finally she spoke. "My daddy knows lots of cops. He knows your boss. The chief."

"That right?"

"Oh, that's right. Well, it's been so good to meet you," Talia said. "I hope your moving back to our little town won't be a disappointment, and maybe, who knows, you might get a chance to—how did you put it?—beat the living shit out of someone."

"Well, there's always a turd or two you have to step over, no matter where you are. But I think, on the whole. I'll be fine. And, who knows, I might just get my chance to beat the shit out of someone. Harry, nice seeing you."

"I must get the name of that perfume," Talia said.

Kayla smiled at Talia, but didn't speak to her. She turned to Harry. "We'll talk later."

Harry, feeling as if he had just been run over by a truck, said, "Sure, Kayla. Real good to see you."

"That toilet water she was wearing," Talia said. "Where in hell would you find that? And darling, it was almost attracting flies."

"It was a little strong, but it was okay."

It was Harry's lunch break, and they were walking from the bookstore to the little hamburger joint not far away. Harry walked very carefully, aware of staying on the path he knew, hoping nothing had changed recently. Like, say, since last night.

Cars drove by and Harry heard every motor, every backfire,

music coming out of car windows, sometimes causing cars with windows rolled up to throb like an excited penis.

In the hamburger joint, they ordered, took a table. Talia reached out and gently touched the bump on Harry's head. "Oh, that's going to look really bad when we're out. Maybe you should put some ice on it, see if you can get it to go down."

"It hurts some."

"You should get it to go down. It would look better if you used some ice."

"Right. Ice."

Talia turned slightly, looked across the way. Harry looked too. He saw she was looking at a guy over by the counter. Harry had seen him before. He was one of the guys he had seen with Talia the second time he had taken her for coffee.

"Good friends?" Harry asked.

"What?"

"That guy and you?"

"Are you jealous?"

"Might be."

"Oh, not at all. We used to date. It wasn't much. He wasn't much. That girl. You and her, did you used to be—"

"We were kids, Talia. I mean, kids."

"When I was twelve, a fifteen-year-old boy showed me how the eel went into the cave. It wasn't so bad, even if I was twelve. So kids, that doesn't mean a thing, dear."

Harry didn't know what to say to that. So he said, "Kayla's all right. She and I grew up together. She's all right."

"I'd rather you not see her, though, hon. People will think she's upstaged me. And I'm not used to that. I don't like to share my men."

"Men?"

"Figure of speech."

"She's all right," Harry said again. He felt all messed up inside, as if everything he had just learned to understand had suddenly gotten scrambled.

"Oh, that's our number," Talia said.

Harry got up to get the burgers.

It was a sweater night up in the hills, or what served as hills in East Texas. Up there, where the night was closer and the stars were brighter and the thick pines surrounded the narrow clay road, they sailed along in his car as if propelled not by the engine and gasoline, but by air.

They went to a little place blatantly named Humper's Hill, way up in the trees where there was a clearing from what appeared to be the landing of a great spaceship, but was most likely the result of a once-terrific lightning blast that blew out the trees and burned a circle.

Talia knew the place, led him up there. He pulled into the empty circle. The moonlight, from a half-eaten moon, was bright and silver and clean.

There was a slight rise, and near the front of the car the rise fell off and there was a dip. Not a cliff exactly, just a slope, and Harry had heard that a car had actually gone off of it once, down into the brush, and no one knew it was there for some three, four years. It was a couple, and sometimes the story said they had been shot, pushed over the side in their car. But no one knew they were down there until years later when hikers found the car and discovered their remains inside.

Somehow the story, true or not, made the place more exciting, that and the tale that a flying saucer had burned the place black.

So when Harry parked, he did it at the peak of the hill, just before it dropped away, his headlights pointing at the sky. And when he killed the beams, there was the moonlight, and after a moment their eyes adjusted and the stars seemed to pop out, sharp, like shiny spear tips falling toward them.

Harry was thinking: She's been here before. Do I say: "Have you been here before?" No. That's not good. 'Cause if she has, I know what she was doing, and she'll know I know, and maybe she just likes it up here, and this lonely place has got nothing to do with passion, maybe she's just a goddamn nature lover, and—

She put her hand on the front of his pants.

—maybe not.

"Get me naked," she said. "Show me the moon."

It was the first time they made love, and it was constructed of writhing flesh, flowing moonlight, and cool fall air; it was ripe with the smell of pine needles and drying leaves and red clay and the acid sweetness of clashing sexual organs.

They changed positions a number of times, went from sweater-cool to naked-warm, and one time, when he was behind her, her head out the window, her midnight hair jumping as he went into her, back and forth, she said, quite loud, "You're my poor boy, aren't you? Fuck me, baby. Fuck me, baby."

Poor boy?

He thought that one over and it tumbled in his head like junk falling down attic stairs, but the feeling was so good and the night was so fine, and the really bad noises, the ones that hid in the texture of this and that, that clanged and whanged and bammed and whammed, had been absent from him for some time now, at least in a big way, and the universe, it was his (when he didn't tangle his feet in roots), and he was long gone from being who he was and how he was, so it didn't matter.

Not at all.

35

Next day, in his apartment, lying on the couch, hands behind his head, contemplating the date with Talia, running it over and over in his mind, especially the parts out there on Humper's Hill, the phone rang. Slowly he got up from the couch, went over, and looked at the caller ID.

It was Joey.

It rang three times and the answering machine kicked in.

There was a pause.

No message was left.

"Damn," Harry said. He picked up the phone and dialed Joey.

"I just called," Joey said.

"I know. I saw your name. I couldn't get to the phone in time."

"Must have been taking a shit. Small as your place is, you can get anywhere under, say, oh, I don't know, two seconds."

"You're right. I was on the toilet."

"The other night, your friend—he don't like me much, Harry."

"Figured as much."

"He tell you about it?"

Harry lied. "No."

"Want to know about it?"

"No."

"He hurt my feelings, man. He didn't treat me like I was your friend."

"Got to admit, Joey, sometimes I got to look real hard to find the love."

"Come on, man. Don't go homo on me. This all got started over some girl. We don't want shit like that to come between us. Thing is, though, I wanted to ask you. You really end up seeing her? Talia?"

"Yeah."

"No joke?"

"No one laughing here."

"She a good fuck?"

"Come on, Joey."

"Is she?"

"I got nothing to say about things like that."

"You must be lousy. That must be the thing."

"Joey?"

"Yeah."

"Blow me."

Harry hung up.

36

A week passed.

It went by like a bullet, because he was seeing Talia, a lot. And all over, and in all kinds of positions. Next to a nonstop flight to heaven with free peanuts, things couldn't have been better.

"You should meet Daddy," Talia said.

"Daddy?" Harry said, not knowing what to think of this. Was it that they were so serious he should meet Daddy? Or was it that Daddy thought anyone dating his little girl should be met?

What was up?

As for himself, was he serious? He certainly thought so. Felt high all the time, way he felt when he drank, but without the hangover.

She had surprised him this morning, when he'd been sleeping in, and he answered the door in his boxer shorts.

"When?"

"Today."

"Today?"

"Now."

"Now."

"Harry. Are you a parrot?"

"Parrot?"

"Now stop. He's out at the shooting range."

He looked at her, sitting on the edge of the couch so only a pin-point of her fine ass was actually making contact with it. She never seemed comfortable there, but it was what he had. And he wasn't nuts about going to her parents' house. He didn't know what it was like, but he knew she had money, and he knew he did not.

"I should clean up then."

"No. You look fine. I like you like you are."

From past experience, he knew his hair was sticking up like a rooster comb, 'cause it always was when he woke up, and he had a couple days of whiskers going, breath that would melt a wax block, and this was brought all the more home because she looked like a million bucks and change. It was a good bracer to meet a girl in a black mini-skirt first thing in the morning, a halter top so tight you could tell her religious affiliation, but it also brought home the fact that he looked like a cardboard-box wino.

"I thought you should meet him, and now's the time. He's out at the gun range."

"Gun range?"

"There's that damn parrot again."

"I don't know, meeting a girl's father at a gun range—it tends to make a man nervous. Especially since we've been doing more than swapping stories."

"He's very cosmopolitan."

"Yeah, but I'm not. Guess I get to comb my hair and put on some clean undershorts."

"If you hurry. Don't bother to shave."

Harry brushed his teeth, changed underwear and combed his hair, and put on the best pair of jeans he had. They were only moder-ately faded, and the cuffs were ragged where he had been stepping on them with his boots. As he pulled on his socks and tied his tennis shoes, he wondered what in hell Talia saw in him. What made him so lucky?

He took one more trip to the bathroom, looked in the mirror, said, "Sure I don't have time to shave?"

"He'll only be there awhile, then he's so hard to find. He has all kinds of meetings and the like, and he doesn't always answer his cell phone."

"This shooting place. They haven't killed . . . anything out there, have they?"

"What?"

"Killed anything. Been any accidents?"

"Harry, sometimes you can be so strange."

She drove them over in a very new and very nice and very red sports car. That was good. New cars were good. They hadn't had a lot of chances to get wrecked, not as much time to conceal bad memories.

The shooting place was a field, really, not far out in the country. There was a gate you went through, and to get through it you had to push code buttons.

Talia did just that, and they cruised in.

They parked near a long, low building, and walked out back. There were three men out there with shotguns, and three younger men pulling the skeet launchers.

They walked back that way, and Harry stole glances at Talia, way she walked, way the short dress sheathed her thighs, and how she stood tall with her breasts jutted out like high beams.

As they neared, Harry saw the young men at the skeet launchers turn to look at her. Two of the older men looked as well. One was a slightly heavy guy with a jet-black caterpillar mustache, hair gone slightly south, wearing clothes that could be called sporting clothes if you could keep them ironed while in the woods. He looked about fifty, but as he got closer, Harry realized he was much older. Sixty-five, maybe even right at seventy. Well preserved. Money could do that. The man gave them a brief glance.

Without asking, Harry knew he was her father.

Talia leaned to Harry, said, "He dyes his mustache, you know."

The others were almost in a trance, watching Talia come toward them.

When they were close, Mr. McGuire said, "And who's this?"

"Harry," Talia said.

"Harry, huh?" the father said.

"Hello, Mr. McGuire." Harry stuck out his hand and Mr. McGuire rested his shotgun on his shoulder and held the stock with his left and shook with his right.

"Nice to meet you. You out of razors?"

"Well, I—"

"I just love him like he is," Talia said. "And he's not like us, Daddy. He doesn't worry about money. Or appearances."

"I don't know I'd say—" Harry started.

"He and I are quite fond of one another," Talia said.

"Say you are?" Mr. McGuire said.

"Very fond."

"That's very nice, dear." McGuire turned his attention to Harry, studied him, said, "You will drop by and visit with us sometime, won't you?"

Before Harry could respond, Talia said, "He works at a book-store."

"That right?" Mr. McGuire said.

"He may come to our party, Daddy."

"Really," Mr. McGuire said, shifting his shotgun, looking off at a ridgeline of trees as if he might have seen a flying saucer pass over them.

"What party?" Harry asked.

Neither Talia nor Mr. McGuire bothered to explain. They were looking at each other now the way gunfighters would, waiting for someone to make the next move.

"Well, nice meeting you, Henry," Mr. McGuire said.

"Harry," Harry said.

"Of course." Mr. McGuire turned his head, said, "Pull."

The man near him, on the ground, looking up at Talia as if she were a work of art, took a moment to understand. McGuire repeated himself, and the young man pulled.

The skeet sailed, and Mr. McGuire effortlessly exploded it.

As they walked back across the field, past the building, Harry looked back. Everyone but Daddy was eyeballing Talia's ass.

Harry said, "That was odd."

"Think so?"

"Well, yeah."

"It wasn't really. He takes his shooting seriously. He's killed animals all over the world. A few endangered species even. He likes to preserve them himself."

"Really?"

"Yes. Really. He's not very strict, you know. I think he liked you."

"Liked me?"

"Sure."

She drove away from there quickly and dropped him off out front of his place.

"You going to come in?" Harry asked.

"No. I have some errands. Be a dear and call me later."

"Sure."

Harry got out and closed the door.

For a long time he stood on the curb looking in the direction in which Talia and her fine red sports car had departed, trying to figure out exactly how he felt about things. Had he just been a dirty pawn in a dirty chess game, or were Talia and her father just odd, like the rich could be?

And if he was a pawn, what exactly was his role in the game?

There was an answer in there, and he thought maybe it bounced up against his head once, but he didn't catch it, and whatever might have been there didn't bounce back in his direction again.

He did ask himself a question, however, and he asked it aloud:

"What party?"

37

My little friendly composition notebook, I come to you having been sharply centered, to now being off the plumb line, maybe two bubbles.

I'm not sure how I have come to be where I am. . . .

No. That's not true.

I don't like how I have come to be, don't like how I am, and yet I don't know what to think or do about it, so pardon me as I write, for this will be, to put it bluntly, a little bit mixed and undecided.

There are upsides to my position. Mostly Talia's backside, bent up and ready, but that's not a way I like to think or a thing I want to live my life for, though, to be honest, it's such a fine thing that one can't help but consider, and I fear—shit, I know—that little pleasure may have departed.

Look at that.

May I say, I'm still clinging to hopes that are unwarranted.

Elvis, my friends, has left the building, and that's all there is to it.

So here I sit. In darkness, except for this one lamp and my journal and pen, and this strange feeling of remorse and sadness, and the awareness that my old demons, the ghosts in the machine, have not gone away and I have heard and seen something horrible, and that true love isn't always true and isn't always love, and that love at first sight is sometimes a harsh light in the eyes.

Most of what plagued me before, the goddamn sounds, has not gone away, but I have been able to frequently put them aside, or, to be more exact, they activate and swim about me like sharks. It is as if I am in a large aquarium, a piece of kelp on the bottom of the goddamn thing, and the sharks are set loose, and as they move the water moves and the kelp moves, and I drift amongst them.

Not a good feeling. But I try to shove it back. Tad says not to do that, not to shove it back, because then I become a depository for those feelings. I am to be like a filter, let them drift through me and out of me. I am to accept our sameness and oneness and move on.

Easier said than done. I'm still trying to figure how they and I are the same. Or even how we're one.

Zen, baby. It do be confusing.

On a good day it is less like the sharks and more like noise heard from construction work ten blocks away. That is a good thing.

But that is not why I come to you today, my composition friend. No, sir. That ain't it. I come to you to tell you of a very bad thing and how sometimes the sounds and images are not from far away, nor are they swimming by you, making you nervous. Sometimes they are close as your skin, your intestines, your brain cells, in there with the beat of your heart.

Alas, I avoid. And for good reason.

Best way to put this, best way to explain this to you, is to start where it starts, not behind some rock looking from afar, wishing for a Winchester rifle.

Here it is, then.

So things were going really well, with a stress on the well, but there were signs, dear friend. Signs and portents, and the advice of Tad, right out there in front of me in my lessons, and all of it has come back to me now, and all I can think is: Weren't you paying attention, asshole?

Once upon a time a poor boy who was afraid of sounds—and for good reason, I might add—got drunk and felt better, but felt less good when sober, and he met a drunk who didn't feel so good himself, so they decided that together they would not be drunk.

Something like that.

Plans were made, deals were struck.

And, sure enough. They began to find the center they had lost. The wobble stopped.

Well, for me, Composition Notebook Journal (I give that to you as a title now), the wobble is back, because I forgot who I was and what was inside me, and I forgot who Talia is and how it's her world, not mine.

Hell. I did not forget. I refused to remember.

My world is the dirt beneath her feet, and her world is the clouds. Way up there in the misty white, spotted with clear blue and all manner of hope and fortune and future.

Me, I'm down here with the worms, maybe loony as a rat in a paint shaker, for in spite of my thought-to-be-centered life, I was always listening and waiting for the trumpet blow, the one that announced betrayal.

Or maybe it was just the trumpet blast that told the truth. How it is on earth and not in heaven, and how it is for the not-so-fine and the not-so-beautiful and the not-so-gifted and the not-so-lucky and the not-so-rich.

And how is it, you ask?

Not good, the poor boy answers. Not good.

Joey is an asshole, and maybe, as Tad says, he is like a monkey who throws his own shit because it's all the ammunition he has, but, that said, he still knows some things; there is still some undigested fruit or nuts in the shit he throws.

38

"It's a very nice party," Talia said. "You want to look nice."

"I have a good suit."

"The one in your closet? Or is that your room it's hanging in?"

"What do you mean?"

"The place is small."

"Yes. Yes, it is. Sometimes I pretend it's large, but when I open my eyes, it isn't."

"Oh, don't be mean."

"I'm just saying. Yes, it's small. And my suit is just fine. And, hey, when I met your dad, you didn't even give me time to shower and shave. So now I'm supposed to look sharp?"

"I wasn't thinking. I just wanted you to meet him while I had him cornered."

"That was it?"

"Of course. What else? But for this, you should look nice. There will be a lot of people there. They will all be very well dressed, and Harry, I've seen your suit, and it's what, from JC Penney?"

"Yeah. Well, maybe Bealls. I don't remember."

"I rest my case."

"What case?"

"The one in your closet isn't the suit you want to wear to the gala. Trust me on that. Everyone will be there, and—"

"It's the suit I got."

"I can fix that."

"Oh, no. I don't want you to buy me anything, and I can't afford to buy anything. Maybe I can rent a tux."

"Those never fit right. Listen, Harry, I want to do it. It's not a problem for me."

"You mean it's not a problem for your daddy."

"Same thing."

"Either way, I don't like it."

"Harry, you have to look nice if you're going to come, and you do want to come, don't you? You and me, at my father's house, and all those people? A lot of them very prominent."

"You mean rich."

"Okay. Rich. So what? Is it okay if we're rich? Is that a crime? You're starting to hurt my feelings, Harry."

"I don't mean to."

"We want to look our best. Want to dress up and look fine, and I can show you off, introduce you to my mother, and later, well, we'll go our own way, and we have our place, don't we?"

"We do. Though we shared it with four other cars last time."

"True, but they weren't in our car, were they?"

"No . . . I don't know about this suit business, Talia. It doesn't seem right, you buying me a suit."

"I want to do it. Everyone at these parties knows a good suit from a bad one, and they'll spot a cheap one right off. And you'll need shoes, some good socks, and I'll pick a tie."

"I feel like a mannequin."

"Don't be silly."

...

At seven in the evening the phone rang, and Harry, dressed in his new suit, socks, tie, and shoes, waiting patiently on his couch, hands in his lap, rose and picked up the receiver.

"Hey, baby," Talia said.

"Hey."

"We're coming around the corner. Come down to the curb."

"Okay. We?"

But she had hung up.

Harry went downstairs and out to the curb. He was no sooner situated then a limousine, black as a crow's wing, came around the corner and glided to a stop.

The driver got out, went around, opened the back door to let Harry in.

"I could have done that," Harry said to the driver.

"Yes, sir," said the driver, "but, unlike me, you wouldn't have gotten paid for it."

Harry climbed in. Talia, in a short black dress, her hair pulled back and up, her dark-stockinged legs crossed, her cell phone beside her on the seat, looked at him and smiled.

Harry's discomfort began to melt away.

"You look fantastic in that suit," she said.

"For what it costs, I should not only look fantastic, I should *be* fantastic, maybe have some superpowers. Good God, Talia, you are dynamite. You are so lovely."

"Thank you, sweetie."

The car drifted away.

Talia's parents' house was off a little road that wound in amongst old oaks and new pines. They pulled up at a gate with a metal box on a pole beside it. The driver pushed a series of buttons on the pole, and the gate opened. They cruised up a hill between oaks, willows, and walnut trees, a sweet gum here and there. As they climbed, Harry could see lights shining brightly through patches of greenery, warm explosions of yellow and orange.

The car window on the driver's side was still down from the driver having worked the buttons on the pole, and Harry could smell perfume on the air, and hear music, a big-band sound, and it all came down the hill in a waft of smell and sound that filled the car thick as taffy. Harry had gotten to where noise, even noise in which the past did not lurk, annoyed him, but this wasn't so bad. It was the sound of another time, and there wasn't any anger or violence in it, not like most of the stuff today.

The greenery divided as the car wound along the concrete path, and now he could see the house up there on a hill, lit up like the pearly gates, so brightly lit that at first glance it appeared to be on fire. The house stood strong and heavy of stone against the night, and outside of it, along the pool, on a large, flat area of tile, well lit up from decorative lights on poles, people danced, and the music was suddenly divided by a voice, the sound of a male singer crooning into an old-style microphone. His voice was rich and strong, and the dark and the lights and all the people were as one, the way Tad had told him the world could be if you looked at it right.

There were cars parked all over, pointing this way and that, like discarded cartridges from big guns, but the limousine slid past them, around to the back of the house, where there was a carport supported by stone pillars. They parked, and with the driver holding the door for them, Harry climbed out first, extended his hand to Talia.

"I thought it would be larger," Harry said.

Talia grinned at him.

They went in the back way, and as they entered the house there was a burst of light and the bright white paint of the walls jumped out at him. The house on one side was free to the outside by open windows and open glass doors, and the music came inside, loud and friendly, filling the giant cathedral room. People laughed and danced. There was a long table full of food of all persuasions: sushi and barbecue and darkly cooked birds, bowls of this and bowls of that, and all manner of wine and beer and soda and bottled water, and there were Latino men and black women in little white outfits, walking this way and that with silver trays, smiling, as if nothing in the world pleased them more than to cater to the happy, indulgent, honky rich.

"Daddy," Talia said, and sure enough it was Daddy coming their way. And tonight he seemed happier, and the drink in his hand was probably the source of it, thought Harry. The suit he wore was just like the one Harry wore, so were the shoes. The only difference was the tie. And maybe the socks. Harry decided not to ask him to extend his leg so he could check.

Mr. McGuire said, "Ah, this must be your date. Barry—"

"Harry," Talia said.

"How are you, Harry? Name's John." And he extended his hand.

Harry shook it. He realized that Mr. McGuire didn't remember that they had met before.

"I'm fine, sir. Thanks for having me here."

"Quite all right. Bird's good. So is everything, but the turkey, it's to die for. Black people are such good cooks, and I've got three or four of them to do the kitchen business. Got to circulate. Host and all. You know how it is. Nice to meet you. Nice suit."

"Thanks."

John went away, and so did Talia. Harry found himself standing in the middle of the room, not knowing where to put his hands. Men and women danced around him in their fine clothes, like drunken moths a-spin beneath a bright night-light.

Harry went over to the food counter, which was as long as the room, looked to see what was there.

A black woman in a maid outfit appeared at his elbow. "May I help you, sir?"

"Just looking."

"Yes, sir."

"What do you suggest?"

"It's all good."

"You know the cook?"

"I am the cook. Me and three others."

"That's quite a staff."

"We cook and wait, us three. You add the whole staff together, all the people work here, there's about twenty. That way, the folks live here don't have to do a lick of work. . . . I didn't mean that—"

"Oh, that's all right. Don't worry about it. I'll have some chicken, a diet cola."

The maid fixed Harry a plate, gave him napkins and silverware. Harry glanced around for Talia, didn't see her. He went outside and watched people dance out there. He found a metal table and a metal chair, sat down, and ate his chicken. When he was finished he wiped his fingers on the napkin and went back inside.

No sooner was he in the door than a woman in a bloodred dress grabbed his elbow. "You all alone?" she said.

She was a very nice-looking woman, maybe forty, with too-red hair and a fine build and a good face full of Botox.

"No. I'm with Talia. She lives here."

The woman laughed. "She certainly does. Some of the time. I'm her mother."

"Oh, glad to meet you," Harry said, and held out his hand.

"I'm Julia," she said, and took his hand and held it softly. Her eyes looked just like Talia's eyes. "I'm a little drunk."

"Yes, ma'am."

"Oh, don't 'ma'am' me. Makes me feel so old. Let's dance."

"I'm no good. Don't know how."

"I can teach you."

Harry shook his head. "I think that would be a waste of your time."

"Oh, there you are." It was Talia.

"Hello, dear," Julia said. "I was trying to steal your date."

"I don't doubt it," Talia said. Mother and daughter sparred with their eyes.

"I'll just get a drink now," Julia said. "You two enjoy. And show the boy how to dance. He says he doesn't know how."

Julia, like a bloodied bird, glided away on the light and the music, dancing as if with a partner.

"She's quite charming," Harry said.

"She's a bitch," Talia said. "She'd fuck you, you know? That's how she is."

Harry didn't know what to say to that. He was beginning to feel as if the world was not in fact round, but awkward-shaped and rare of gravity and hard to stand on.

"But don't feel too proud," Talia said. "She's fucked the waitstaff before. Both the men and the women. Whoever was willing and didn't mind a little extra money."

Harry looked in the direction of the waitstaff, standing by the counterful of food.

"All of them?"

"No. She fucks them, pays them, and fires them. This is a new lot. Some of them won't appeal to her. Though she has a taste for almost anybody."

Harry didn't know what to say to that either, but it didn't exactly swell his pride.

"Let's get a drink," Talia said.

"I don't drink."

"Just tonight."

"I made a promise to someone."

"For me."

"Nope. Not even you. I'll have a soda, some iced tea maybe."

"You're starting to be a bit of a stick-in-the-mud."

They got drinks, Talia a beer, him a soda, and pretty soon they were dancing. Harry wasn't good at it, but Talia helped by dancing very close and giving him pointers. Before long she was back at the bar, getting another drink. As the night wore on and she drank more, her dancing got wilder. By midnight she was riding his leg like a horny dog.

Once, over by the food counter, Harry saw one of the boys he had seen that day on campus with Talia. Kyle. That was his name, When Harry turned back to Talia, he saw she was watching the boy as well, and he felt a little twist inside. Nothing big, just a little one, like a washerwoman had twisted a wet rag sharply to wring out the water.

"Let's get some air," he said. "Out back, away from the band."

"All right. Oh, I'm tipsy."

"Honey. You're drunk."

"Just a little."

They went out the back way, through the big carport, and looked about. The stars lay down on the tips of the pine trees and the glow from the front field lights fled over the top of the house and dissolved into a silver film before reaching the trees.

"There's a place I want to show you," Talia said. "It's kind of cool."

"We're leaving?"

"No. It's out back, down the wooded trail. I used to play there. It's a kind of a root cellar, or storm cellar. Not that we need one or use it for that. But Mom and Dad liked the idea, and it was a playhouse for me. When I got older, Daddy took it over."

She took his hand began leading him across the yard, toward the woods. "He goes there to get away from my mother. He and some of his friends go there to play cards. Or used to. He hasn't been there in ages now."

"Won't it be kind of worn down? Dangerous?"

"It was well made. Sealed tight so water doesn't get in. Oh, shit."

Talia tripped. Harry caught her.

"Maybe I did drink too much," she said.

"Just a little. You're not full-fledged drunk. You want to go back?"

"No. Not at all. Come on."

The shelter was out in the woods. It was standing partially out of the ground, made of thick concrete. The entrance looked like a tomb.

Talia took hold of the door handle and tugged.

Nothing happened.

"It's a little heavy and I'm a little drunk."

Harry pulled. It slid back smooth and easy. "It's been recently oiled. I can smell it."

"Like I said, Daddy keeps it up."

"Don't we need a flashlight?"

"It has electricity."

Talia reached inside and hit a switch and the place lit up. It wasn't a bright light, but it was light. It hung down on a long black cord, and there was a bulb contained within wire mesh, and the light through the mesh made the room appear as if it were contained within a spiderweb. The light showed a drop of stairs, and Harry could see a bed against one wall, and he couldn't see much else.

They left the door open, and as they went down he was surprised to discover it was quite roomy. There was even a bookshelf and some books. There was a doorway that led somewhere. There were spiderwebs, and one wall was crumbly. A roach ran under their feet, and Talia made a noise and jumped.

"I can stand snakes, spiders," she said, "but I can't stand a roach. Oh, I'm dizzy."

Talia sat on the narrow bed.

"What's through the door?"

"The generator. Runs on kerosene. There's a toilet too. It's got a big septic tank. You wouldn't believe. Daddy wanted to make sure everyone got to shit. A lot."

"Kerosene?"

"It's old-style."

Talia patted a place beside her. Only a little dust came up.

"Your dress is going to get dusty, and this suit you bought me."

"We'll dust each other off. If you know what I mean."

Harry sat.

Talia leaned to him, and they kissed. Her lips tasted like what she had been drinking, but it wasn't bad. Her perfume reminded him of orange blossoms. She ran her hand under his coat and pushed at the inside of it. He removed it, laid it at the foot of the bed. He slipped the straps of her dress down. She wasn't wearing a bra. She didn't need one. In a few years, probably, way she was built, the size of her breasts, she would, but right now—perfect. As he kissed her again, he took hold of her left breast and gently squeezed it, let his thumb and finger play over her nipple, felt it go stiff.

A breeze came. The door was caught by it. It slammed and the light cord shook—

—and the world went to pieces and so did the kiss. Colors leaped into Harry's head, and the colors screamed.

39

Puzzle pieces, like a Picasso painting, flew through Harry's cranium, wrestled together briefly, then there was light and the light went back and forth and the shadows did the same.

It was the light on the cord, and the room was fresher-looking. There was a large man coming down the stairs, and Harry knew then that the slamming door had shaken the bulb on the wire. The room leaped from bright to shadow and back again as the bulb went this way and that. The man on the stairs was carrying something bundled in what looked like a blanket. The blanket moved.

Harry was looking up the stairs, and in another way he was overhead and looking down, but he couldn't see the man's face because he wore a hat and it was low on his forehead and the collar of his long coat was turned up and the bundle he carried, which he carried as if heavy, was partially in front of his face. As he worked his way downstairs, turned at the bottom, one end of the bundle struck the bulb sharply, and it swung harder and hit the wall and exploded against the wire mesh of the fixture and the shelter went dark.

A pause and silence.

A snapping sound.

A burst of flame.

A match had been struck.

In the glow Harry could see the bundle on the floor. The man bent over it and the flame licked his face, but even in the match light it was still too dark to make out his features.

The match went out.

Another was lit.

The man went across the room to a shelf. He walked as if his foot hurt. He took down a candle and lit it. The candle wavered and the light in the room wavered. The big man opened the bundle. A young man was inside. Not a kid, but a little guy. Even in the dim light Harry could tell the man was redheaded and freckle-faced.

The young man had a rag in his mouth—no, a sock—and his hands and legs were tied with what looked like wire. His head had a large red raspberry on it. Harry knew then that the big man had slammed the redhead's head against the door outside, and the whole thing had been recorded. He watched as the frightened young man, out of the wrapping, tried to scooch away on his butt. He didn't get far. He came up against the wall.

The big man stood, his shadow falling over the young man like a tar-covered slat. He bent, dragged the kid to the center of the room by his feet, spun him on his butt, wrapped his left arm around the kid's neck, hooked his hand into the bend of his right elbow, slid his right hand behind his victim's head and began to choke—

"That hurts . . . too tight, Harry."

—and the room was full of colors, the sound of the young man struggling, trying to free his neck arteries from being crushed. All of this, the nerves screaming, the muscles snapping, these sounds were as loud in Harry's ears as firecrackers popping. Then the young man made a spitting sound, and his feet, tied together, rose up and hit down, and did it again, and went still. The big man continued to squeeze, and he bent forward, putting his weight on the back of the young man's neck—

"For God's sake, quit it."

—and there was a snapping sound so loud it made Harry feel as if his eyes would bulge out. The big man let out a breath that reminded him of a tired man lying down to rest, then all was—

—bright light and Talia screaming, "You're scaring me. Stop it! Stop it!"

Harry snapped back. His fingers ached and his mind felt drunk. "You're hurting me."

Harry had hold of Talia's arms, and he was squeezing hard, so hard his fingers hurt, and he was hanging on as if for dear life. Her dress was down and her breasts swayed in the light as she struggled.

He let her go.

"Sorry . . . Sorry. My God, Talia. My God . . . There was a murder."

"What?" Talia said, standing, slipping her arms through the dress straps, looking at Harry as if he had fallen out of the sky dressed in a gold lamé jumpsuit.

"Right here," he said. "In this room. There was a murder."

"A murder? What are you talking about. . . ? You hurt my arms, you son of a bitch."

"And I think your father did it."

PART FOUR

In the Hungry Belly
of the Beast

40

Outside the air was easier to breathe and the sky was full of all those shiny yard lights. The backyard was stuffed with people, because Talia, mad as if she had been dipped in acid, had burst out of the shelter screaming, running toward the house, leaving Harry, coatless and confused.

She brought the crowd back with her. She was no longer drunk. She had snapped out of it.

So now he stood there, out of the woods, away from the shelter at the edge of the yard, watching as they swelled around him like a great flood of well-dressed water.

"What are you doing to my daughter?" Talia's dad said. "She said you hurt her."

"I didn't mean to," Harry said. "It was an accident. I swear. I had . . . I had a vision."

"Do what?" her father said.

"A vision."

"He's crazy, Daddy," Talia said. "I didn't know he was crazy."

"It's okay, Talia." It was the boy who had been in the crowd at school, at the burger joint, the one he had seen Talia look at while dancing. Kyle. All sorts of ideas and questions, and even some sad answers, came to Harry as he watched the boy slide up and put his arm around Talia's waist.

"She wanted to show me the storm shelter," Harry said.

"I did," Talia said. "And then he was all over me. Look at my arms and wrists. . . . Well, you can't see them in this light, but they're bruised. Bad."

"I ought to beat you down, boy," her father said.

"It was an accident, I swear."

Talia's mother arrived. She wobbled out of the crowd and looked at Harry and smiled. "You're cute, you know it?"

"Oh, shut up," Mr. McGuire said. He reached into his pocket, pulled out his cell phone, punched buttons. Then to Harry: "I'm calling the police."

"The police?" Harry said. "I didn't do anything."

"He said you killed someone, Daddy," Talia said, clinging tightly to the boy.

"What?" Mr. McGuire said, then, into the phone: "Oh, police. Yes. Yes."

He gave his name and address, clicked off the phone, dropped it into his front pants pocket.

"Killed someone?" Mr. McGuire said. "Me?"

"He said he thought you killed someone," Talia said. "You, Daddy."

"In the vision," Harry said, "he looked like you."

"Killed who?" Mr. McGuire said. "What in hell are you talking about?"

"I don't know, a redheaded man, had freckles."

"No shit. A redheaded man with freckles. Did he have on a funny hat? Maybe some goddamn galoshes?"

"No," Harry said. "The man, the one big as you, he had on the hat. But it wasn't funny."

As they talked the crowd had begun to mumble, and now they came closer and closer to Harry, and he felt as if he were going to faint, as if he were tucked too tightly in cotton and all the air was being sucked out of the universe by God's own vacuum.

"I killed someone, and I had on a hat?" Mr. McGuire said. "A redheaded man with freckles?"

"He might have been you. The size he was . . . I don't know. Maybe it wasn't you."

"Now you're not sure. Son, you need to make sure you stay on your medicine."

"I think you might be right," Harry said.

Mrs. McGuire said something, but Mr. McGuire yelled her down. She said, "You're always such a shit. I'm going back to the house."

And away she went, adrift and a-stumble toward the house.

They all stood there, Harry in the center, the crowd talking amongst themselves, breathing alcohol into the night air, and Harry, like some kind of sculpture, waited while they looked at him.

About ten minutes past forever the sky began to vibrate with red, blue, yellow, and white lights that wrapped around the golden light from the front yard and twisted it into a knotty rainbow.

The police cars had arrived.

With lights flashing, no sirens, three cop cars pulled into the back driveway and parked, doors opened, and cops poured out. The crowd split and the cops came up beside Mr. McGuire.

One of the cops was Kayla.

41

"Before we go any further," the sergeant said, "my name is Sergeant Tom Pale. This scar on my face, I know it can be distracting, so I'm gonna tell you how I got it, so maybe you'll quit wondering, 'cause I know you are. Everyone does. I want your mind on the business at hand, not this thing. A naked guy on PCP was using a Sheetrock knife on cars in a parking lot, scratching them up. I was on call. We got into it. I arrested him. By myself. Which was some real work. So that's where the scar came from. I got the cut, he got his nuts squashed and lost hearing in his right ear. So that's the scar story, all right?"

Harry said, "All right," because the sergeant was correct; he had, in fact, been focusing on the scar. It was quite a doozy, ran from the sergeant's left eyebrow under his eye, across his cheek, and cut deep into his lips. It had a kind of leathery look, and a shine like a sugary doughnut. It made the sergeant's left eye look a little squinted.

The sergeant said, "So let's go at the important business again. He lit a candle that wasn't there, this big guy in the hat and coat, and he strangled the redheaded guy who was all trussed up? That right? After he lit this candle?"

"Yes, sir."

"Strangled him dead?"

"I believe so. Yes, sir."

"He lit a candle? That's what you're telling me?"

"Yeah."

"But there weren't any candles in the shelter. What did he do, put it in his pocket, take it with him?"

"The candles were there when it happened."

"But not now?"

Harry shook his head.

The sergeant pursed his lips, brought his fingers together, steeple-style. "And he had on a long coat, collar turned up, and was wearing a hat? It ain't that warm, son. That don't sound right, him dressed like that."

"I know how it sounds."

"And the guy, what'd he do, crawl through a crack in the wall, hide under the bed? He didn't come out with you, did he? Didn't say anything to you?"

"He didn't know I was there."

"Ah. Because . . . ?"

"It happened in the past."

"That's what I thought you said. Just wanted to be sure. So this guy from another time—"

"The past. And it was the memory of him, not actually him, that was there."

"That right?"

"Yes, sir."

"So the guy from the past, he wasn't really there, except in the sounds, which only you can hear?"

"Afraid so."

"You see the killer's face?"

"Not really."

"You're sure?"

"Yes."

"And you didn't dream it?"

"I didn't dream it."

"This kind of thing, you said it has happened before?"

"Yes, sir."

"You on any kind of medication?"

"No, sir."

"Spent any time in, you know, hospitals?"

"I suppose you could say I've seen a few doctors. But, no, outside of tonsils, no real hospital time."

The sergeant considered this silently, as if trying to mentally phrase his next question before asking it.

Kayla came into the room. When she came in her perfume came with her. It was strong and unique, just the way it had been when they were kids. The room had a long table and a couple of drink and snack machines, a short table with a coffeepot and a microwave on it. There was also an empty box of doughnuts—ambrosia of the law—on the counter.

Kayla poured coffee into a paper cup, sat at the table.

The sergeant looked at her. Harry wasn't sure what the look meant, but it meant something.

Kayla sat prim and straight. There were no wrinkles in her cop clothes. There was no expression on her face, but from time to time she looked at him. Her eyes were so green they appeared to be gems.

"All right," the sergeant said, "Here's the recap. This guy, one you saw, he killed someone in the past, exactly when, you don't know, but he did, and you saw him, because you see stuff that's in sound? That right?"

"That's about it."

"Sound?"

"Yep."

"And I'm supposed to believe it?"

"Doubt you will, but that's it."

"And you're saying the guy did it was Mr. McGuire."

"I thought so. Now I'm not so sure. But someone was murdered there, and the memory of it was trapped in sound."

"How long ago you think this murder happened?"

"I don't know."

"So you didn't really see him, but you saw his ghost—"

"Impression, actually. He could be dead or alive. If it's Mr. McGuire, he's definitely alive. I probably shouldn't have said it was him. It's just who came to mind, because the killer knew the place, knew where the candles were. Guess that's why he came to mind. Shouldn't have said it was him, though."

"You're right. You shouldn't have said it."

Kayla said, "I got a question, it's okay with you, Sergeant."

The sergeant lifted his eyebrows, said, "Okay."

Kayla leaned across the table toward Harry. She really did smell good. "The redheaded guy, can you describe him?"

"Him I saw very well. Redheaded, freckle-faced—"

"In match light?" the sergeant said. "In candlelight?"

"The light was on his face," Harry said. "He wasn't a big man. He wasn't a kid, exactly, but he was young. Maybe my age, maybe some younger. He was as small as a child. The killer was strong though, guy that carried him. Way he carried him, coming down those stairs and all."

"So the guys you dreamed," the sergeant said, "the big guy had a coat and hat and the little guy was redheaded and freckle-faced."

Harry was getting tired of this. He needed a drink. A tall drink.

"Yeah," Harry said.

"Sure you didn't try and encourage Miss McGuire to give you sex; sure you didn't try and rape her?"

"I didn't."

"Got to wonder, a story like that. Sounds like something you would make up off the top of your head—"

"It's not," Kayla said.

The sergeant shifted in his chair to look at Kayla.

"I know Mr. Wilkes," she said. "He's always believed this sound business. He might have some kind of condition, but he's telling the truth as he sees it."

"Really?" the sergeant said.

"Yeah, really," Kayla said.

The sergeant ran a hand through his hair. "Let me explain some things to you, son. What happened tonight, it could get your ass thrown in jail. And I don't take kindly to men who mistreat women. I don't take kindly to that at all."

The door opened. An officer came in, beckoned the sergeant out. "One minute," the sergeant said. He got up and went out.

Harry nodded at Kayla. She nodded back. Neither of them spoke for a few moments, then Kayla said, "When this big man came into the shelter, he just let the door slam?"

"Yes."

"Didn't seem surprised by the sound?"

"No. The house isn't that close, though. You could slam it a lot and it not be heard."

Kayla nodded as if she already knew that. She had been there, the house and the shelter.

"You smell good," Harry said.

"Yeah." She broke her professional demeanor, smiled. "I'm not supposed to wear perfume on the job. But I can't help myself. I'm addicted to it. Made it myself. From other perfumes. I wear too much, don't I?"

"Not for me, you don't."

The sergeant was back; his attitude had changed. "I'll make this quick. That was a call from the chief. He wants me to wrap this up. Chief got a call from Mr. McGuire, and he's not going to press charges. His daughter isn't either. They just want you to stay away from them and their daughter. Way they see it, some head problems got the better of you. I'm not saying that, but that's what they say, and the girl, Talia, she says you scared her, but she thinks now you didn't mean to hurt her. But she doesn't want to see you again. Said you have a suit she bought."

"The coat is still in the shelter. I'm wearing the rest of it. I'll have it cleaned and returned. I'll give you the tie, cuff links, stuff like that right now."

"She bought all that for you?"

"Yes, sir. She didn't like my Bealls suit. And, just for the record, she doesn't like JC Penney either, and I'd guess she's not crazy about Sears."

Sergeant Pale studied Harry for a long moment, nodded slowly.

"Remember this. McGuire and the chief, they're friends. Very tight. Hang together. Getting my drift? You're getting a favor done here."

Kayla walked Harry outside.

"Hey, great to see you," Harry said. "Now if I could just throw up and shit my pants out here in the parking lot, it would be a perfect day. . . . Sorry—I talk stupid when I'm embarrassed."

"That story you were telling, all of that sounds a little stupid."

"I know. But that's how it is. You've heard a similar story before."

"I said as much."

"And I thank you for that. Frankly, I'm kind of used to being thought an idiot."

"You said you didn't do that anymore."

"I lied. I hadn't seen you in a while, and I didn't want to touch on the fact that I might be a fucking nut."

"We could always be honest with one another, Harry."

"I haven't seen you in a while."

"Not so long. Not really. You know what I think?"

"What?"

"You need a better class of friends. Girlfriends, for that matter."

"She wasn't very nice when you met, was she?" Harry said.

"You didn't exactly rush in to support me."

"No. No, I didn't. I should have. I feel like the biggest dumb cluck in the world. Joey was right. She didn't give a damn about me. I think she was using me to make another guy jealous. I'm slow on the uptake."

"You're trusting."

"And how kindly that trait has treated me."

"Wait a minute. Joey? You mean Joey Barnhouse?"

"Yep."

"He was always such an asshole. I thought he'd be dead by now. Maybe shot while stealing beer from a convenience store."

"You'll be happy to know he hasn't changed. . . . You know what, Officer? I don't know how I'm going to get home."

"I'm going to drive you."

On the way to his apartment, driving slowly down dark streets, Harry said, "Questions you asked, I get the feeling you might believe me. Not just believe I believe, but that you might think there's something to it."

"I've thought a lot about what you told me long ago. About the sounds."

"And?"

"I'm still thinking about it."

They drove a distance in silence. Harry was thinking about what he had read in the newspaper those long years ago, about Kayla's dad hanging himself. He didn't want to bring that up, but he certainly thought about it. Instead, he said, "How was Tyler?"

"Too many churches. Not enough Christians."

"The school all right?"

"Pretty good."

"You probably don't know about it, but my dad died."

"No. I didn't. I'm sorry. He was a nice man. Recently?"

"A while back. Heart attack. Died at home."

"You probably know about my dad."

"Saw something in the paper."

"Pink."

"What?"

"Nothing."

When they arrived at Harry's apartment, Kayla pulled to the curb. "It's the one on top," he said.

Kayla nodded.

"Maybe we could talk," Harry said. "Have some coffee some-time. It's been a while."

"Sure."

Kayla wrote down her phone number, gave it to Harry. "Old times," she said.

42

His apartment seemed a place of long ago and far away, but it had been only a few hours since Harry had sat on the couch waiting for Talia's call.

No sooner was he in the door than he stripped off the clothes Talia had bought him, draped them over a chair. He put the shoes and socks together and put them under the chair. He sat on the couch in the silk underwear she had bought him and decided to keep them.

He figured, what he'd been through, he'd earned that much. Besides, they were really comfortable. He decided if he gave them back, he was gonna make sure they had a skid highway in the back, something she could remember him by. But no. He was going to keep them.

There was a knock on the door.

Harry got up and went to the window and looked out by moving the curtain slightly. A big man was looking right at him, and next to him, in front of the door, was Mr. McGuire. Still in party clothes.

Harry dropped the curtain.

"Open up," said McGuire. "We just saw you at the window."

Curses, thought Harry.

"Open the goddamn door, or Jimmy here will kick it down."

"I'll call the cops," Harry said. "Fact is, I'm doing it right now."

"Go ahead. I know the chief. He knows I'm here. Count of three, the door comes down," McGuire said.

Harry opened the door.

McGuire and the moose named Jimmy pushed inside. Unlike McGuire, the moose wore blue jeans and a flannel jacket over a T-shirt.

"What a crummy place," McGuire said. "You brought my daughter here?"

"Actually," Harry said, "she preferred the backseat of the car."

McGuire slapped out at Harry, and Harry stepped back and the slap passed by, and Harry thought: Cool, I'm really starting to learn something. I knew that was coming. I got out of the way, smoothly.

McGuire slapped him with the other hand.

It hurt.

Harry put a hand to his face. Thought, note to self: When you do something smooth and cool, best not to become too caught up in it. 'Cause then you get decooled in the following moments.

"I want you to stay away from my daughter," McGuire said.

"Hey, I'm through."

"Others have said as much, and they kept coming around. I know she's always in heat, but you keep your dog nose out of her ass. Got me?"

"Promise you. I'm done."

"You're not done. Jimmy here, he'll make you done. Like way fucking overcooked."

Harry glanced at Jimmy. Jimmy didn't seem too interested. He looked as concerned about this meeting as a pig might be over the proper use of dinner china. He probably had an overdue date with a beer, a nudie magazine, and a handful of Vaseline.

"Jimmy can really fuck you up," McGuire said.

Jimmy slapped a big fist into a big open palm.

"I don't want to be fucked-up."

"Thought not," McGuire said. "And don't be spreading lies about me killing someone in the shelter. Visions, my ass. You were trying to impress my daughter and it backfired."

"I saw something."

McGuire studied Harry. He put his face close to Harry's.

"You saw shit. Now forget it. You go around saying things like that . . . well, I won't bring Jimmy. I'll just bring me. I like to have someone else do my dirty work, pay them well. But for you, I might make an exception. Dragging my name through the dirt, that isn't good. And as for cops, forget it. I could kill your ass and throw you in the riverbottom, bury you out back of the fucking Coke plant, and no one would look for you, and if they found you, one word from the chief and they'd put you back. Got me, pencil dick?"

"Loud and clear."

"Jimmy, show him something."

Jimmy came forward quickly, and Harry thought, I ought to do something. I ought to do something Tad taught me, except mostly what I've learned so far is concentration and don't fall over roots. And then Jimmy sent an upper cut into Harry's belly, and Harry folded with it, tried to relax, and did. It was a good shot, and he felt it, but not like he would have before. He let his breath out and went limp and the punch picked him up some, and when it was over Harry straightened and took in a deep breath. He was hurt, but not destroyed.

Jimmy and McGuire both looked at Harry for a long, odd moment.

"Tougher than you look," McGuire said. "But nobody's as tough as they would need to be if I get after them. You got me?"

"I still got you."

"Good. Now, no more business about the shelter, and stay away from my daughter. Buy you a watermelon, drill a hole in it, fuck that. It's more fitting to your station in life, which is just under the fucking dirt, southwest of nowhere. Good fucking night."

They went out then and shut the door, and Harry sat down, feeling the pain in his stomach. Kind of proud of himself, really.

"Nighty-night," he said to the empty room.

Harry glanced at the suit pants, the fancy shirt on the back of the chair, thought, damn, there was my chance to return that shit. Then he thought: You were just a pet, you idiot. And not even a loved pet. Just a dog she liked for a while, got tired of, was ready to send to the animal shelter. She's already, this very night, petting another spaniel's head. A full-blood. Not some mongrel.

He asked himself: In the long run, what did I get out of it all?

Well, yeah. There was that. That was something.

Still, those memories didn't make him feel as good as he would have liked to have felt. And, of course, seeing someone murdered in the past inside an old shelter—well, really inside his head—squeezing Talia till she hurt, that didn't work out so well.

Of course, he had met Jimmy. He was starting to get out and meet people. That was a kind of plus. Getting punched by a hired thug. That was new in his life.

He felt emotions wind up in a ball and bounce off the inside of his head, and they weren't his emotions. They may have been released by his own, but these belonged to time travelers of a sort. Banged and battered, murdered, and in some cases self-destructive souls, released by sound, reverberating in his skull, flashing at the corners of his eyes, knotting up his nerves, squeezing all the juice out.

He hung his head between his knees, then slowly lifted it.

He had done well for a moment there. Took a punch, avoided a slap. But now he was feeling weak. Feeling a lot like he had always felt. And he thought about the sounds lurking. More bad memories and painful emotions ready to leap into his head and ride around on his nerve endings.

Sucked.

He looked about, considered putting the cardboard and egg cartons back. Except he had disposed of them. Maybe he could get more, starting tomorrow. He would have to consult his book, maybe do some research, as he hadn't been to the Wal-Mart lately, and out back of it was where you found all the good boxes.

But there might have been an accident somewhere near there, so he had to watch that.

He paused.

Nope.

Not going to do that. Won't slip back into the old ways. No, sir.

I'm one with the universe.

Except for this little snag, of course. It's not every night you can lose your girl, accuse her father of murder based on visions from the past, get arrested, released, get the cop's number who drove you home.

That part wasn't so bad.

Course, Kayla was just being friendly. Old times, she said.

Pink?

What did that mean? What was she talking about? Did he misunderstand her?

No. He was fairly certain she had said, "Pink."

He thought on matters awhile, decided the thing to do was go for a walk. He got dressed and went along the way he knew best, way out along Pecan Street, strolling briskly, hands in pockets, a cool wind on his face. It was the long way to go, not the short way, but the last time he had checked, written in his book, this had been a pretty safe place.

He walked along the familiar route and came to the liquor store and stopped in front of it. He looked at his watch. The store closed in fifteen minutes.

Sometimes you had to break the rules. *Shit.* He had earned a drink, the day he'd had. He'd earned two drinks. Maybe a whole bottle. Bottles. Beer, that might be the thing. No gin, whiskey, anything like that. *Rio Bravo*, baby. He could handle it the way Dean handled it. Beer instead of the hard stuff.

He walked inside the store and the counterman looked up, said, "Hey, haven't seen you in a while."

"I know."

"I was thinking you gave it up."

"No."

"What's it gonna be?"

Harry stood his ground, looked around. All the bottles were so bright and inviting; it was like he expected to find a genie inside, one that could grant him the wish of oblivion.

One with the universe. Yeah. He got a few beers in him, that's exactly how he'd be. Tad was wrong. He had been one with the universe when he was drunk. It was the sober part that fucked him up.

Harry picked up a six-pack of Bud and put it on the counter and took out his wallet. There wasn't much inside. A few bucks. Enough for this, though. He looked up and the counterman smiled at him. He didn't know the man's name, but the man knew him, knew what he wanted. Over the counterman's shoulder, he saw his reflection in a mirror on the wall.

He looked frantic. His tongue was sticking out of his mouth a little and his face was flushed, and the grin that was around his probing tongue looked to him to be the grin of an idiot.

"One with the universe, my ass," Harry said.

"What?" said the counterman. "What did you say?"

"Nothing."

Harry left the beer, turned, and went out and back along the sidewalk. He went a way he knew that led toward a little street that passed between a grove of pecan trees. He went that way because it was a shortcut that had always been safe, nothing horrible in any sound he had ever found.

Went along knowing that the street connected to another that would lead him to Tad's.

Tad was the man. Tad had some answers.

Kayla unlocked the door to her little house on the shadowy end of the street, hoping that damn dog Winston wasn't loose in the yard. He was big, a Great Dane, and he loved to stick his nose in her ass, as well as stand on her car. Anyone's car or ass, for that matter. He must have thought he was a cat. If she didn't like the silly dog so much, she'd turn in his owner for not keeping him on a leash.

Winston didn't show.

She went inside, moved slowly through the dark. She didn't need a light. There wasn't much to figure out. Furniture was minimal.

When she got to the den, which she had transformed into an office, she turned on the light. There was a clutch of darts sticking up in a block of wood on top of a large carved wooden bear. The bear had been her father's. He bought it for her when she was ten. They had been driving along on their way to visit relatives in Houston, and there it was, along with a bunch of other chain saw–carved critters. She had squealed so loudly he had pulled over and bought her the bear, right there on the spot, had to rent a truck later to come back and get it.

The block of wood fit right between the bear's ears.

Kayla picked up the block, pulled the six darts out of it, put the block back between Harry's ears. That's what she had named the bear. Harry.

After all these years she hadn't forgotten Harry, and of course he remembered her too. A little. Had asked for her number. Just to be friendly, most likely. A sort of I'll call, we'll do lunch. That wasn't exactly what she had in mind. It wasn't the way she dreamed things would be. She thought she would grow up and see Harry again and he would fall madly in love with her and they would marry.

Two interlocking pieces of the same great puzzle. Hadn't that been the way they talked that time so long ago?

Tonight hadn't quite been the vision she had imagined.

Course, she had a lot of other things in mind, and nothing had come of any of those either. Like solving her father's murder for one.

Suicide they called it, not murder.

Well, strictly speaking, no one back then thought it was a suicide. Autoerotic accidental death. That's what was thought. But her dad had been a cop, and the police force didn't want that out, the stuff about the autoerotic business, and they spared her and her mother from having that in the paper.

Suicide.

That's how it read.

It wasn't.

And it was no accident either. She didn't care what the cops thought or what it had said in the paper.

It was murder. She was sure of it.

There was a target on the door across the way and she threw the darts one by one at it. Three of the darts stuck in the door. She was going to have to replace that door pretty soon. It was pocked with holes. The landlord found out, he'd be pissed. Maybe, she thought, I can get some cork board, cover the whole door, that way I miss, no damage.

She collected the darts, tried again from a closer distance. She hit the board five out of six times. A couple of them landed in the general vicinity of the bull's-eye.

When she gathered them up a third time, she picked up the block of wood, stuck the darts in it, replaced it between Harry's ears.

So much for sports.

She turned on some music, doo-wop, her favorite.

She fixed a cup of instant coffee, heating it in the microwave. It tasted dreadful. She sipped it, standing at the kitchen sink, thinking about the events of the night, about what Harry had said about a red-headed guy, thinking this while she listened to the Tokens sing about the lion in the jungle.

She sat down at her desk in the den with her cup and used a key under her chair cushion to unlock the central desk drawer.

She took files out of the drawer, placed them on the desktop, shuffled them open. She looked at the photocopies of the crime photos inside.

Her father. Hanging. Wearing lipstick, a bra, lace panties, and fishnet stockings with leg hair poking through.

You couldn't tell it in the photos, but the panties were pink. They really didn't go well with his skin color, and they certainly didn't match the bra, which was white and rather loose-fitting.

Nope. Didn't look good. Loose bra. Hair poking through the stockings. And those frilly pink panties. Just didn't work. Especially in the bug-smeared light of his garage. Bad atmosphere.

It was an atmosphere she remembered very well.

She was the one who found him.

43

Harry found Tad's door wide-open, and when he went cautiously into the house, turned on the light, he smelled something that he recognized immediately.

Liquor. Alcohol. A lot of it. You could have given about fifty fat people a full-fledged rubdown with just the smell alone.

Damn, thought Harry. Damn.

Tad's feet were poking out from under the kitchen table, cans and bottles were spread all over. Two empty bags of honey-roasted peanuts lay ripped open nearby.

Harry got Tad by the feet and pulled him out from under the table. Tad groaned, threw an arm over his eyes. "Turn off the goddamn sun," Tad said. His voice was so slurred, it took Harry a moment to understand what he meant.

"It's a lightbulb, Tad."

"Goddamn bright."

Harry dragged Tad across the room, down the hall to the bathroom, by his feet. By the time Harry got him there, Tad was out cold again.

Harry hit the light, bent Tad over the tub, turned on the shower, gave Tad's head a good dose of cold water. Tad came up sputtering. Harry had a hand on Tad's shoulder, and before Harry could figure how it happened, he was in a wristlock that hurt all the way to his spine and caused his head to touch the floor.

"It's me, Tad," Harry said, his face against the tile. "Harry. You remember Harry."

"Oh," Tad said, letting him go, falling to a limp sitting position against the wall. He put his arm over his eyes to fend against the bathroom light. "Any more peanuts?"

"I think you ate them all. You fucked up, Tad. You fucked up big-time. We had a deal, and you blew it."

Tad didn't move his arm from over his eyes. He seemed suddenly sober. "On this day they died. Don't seem that long ago to me, though, Harry. It's like fucking yesterday. My boy, he'd be your age, I'd been on time. Shown up when I was supposed to."

"It happened on this day?"

"Today, so many—but not so many—years ago," Tad said, and began to cry.

"Damn," Harry said, reaching out to gently touch Tad's shoulder. "Damn. I should have been here. You should have said."

After about ten pass-outs and two pots of coffee, and with morning near, Tad was sober, or at least something that passed for it. They positioned themselves in lawn chairs in the backyard with large cups of coffee. The only light in the yard was starlight, and there wasn't much of that, but there was a glow from the next-door neighbor's yard light as well. The wind was blowing gently and so were the leaves, dry now as mummy wrappings.

"My boy, he would have been your age, Harry."

This was something Harry had heard a lot. Tad had repeated it both drunk and sober all night.

"I know, Tad. I'm so sorry."

"Knew the day was coming. The anniversary of the event.

Thought I had it by the balls. Really did. Then it came, and I got to thinking, and you weren't around—"

"Sorry."

"Not your fault. I was kind of glad you weren't, because I wanted to feel miserable and sorry for myself. And I knew I was going to do it before I actually went to do it. About dark I drove down to the liquor store, bought all manner of knock-down juice, and well, you see the results. I'm not proud of myself. To put it simply, tonight has not been a good night for our hero."

"Not on my end either."

"Oh?"

Harry told him all about it, Talia, the shelter, Kayla, his own trip to the liquor store, his close call there, whole ball of wax.

"Damn," Tad said. "Your day really did suck the big old donkey dick. I'm sorry about Talia."

"Me too. Sort of. I should have known better. There was plenty there in the way of signs to tell me I was getting jerked around, and then . . . the shelter . . . what I saw there."

"Hey, you got to cast your line in the water, try and drag something in from time to time. Now and again, you do that, you get a stinker. But what about this cop, Kayla? You know her, she gave you her number. Said you used to have a crush on her."

"I think she gave me her number in a friendly way. You know, old times."

"No, she didn't."

"You don't know, Tad."

"Sure I do. She wouldn't have given the number to you if she didn't want you to call."

"We were neighbors, old schoolmates. That's all it is."

"Old schoolmates can talk. So what's wrong with that, talking?"

"Nothing, I guess."

"Darn tootin'."

"Tad, got to tell you, when I thought about getting drunk tonight, what you taught me helped me block the urge, fight the sounds. Got to admit, I'm not living with them so much as I'm hiding in plain sight. But it's something. They aren't chasing me around like before. Well, not as much. Some. But not as much. And thinking on that, trying to pay attention to what you taught me, I didn't drink. Didn't lose my head completely."

"And I did. Some fucking role model I am. Told you from the start, kid. I'm great at giving advice, not so good at following it."

"You're doing what you can. In spite of this, you're doing better."

"Good to have a friend. I forgot what that was like."

They sat silent for a bit, sipping coffee, then Harry said, "Tonight, down in that shelter, cellar, whatever the hell it was, that wasn't little stuff. It was murder. I know it sounds crazy—"

"I believe you."

"You do?"

"At first I thought you had been dropped on your head, or that the mumps infected your brain, wiped out some cells. But now I think if you're crazy, well, I'm crazy too."

"Means a lot coming from you. You may be the only one who believes me. And maybe Kayla. Hard to tell. But someone was murdered there in that shelter, and I have a hunch they were never plucked for the crime."

"Said you thought at first it was Mr. McGuire? But now you sound like you're rethinking it."

"Don't know what I think. I quit saying it was him at the police station, 'cause I wasn't sure. Tired of being in trouble. I was lucky McGuire dropped the charges—"

"But that makes you suspicious."

"Another thing. More I think about it, Kayla, she probably does believe me. She asked about the redhead, and the sergeant didn't. Not really. He asked me for a description to kind of mock me, I think. But she seemed to believe me."

"I tell you, she likes you."

"Maybe."

"Gonna call her?"

"Maybe."

"Want to move a bit across the yard? Show you some new moves? Think I'm up for it. It's the kind of thing that can get your head straight, moving around, meditation in motion."

"You sure get over a drunk good."

"Hey, boy. I've had a whole lot more practice than you. And who said I'm over it?"

"What about next time?"

"You mean next year, same time, same station?"

Harry nodded.

"Don't know. I'm worried about tomorrow. And the next day. It's like they say in AA, one day at a time."

"You belong to AA?"

"Nope. Tried a few years back. Never could accept that shit about letting a higher power have the hold of things. Don't believe in a higher power, so that wasn't for me. I think you live, you die, and that's it. Heaven to me is a fairy tale, like the tooth fairy, Santa Claus, and the Easter bunny. But the double-A drunks, they're right about that one-day-at-a-time stuff. All you can do. Got to think about now, not tomorrow. I'm proud of you, Harry. For having more balls than I do. For not getting on the liquor wagon tonight. Especially after those goons came by. That takes a tow sack of nuts, friend."

"I don't think my fucked-up love life, a slap, and a punch compares to what you've been through."

"It's not a matter of degree, Harry. It doesn't matter what the reason is. Drinking compounds the problem. Want to know something, Harry?"

"Sure."

"Before I met you, I knew I was unhappy, but I didn't know just how lousy I made myself. Really was no fun being a drunk, and tonight didn't help anything. I want to keep trying to quit . . . I am going to quit. That's final."

"I believe you."

"Good. 'Cause me, I'm a little uncertain. . . . You sticking around for what's left of the night, or going home?"

"If it's okay, I'll stay."

"You know where the spare room is."

"Sure."

"Like to think my boy had lived, he would have been a lot like you."

"That's a special comment."

"I got you something. It's in the house. It's a cell phone."

"That's nice, Tad, but the bill—"

"I'm covering that."

"You can't do that."

"Listen, I want you to have it so we can be in touch, so next time I get the urge to go stinking, I can call you, or you can do the same. It's got like, what do they call it, text messages. Where you can write me on the phone, don't have to call. We can even take pictures and send them to each other. And here's a real extra. You can use it as a phone. That's pretty fucking uptown, I think."

"Tad . . ."

"It's as much for myself as it is for you."

"Sure, Tad. That's great. Thanks."

Tad cleared his throat. "Now let's get up and move."

They moved in the starlight, soft and light, and the crickets chirped, and somewhere a frog bleated. Harry felt as if the night and the stars, the sounds, were an extension of himself, gliding through the dark, sucking it up, deep inside the absolute where he was part of the ebb and flow and pulse of the earth. Most important, he was connected to the universe without seams, gently breathing, gliding along, out and away, the sun rising slow and red and hopeful, gradually blazing out the night and the stars.

44

Fall flowed by and winter flowed in, and it was a cold one, and wet. Harry thought of what he had seen down there in the McGuire shelter, but there was nothing to do with his thoughts but wonder.

Tad believed him, but so what?

There was not a thing they could do about it.

The police were reluctant to investigate ghosts.

In time, Harry let it all slip to the back of his mind, tried to keep on keeping on, studied for finals, worked as much as possible, spent time with Tad, practicing, learning.

He spent less time at his apartment, and never answered Joey's calls, which kept coming, filling up the answering machine. He played them back, he got a series. They sounded like someone trying to patch things up with his lover.

Beep.

"Came by. You weren't there."

Beep.

"See you soon."

Beep.

"I'm gonna drop by."

Beep.

"Call me," all the messages ended.

But Harry didn't call.

He thought about Kayla.

He thought about Talia. How she had looked that night when she had dragged the crowd after her, out to where he stood under the great lights, waiting for the cops. He remembered the way she had held Kyle tight, like it was all she ever intended to do in the first place.

But, damn. She sure had looked good.

He hoped she got the suit he sent back to her, sort of hoped she might hang herself with the tie.

In November he voted in an election, but his man lost.

It was Tad's man too.

"Such is it always for the righteous," said Tad. "Way you got to look at it is, the people have spoken. The goddamn ignorant cocksuckers."

At school Harry found himself creeping around again, but it wasn't so much the sounds that freaked him, it was Talia. He didn't want to see her. Started going to class the back way, so he wouldn't cross her path coming out of the building, wouldn't see her on the spot where they had first met.

And it worked well. He saw her only once in the next few weeks, and from a distance. He started missing a lot of classes, studying out of the book. Talia had been right about that. The tests were out of the book more than the lectures. At least there was that good thing about their relationship, him knowing how the old man graded.

On the way to his other classes he was cautious too, just in case she changed her path and he came up against her, like a surprise meeting with a panzer division.

But she wouldn't do that. He knew better. That wouldn't be her way. She would know he would change his route. She was that confident. He was certain of it. Must be a good feeling, being that confident, that certain.

He had almost been there. Right in the middle of Confident Town. Almost. Once. And maybe some of the confidence he had learned had returned of late. He flowed better and better, and now Tad was attacking him, and he was defending, and once, just once, out back of Tad's house, during the middle of a cold day, he had managed to touch Tad a bit, right close to the jaw.

Then he had gone unconscious.

When he awoke, Tad said, "You got to watch both hands. Most guys, they got two."

So he was getting better. Not where he'd like to be, but better.

Of course, he had put the egg cartons back up, the cardboard. There wasn't any use being silly.

One day at work, shelving books, lost in his own world, not thinking about Talia or school or the sounds, or anything like that, a female voice said, "Hey."

It was Kayla. She wasn't in her cop duds. Had on a loose T-shirt, blue jeans, tennis shoes, an oversize coat, her hair tied back, little to no makeup. She was smiling. He loved the way she smiled. She had a wide, expressive mouth, and seeing her smile made him do the same.

"I was softer this time," she said. "So you wouldn't bump your head."

"No. I'm good."

"Ever get a break?"

Harry looked at his watch. "I get off in five minutes. Just work mornings, two to three hours."

"Could you take a girl to coffee?"

"I could. I would. I want to."

"Remember how Joey was always taking a beating?" Kayla said.

"Never really had much of a chance, did he?"

"Guess not."

"Why I've sort of stayed friends with him, I guess. We're not exactly talking right now, but I know we will. I always go back. He's just such a part of me."

They were in Kayla's car, and as they pulled into her drive a large deer sprang into the yard and leaped onto the car.

No. Not a deer. A big-ass dog.

"Good grief," Harry said.

"That's Winston," Kayla said. "He's part Great Dane or something."

They sat inside the car and studied Winston. He had his paws on the front of the hood, his tongue hanging out of his mouth, saliva dripping all over the place.

"He's actually a baby," Kayla said. "He has nuts the size of baseballs, but he's a baby. Belongs to my next-door neighbor. Winston likes to walk on cars."

"No joke?"

"Also likes to put his nose about six inches up my ass every time I go to the door."

Harry thought, Well, he's got that in common with a lot of males. He said, "That's not good."

"Depends on what kind of mood I'm in," Kayla said, and looked across at him and smiled.

"Can we get out?" Harry asked.

"We can. But it's best to let him sort of finish with the car."

After a moment Winston struggled up to where he could stand on the hood, looked directly into the windshield, making dog nose smears on the glass. From that angle, Harry confirmed that Winston did in fact have nuts the size of baseballs.

"This can't be good for your car," Harry said.

"Thankfully, it's a piece of junk. I love driving the squad car. That baby will run. This one limps."

"I have a similar ride," Harry said. "The limping one, I mean."

Winston sprang off the hood of the car and dashed across the yard, stuck his nose under an overgrown shrub, and started noodling the dirt aside with his snout. A moment later he was snapping his jaws together with a kind of ecstasy that, if he weren't a dog, might indicate drug use.

"Cat shit," Kayla said. "He digs it out from under the shrubs. Standing on cars, nosing asses, eating cat shit. That's his life. Simple, but somehow poetic. Don't you think?"

When they got to Kayla's door, Winston ran over and gave them a sniff. "Go on, Winston," Kayla said.

The dog looked as if he had been insulted, then bolted back across the yard.

"I'm always afraid his big dumb ass is going to get run over," Kayla said, working her key in the lock. "As a cop, I could make a stink of it, but I'm afraid Winston will end up at the shelter, get the needle. Around here most of the neighbors kind of put up with him."

Inside, the place smelled faintly of incense and Kayla's intense perfume. "Thought we'd just have coffee here," she said. "Besides, there's something I want to show you."

"So much time had gone by," Harry said, "I thought you had forgotten me."

"Hey. You had my number."

"I mean after you moved."

"Oh. Well, I meant now. I was waiting for you to call. And when you didn't, I was a little pissed. But I cut you some slack. You breaking up with your girl and all."

"I don't know she was ever really my girl."

"Oh," Kayla said. "That's just terrible."

In the kitchen there were a couple of bar stools at the counter. Harry sat on one while Talia made coffee. While it perked, they talked about this and that, old times mostly. When the java was ready Kayla poured them cups and they moved into the living room.

"Think you and Talia might get back together?" Kayla asked.

"Only if our cars collide."

"You'll drive safely, won't you?"

"Absolutely."

"I've thought about you over the years."

"My handsome face, I suppose?"

"You look all right. I've thought about you. I always thought you were . . . sweet."

"That's what every red-blooded American boy likes to hear, how they're sweet. Sometimes we like to be thought of as a little dangerous. Sometimes, when I'm at work, I stack some of the books a little crooked. Who knows if they might fall?"

Kayla sipped her coffee, watched him over the cup.

"No joke?" she said.

Harry crossed himself. "Gospel."

"I don't want you to think I only brought you here because I need help."

"Help?"

"Yeah. Harry. I believe your visions. The sounds. I do. I did when we were kids . . . Well, for the most part. I've been thinking about it for a few days, and what you said about the redheaded guy—"

"You want help?" Harry had a sudden sinking feeling. Maybe women saw him as some kind of temporary utensil, like a plastic fork. Use it and toss it. The coffee turned sour in his stomach.

"Yeah. I mean, I want to see you. But you talking about the sounds, your visions, that's what got me really excited. Let me tell you something. Back when my dad died, the papers said it was suicide. It wasn't. Even the police knew that. They were giving it what they thought was a good spin."

"How do you spin suicide as good?"

"I found him, Harry. He left the force, had his own garage, like he always wanted. I had come to visit him for a few days. When he didn't come home at dark, I went down to the garage. It was walking distance from the house. Went down there and found him. He was dead all right. He was hanging from a door and had a lamp cord around his neck and he was . . . Shit, this is hard. Not many people know this."

"You don't have to say any more."

"I want to. I think you can help me."

"I don't know, Kayla . . . I mean, if you're going with this where I think you're going—"

"He was hanging from the office door and he was wearing a bra, fishnet stockings, and pink panties."

"Pink panties?"

"With lace."

"Ouch."

"Oh, yeah."

"Last time we were together," Harry said, "I asked you about your father. You said, 'Pink'."

"I did?"

"Yeah."

"It was on my mind. Those goddamn pink underpants."

"Go on."

"So I called the cops, and they came out, said he died of auto-erotic strangulation. You know what that is?"

"I think so."

"Said he was, well, masturbating, and that the choking heightened the sensation. That he went too far. Cord got too tight and he died. Happens all the time. You can even buy special rigs for the operation. Devices hang you for a certain length of time, then the rigs let go. Daddy didn't have a rig. Had a lamp cord tied around his neck, stretched over the door, and tied to the doorknob on the other side.

"Cops took pictures, made an investigation, decided he accidently killed himself. Being as he had been one of their own, they called it suicide so as not to embarrass me or my mother. But the crime photos, the case—it went into the files. Way deep in the files."

"You don't believe he died of autoerotic asphyxiation?"

"No. I know kids don't know everything about their parents, but I don't believe that. That wasn't anything like my father. He didn't even like to hold my mother's purse when she was in the store—you know, macho thing. So him dressed up like that, I don't think so. And there are other things.

"One: The bra didn't fit. He was going to do that, cared about it, don't you think it would fit?"

"Gee, Kayla, I don't know. That's kind of out of my league."

"Two: His feet were a foot off the ground. If it was autoerotic, and he didn't intend to die, don't you think he would have worked that out better? So he could get loose of the situation when he wanted?

"Three—and I don't even like to talk about this, but—his penis was in the panties. He didn't have it out. He wasn't, you know . . . stroking it."

"Maybe he hadn't had time. . . . Just being devil's advocate. You know, things could have gone wrong, and it was all over before he got to that part."

"Maybe. But there are other things. Four: the wire around his neck. It was cut off a lamp from the office. He was gonna do it, don't you think he'd have had rope, or another wire? I don't believe he suddenly thought, Damn, I got to have me some of that pleasure, so I'll just take this long lamp wire and cut it and use it. That doesn't seem right. And five: The door to the garage wasn't locked. The lights were out, but the door wasn't locked. Back door was open too. I know. I ran out of that one. I ran all the way to the house to call before I realized there was a phone in the garage. He was going to do something like that, don't you think he would have locked the door?

"Six—and this one I didn't know until I looked at the photographs—he was all bruised up around the eyes, the jaw. You can see the bruises in the pictures. Look."

Kayla went to her desk, took a key from under the chair cushion, unlocked a drawer, and pulled out the files. She took them over to where Harry sat, opened them, gave Harry a look.

Mr. Jones certainly didn't look as if he was the kind of guy to deck himself out in bra, panties, and fishnets. He was a big, burly guy. But hell, it took all kinds.

"Seven: Look at his wrists. Look at the marks. Looks like they were tied so he couldn't get himself loose. When it was over someone cut the bonds, left him hanging to make it look like an accident."

"Why exactly are you telling me all this, Kayla? I appreciate your confidence, but . . . no offense, I don't hear from you in years, and all of a sudden you're telling me about your dad in panties and fishnets, and you're showing me very private photographs."

"Do you see the bruises? They show up good here."

She handed him a photo.

"Could be bruises, I guess."

"Look at the next one, Harry. It's a close-up of his face."

Harry didn't like the photographs. The close-up especially, way Mr. Jones's tongue was poking out of his mouth, his teeth clenched into it. But he did see the bruises.

"I see them," he said. "But I still don't understand what this has to do with me."

Actually, he had an idea, but didn't want to suggest it.

"Eight: the redhead, Harry. One you saw in the shelter? Way you described him. It fit with something. I think that was the guy who worked for my father. Young guy learning the mechanic trade. I didn't know him well. I met him during my visit with Dad. But the other night you described him to a T. His name was Vincent Something-or-another. I'd have to look at the files to see. I have more in the drawer there. I'm not supposed to have them. I slipped in and copied them. They're not part of my bailiwick as a new cop, but I copied them anyway. Vincent was there that night, earlier, because I saw him when I came down to see Dad the first time, but he wasn't there when I found Dad."

"You think the redhead did it?"

"He was never found. Just disappeared. Never went home."

"So it looks like it was him."

"Don't think so. You know what I think? I think someone did that to my dad to make it look like an accident and not murder. As for Vincent doing it, he couldn't have rolled my father over if he was dead. He was too small, and he adored my father. You could tell. Dad was, I don't know, a kind of uncle to the kid, or father figure. This is stuff I've figured out after the fact, based on the way I remember things."

"Sometimes we don't remember as well as we think. Or we remember the way we want to."

Kayla tapped the photo with the tip of her finger.

"What I believe happened is someone—probably more than one, because I think those bruises show my father put up a fight, did this to him. And to keep the murder from being investigated, maybe to embarrass him in death, they dressed him out in women's clothes."

"Why would they want to embarrass him?" Harry asked.

"I don't know."

"What about the redhead? He didn't do it, what's his connection? Where is he?"

"I think he was there that night when it happened," Kayla said. "I don't know where, but I think they may not have known it right away. When they found out he was there, their plan was snapped. They had to get rid of him. They killed him because he was a witness. Couldn't let him be found dead in the garage, that would mess up their plot, so they took him somewhere where he could never be found and killed him."

"The shelter?"

"I think so. The golf course McGuire owns, it's right behind his house. There's a thin line of woods between the course and his property. The garage is on the far side of the golf course. What I'm saying is the garage, the course, and my dad were not that far apart. I'll throw something else in: Joey's dad doesn't live far from there, and that's one of the reasons my mom and dad split up."

"Joey's dad?"

"Joey's mom. Dad, he was seeing her. He was more than seeing her. Mom found out about it, and . . . well, it started coming apart. Can you imagine that? Joey's mom."

"It surprises me. You believe it?"

"Yeah. He admitted it to Mom when she found out. Why they split up. Why he lived here and we lived in Tyler when I was growing up. Me and him, we got okay again, though. That's why I was down to see him when he died. Trying to do the quality-time thing. But all this, and Joey's dad being nearby, and him maybe finding out, probably knowing all about it, and him being the way he was . . . he could have been in on it. It all links up like boxcars."

"But where's the body? Why would they take him there? Why the shelter?"

"According to you, whoever did the murder knew that shelter. Right?"

"Seemed that way. Still, what about the body? Where is it?"

"Haven't figured that part. There are a number of things I haven't figured. You see, Harry, the house my dad lived in, it's sold, but the garage is still there, locked up. It belongs to me. It was in some kind of will or trust or something. It's mine. I've been there several times, and—"

"You want me to go there?" he said.

Kayla nodded. "You have a unique ability."

"God, Kayla . . . It's not easy. It's not like watching a movie. I get . . . sensations, feelings. I've just now gotten to where the little stored-up things, accidents and fights and arguments that I hear from some bang or clang trapped in a car, a stone, or whatever . . . It's just now that that stuff doesn't drive me crazy. I've been working hard on that. I don't want to dive right back into it."

"It's a lot to ask—"

"More than a lot."

"—and I don't want you to think it's the only reason I'm glad to see you, but . . . it's important, Harry. Don't you think? Solving a murder? My father's murder?"

"Jesus, Kayla. You don't know what you're asking."

"I know what I'm asking. I'm asking for you to help me know what happened. He was murdered. I'm sure of it."

Harry sat and thought for a long time. When he looked up, Kayla was watching him intently.

"I don't think so," he said.

She looked as if she had just been pushed off a cliff. She nodded. "All right . . . I'll give you a ride home."

45

Lying on his couch in his undershorts, Harry listened to the afternoon wind wrap itself around the apartment. He wondered why wind didn't carry all manner of messages. Seemed as if all the horrors and terrors and bad things of the world would be on the wind. Was it just too flexible to hold it all?

He wondered why the big, bad sounds hid in rocks and wood and plastic and stone. He wondered why people his age liked rap music. He wondered why cats were popular pets. He wondered why in the middle of the day, even when he felt tired, like now, he couldn't go to sleep. He wondered if Jimmy was beating someone up right now, or if McGuire might be in on some kind of kill. He thought about all manner of shit to keep from wondering about Kayla.

She didn't know what she was asking. Not really.

If she did, she wouldn't ask.

Or maybe she would.

If it were his dad died that way, would he put himself through this business? Would he?

Course he would.

Harry sat up in bed and looked around his room. His prison cell.

Shit. I'm gonna be sick and scared and miserable and keep telling myself how goddamn good I'm doing, I might as well turn it all into something positive.

He got up and found his pants and pulled his wallet out and got Kayla's number out of it. He called. She answered right away.

"One condition."

"Name it."

"I might ask for your body."

"I might give it to you."

"What I want is to bring a friend along. Someone I trust and who can sort of help you watch after me, because I may need it."

"That's not saying much for my body."

"Your body is just fine, and, frankly, I wouldn't mind having designs on it. But not for a favor."

"Not really offering, Harry."

"Got to understand, this is some scary shit to me, Kayla, and I don't want to do it, but I think maybe I should. Think it's the way I can find my way out of all this, or at least find some kind of goddamn point to it all. Understand?"

"Mostly."

"About the friend?"

"Bring him."

Harry called Tad and drove over to Kayla's place.

When Tad arrived, Kayla opened the door. Tad said, "There's a goddamn dog standing on my car. That your dog?"

"Nope. That's Winston. He belongs next door."

"He's on my Mercedes."

"He doesn't stay long."

"Damn well better not. Sorry. You must be Kayla."

"Yep."

"Nice perfume. Plenty of it, but nice."

Tad looked back over his shoulder. "Now he's on the roof," he said.

"He'll do that," Kayla said.

"He's lucky I like dogs."

Tad came inside and shook Kayla's hand. "You are just as pretty as Harry said you were."

"He said that?"

"If he didn't, he should have. He also said you smell nice."

Kayla closed the door and looked at Harry, who stood embarrassed nearby. After more formal introductions were made and more coffee was prepared, Tad wandered nervously about, said, "I see you play darts. Mostly you miss. Your door looks like Swiss cheese."

"Do you play?"

"With others not so well, but darts, some. My guess is, though, you didn't bring me here to play darts. Am I right?"

"No," Harry said. "We didn't."

Tad strolled over to the bear with the block of darts between its ears. He pulled the darts out, swiftly tossed them at the target. He rapidly shifted the darts from his left hand to his right. He seemed to merely flex his wrist. The darts crowded the bull's-eye.

"Good grief," Kayla said.

"Martial arts," Harry said. "This guy is good."

"Thank you," Tad said.

"He doesn't just know how to whip your ass, he knows how to throw things at you. Incidental weapons, he calls it. Isn't that right, Tad? Darts. Rings. Blades."

"That's right. And I do a pretty good Jimmy Durante impression."

"Who?" Kayla asked.

"Well, one thing," Tad said, "I don't do a good one, you wouldn't know. . . . Before your time, gal. Almost before mine. Forget it."

"You can have the darts and the board, you want them," Kayla said. "Me, I'm just sticking them in the door. I'm serious, you leave, take them with you. They just tempt me."

"Thanks," Tad said, and dropped the darts into his coat pocket. "So now do we discuss dominoes or tiddlywinks?"

Harry shook his head. "What I need, Tad, is a little favor."

"Name it, kid."

46

Darkness was creeping along the edge of the skyline, sliding shadows through the trees, when they arrived at the garage in Tad's Mercedes.

It wasn't much. Just a big tin building. There weren't even any electric wires attached to it. It sagged on one side.

When they got to the door, breathing cold air out in white blasts, Kayla gave Harry her flashlight, used a key to open the padlock, and, with Tad's help, slid the door back.

It was dark inside and very cold and it smelled like dried grease and dust. The last of the day's light dropped inside like a dead man falling. Kayla took the flashlight back and flashed it around.

There were long tables with car parts and fan belts and rubber hoses on it, a grease rack to the right, and a pit beneath it. The beam filled with dust motes. She poked it at the grease pit. It was as Harry expected it would be: dark and greasy. Roaches scattered.

"You're asking a lot, lady," Tad said. "The kid's got enough bugs in his head without you helping to put more there."

"I realize what I'm asking," Kayla said.

"Yeah," Tad said. "I'm not so sure."

"It's okay, Tad," Harry said. "Got this problem, ought to do something with it besides be afraid all the time. Turn it into a gift if I can. That's a good thing, isn't it? Gives me some kind of meaning."

"Your call, kid," Tad said. "Just think Kayla ought to know what she's asking."

"I know *why* I'm asking," Kayla said.

Tad took a deep breath and let it out, and, made a little mushroom cloud that floated off and broke apart.

"How does this work?" Tad said. "This vision business. You've told me about how you got to get some kind of noise out of things. But I don't know that I really get it. Not totally."

"Have to find the sound," Harry said. "Kayla's dad died, and it was violent, most likely he raised a ruckus. That leaves an imprint, and I'm the conduit. Show me the door where he was hanged, Kayla."

Kayla took his hand. He liked that part. She pulled him into the darkness and flashed the light on a door. It was open and led into a small office that had a glass front. The glass was cracked.

They didn't go inside.

"Here's another thing," Kayla said, letting go of his hand. "Look down low on the door."

Harry looked. It had dents in the wood.

"That's where he was kicking his heels," she said. Then she swallowed big, adding, "Shit."

"Kayla," Harry said, "I do this, tell you what happened, it might not be what you want."

"I know."

"Kid," Tad said, "you sure you want to do this? You nearly shit your pants just worrying about running your car into potholes where there might have been an airbag went off."

"I'm not as bad as I used to be."

"Yeah, but this is the big time here."

"Just want the two of you to watch me, make sure I'm okay."

"You got it, kid."

"What I'm gonna do, is I'm gonna pull this door back, slam it, see that does anything. It does, I'll be gone. Just make sure I don't hurt myself. I might not be able to stand up. Sometimes it's like getting hit by a train full of emotions. Runs me over, drags me down the track. After a minute, Tad, pick up something, start beating around the parts table in different places, smack the walls—there's a rubber hose, a fan belt on the table. Use one of those."

"Hit stuff?" Tad asked, as Kayla played the light on the table.

"Yeah."

Tad found a rubber hose, slapped it gently in his palm. "I'm ready, kid."

"Good. Kayla, you keep the light on me. Make sure I'm all right. Gets too much, you two pick me up and carry me out of here. Farther away I am from the event, quicker I'll get over it. Understood?"

"Got you," Kayla said.

"Just start whacking shit?" Tad asked again.

"Yeah."

"This reminds me of that time in the honky-tonk," Kayla said. "Looking for ghosts."

"Thing that was different then, I didn't really think we'd find one. . . . I need to concentrate a moment."

Kayla squeezed Harry's hand, let it go.

The sounds always surrounded him, ready to swoop in and take hold and twist him into a knot, but he told himself what he had been telling himself over and over with mixed results for some time. He found he could keep the sounds pretty much at bay. At least they didn't leap at him pantherlike anymore if he disturbed one of those imbedded rumbles. They reverberated gently, and the images they held fluttered at the corners of his mind like vampire bats in the shadowy edges of a poorly lit tunnel. He could feel them and almost see them in the creaking sounds that the wind made in the old building, in the shifting of the aluminum siding.

There was something here, all right.

Waiting.

Harry took hold of the door, moved it gently at first to make sure there was play. It moved creaky on its hinges, but it moved. He swung it back and forth a few more times, then pulled it forward quick, slammed it toward the wall—

—sound vaulted out of it and with it came all the colors of the world, and then some, and they felt wet and heavy and they jetted into his head and made it swell until it exploded with—

Darkness flapped through his skull, dragging damp wings.

Thud, thud, thud.

A man formed out of the darkness and hung from the door Harry had slammed. It was Kayla's father, dangling there in bra and fishnet stockings, pink panties with lace, his heels beating a tattoo against the door, his tongue, thick and dark, thrashing like a snake tongue tasting air. The wire around his neck bit deep into his flesh. His hands were tied. So were his ankles. He kept kicking back with his legs, striking the door hard with his heels.

The dark tunnel view broke down, widened.

Another man stood to the side of the door, his head tossed back as he observed. He had on a thick coat and hat. White puffs of cold came out of his mouth in what seemed like slow motion, looked like wads of cotton being pulled skyward on an invisible string.

As the man hung there, another man stood in the shadows, by the worktable that contained the parts. He was in darkness, his face not clear.

The man in the hat slowly took a cigarette out of his coat pocket and put it in his mouth. He produced a lighter from another pocket, lit the cigarette, and there was a snap as the sound of the lighter came alive. Harry could hear Jones's heels beating big-time; he could even hear the hatted man let out his breath as he released his first drag of smoke. And this time, Harry clearly saw his face.

It wasn't anyone he recognized.

Slap.

Slap.

Slap.

Harry couldn't figure where it all came from, the slapping sounds, and the slaps kept coming, the sound slightly different after the first three, as if something different had been struck.

And then it came to him.

Tad.

With the hose.

And the vision wadded up into a black ball and went away, and Harry was facing the office now, and he saw Tad bring the hose up, strike the side of the office, just under the glass front—

Slap.

—the redheaded guy he'd seen before, one in the shelter, it was him, and he was being thrown against the glass by the hatted man, the back of his skull hitting it, cracking it, spiderwebbing it, and he was twisting free of the hatted man's grasp—

Slap.

—a pocketknife flashing open in the redhead's hand, cutting at the hatted man's face. A little dark line of blood spat out of the hatted man's cheek, hit the glass in beads. The redhead broke free, darted—

—all of it wadded up again, and—

Slap.

Slap.

—leaping images, some of them ghostly and overlapping, not entirely discernible.

The redhead hit the back door with his hands and it flew open. A rectangle of silver light burst into the garage and the redhead ran into it, out the back, up the hill and—

—faded.

His last vision was of the hatted man grabbing at a phone in the office, popping his own knife out of his pocket with a flick, cutting at the phone wire . . . and then—

Nausea, pain, a twisting of emotions, a crumpling of darkness, a flash of light and the most horrible sensations he had ever experienced, then he was rushing along some bat-ass dark corridor, things reaching out to touch him. He saw light at the end of it all. The light was not very bright, and it was punctuated by little silver dots, and after a moment Harry realized he was lying on his back at the rear of the garage looking up at the stars, gasping in cold air, and then the moon—

—no, Tad's face dropped down over him, and Tad said, "Kid, you went someplace fucked-up, real quick and real bad. You stopped breathing. Kayla gave you mouth-to-mouth. Just consider, it could have been me, and I need a breath mint."

Thank goodness for small favors, Harry thought. Then he realized that he was not lying on the ground, but on Kayla. She had his head in her lap. He had been here before. Years before. He liked it then and he liked it now.

She bent forward to look down at him. A tear fell from her eye and landed on his forehead. It felt good and warm out there in the cold air.

"I thought you were dying."

Finally, after a struggle, Harry said: "Me . . . too."

"You were going bug-shit, spinning in a circle."

"It's okay," Harry said.

"Did you see?" Kayla asked.

"More than I ever wanted to see."

"And?"

"Your father was murdered. Same man that killed the redhead."

Harry tried to sit up. Kayla and Tad helped him. Harry looked up the hill behind the garage. "The redhead, he got away. He ran out back, started up that hill, then faded out on me."

"Toward the golf course?" Kayla asked.

Harry nodded. "Think so."

"And toward the McGuire property, the shelter?" she asked.

"Maybe."

"You actually saw it all?" Tad asked.

"In a fashion," Harry said. "In a horrible fashion."

47

Harry wobbled along.

He was between Kayla and Tad, and without meaning to he leaned first on one, then the other as they walked. No wonder he had an alcohol problem. This was just the thing he tried to avoid, the horrors in the sounds of the past, but tonight he had done it to himself on purpose, and it hadn't been pretty.

They were walking away from the garage to the top of the hill. The hill seemed like something out of a fairy tale, the dead grass at its peak glowed silver in the starlight.

When they reached the top, Harry took a deep breath. The air was cool and burned his throat. When he let his breath out it was white.

Kayla pointed with the flashlight. "He went up here?"

"Saw him run out the door. Up the hill. Then it all faded. He ran outside the realm of the sounds, I guess. When he hit the back door—Correction. When you hit it with the hose, Tad, you revived him hitting it with his palms. He was scared to death, running fast as he could go."

"Poor Dad. Poor Vincent. But why?"

"And who?" Harry said.

"Did these men go after him?" Tad asked Harry.

"I saw the hatted man kill Vincent in the shelter. He obviously caught up with him, tied him up with a wire from the phone."

"This is some creepy shit," Tad said. "And I, for one, don't want to see you do that bullshit again. Your fucking eyeballs near popped out of your head. You hit that floor in there, I was afraid you broke something."

"My shoulder hurts, but I'm okay. I feel weak, kind of sick."

"I was right," Kayla said. "Dad was murdered."

"I didn't actually see them put the cord around his neck, dress him up, boost him on the door. But what I did see certainly made it seem that way. He still had the ties on his hands and feet. The hatted bastard was smoking a cigarette."

"Why would they do all that, the bra and stuff?" Tad asked.

"Like Kayla was saying," Harry said. "They wanted to discredit him. He's found like that, they don't question much else. And the redhead . . . like you thought as well, Kayla. He must have been in the office, heard what was going on up front, panicked, hid in there, then the guy with the hat saw him, and there was a fight. The redhead cut him a little with his knife, broke for the door, went up the hill."

"Didn't you say when you saw the redhead in the shelter, he was tied with wire?" Kayla asked.

"Think so," Harry said.

"Wrapped in a blanket or something?" she asked.

"That's how it looked."

"But you saw the face of these guys? The guy with the hat this time?"

"The guy I saw before, in the shelter. I saw his face. But I can't say I recognized him, though he seemed familiar."

Kayla took a breath, said, "It wasn't Joey's father, was it?"

"No. It wasn't."

"The other guy? What about him?"

"Couldn't really see him to say yes or no."

"Could it have been Joey's dad?"

"It could have been almost anybody. In the dark like that, it could have been fucking Batman."

"Let's follow the likely path," Tad said. "Way the redhead must have had to run to end up at that shelter. You up to it, Harry?"

He wasn't. Harry felt as if his body had been dampened with vinegar and run through a wringer, hung out to dry, and beat with a duster paddle.

And that was the good part.

Inside his head the images came back to him and moved around and shifted the furniture of his mind in new arrangements that he didn't care for.

"Do you?" Kayla said. "Feel up to it?"

Harry thought he might be lying when he said: "I can do it."

Dogs were barking. Lights were on in houses. They stood for a moment looking at the backyards, the clotheslines.

"Clotheslines," Tad said. "You don't see as many of them as you used to, but this is a poorer neighborhood, not as many dryers."

"I beg your pardon?" Kayla said.

"The clotheslines. The blanket the redhead got wrapped in. That's where it came from. It was hanging out to dry. The hatted guy, he grabbed it, thinking he'd wrap the redhead in it, hold him down. Blanket makes a good weapon. This guy, he might have known what he was doing, or just had a brain flash. You get someone's arms and legs pinned in that, you can hold them pretty good. And this Vincent, you said he wasn't a big guy?"

"No," Harry said.

"Fits," Tad said. "This hatted guy, the killer, he grabbed a blanket off one of these lines, went after him with it. Got him down, then used the wire he cut off the phone—was the phone, right?"

Harry nodded. "One of the old-fashioned kind."

"Used that to bind him," Tad said. "Fits together, don't it?"

"Why didn't Vincent just run to a house?" Kayla asked.

"He was so scared," Tad said, "he just hauled some serious ass, looking for anyplace to hide." Tad pointed to a line of trees at the bottom of the slope. "Down there would be good."

"Fits right in," Kayla said. "Golf course is on the other side of those trees."

"Figure the redhead had a good lead," Tad said. "Might have come close to getting away. "Might have thought he could hide down there in those trees. Maybe in the creek bed. I can tell there's a creek, way the trees grow. Right?"

"There's a creek," Kayla said. "Me and Harry and Joey used to play there."

"My mother's house isn't far from here," Harry said. "And Joey's dad's house is the third one on the right."

"And my father's house is long bulldozed under," Kayla said. "Sorry, Tad. A bit of nostalgia. You were saying about the redhead?"

"He hadn't stopped to hide," Tad said, "he might have gotten away. Or had he found a better hiding spot he might have gotten away. But it wasn't his night. Just guesses, but it seems logical, doesn't it?"

"What about the other guy?" Kayla said.

"He maybe did some last-minute touches on your father's body," Tad said. "Cut the bonds. Whatever. Finished, maybe he went in another direction, looking for Vincent. They could have split up, trying to find him. But it was the hatted guy who came across him."

Kayla said. "You'd make a good cop."

"Martial arts I studied also taught psychology and strategy. Some of it stuck with me."

"I'm beginning to think all of it stuck with you," Harry said.

"Thing that throws me is, why didn't the original investigation turn up the missing phone wire, the lamp cord?" Kayla said. "All of that."

"Because they already had their minds made up," Tad said. "It looked like death by misadventure, and they accepted it as that. Case closed."

They followed across the backyard lawns and down the slope and came to the stretch of trees that bordered the creek.

When they reached the other side of the creek they were on the edge of the golf course. They followed it until it came to a burst of woods and a trail. Alongside the trail were gullies, and the water had washed them deep and there were all manner of trees and vines alongside of them.

Harry said, "The shelter has got to be nearby."

They walked a little more, then they could see lights and the great house of the McGuires. They stood at the edge of the woods and looked at it.

Tad said, "Nice digs."

"The shelter is over there," Harry said.

They eased along until they came to it, gently pulled the door back, went down inside. It was cold in there, but warmer than outside. Kayla flashed her light around. There wasn't really anything to see.

"Question is," Kayla said, "what happened to the redhead's body?"

"I'm thinking it's near here," Tad said. "Hatted guy had already taken a chance chasing the guy, and he didn't want to be seen dragging out a dead body. He was strong enough to do it, that's for sure, but that wouldn't be wise, exposing himself even more."

"You think it's here, in the shelter?" Harry asked.

Tad shook his head. "Don't think so. This guy knew this place, so he probably knows McGuire. Hell. It could *be* McGuire. Whoever he was, he obviously didn't leave Vincent here. There's really no place to stash him. Under the bed, someone would have noticed when it started to stink."

"So he got rid of the body outside," Kayla said.

They went outside and walked along.

"May I see the light?" Tad asked. Kayla gave it to him, and Tad kept talking. "Way I see it, he killed the guy, dragged the body back out, and if I'm thinking the way he was, he disposed of it pretty quick."

"I don't see why he didn't just leave it in the shelter," Kayla said.

"Because he knew the guy who owns the place," Tad said. "Or he *was* the guy owned the place, and didn't want to take the chance of tying himself to it. If it was McGuire, wouldn't be cool his daughter brought some date out here and they found Vincent propped in a corner, drawing ants.

"There's some other thinking going on. Your dad's dead, Vincent doesn't show up, it points the business to him. Him being there was actually a lucky break. Kayla, you know anything about Vincent's family?"

"Checked," Kayla said. "Didn't have one. They died when he was young. He was pretty much on his own. Worked in Sheetrock, was learning the mechanic business from my dad."

Tad shined the light into the woods. There was a tire-track trail there.

"Where does this go?" Tad said.

Neither Harry or Kayla knew.

They walked down the trail a ways. Finally it broke out of a patch of woods and onto a little road that wound its way around a curve of trees.

"Hatted guy probably dragged him out here, other fella drove their car down here, loaded up the corpse, took him somewhere else to dump," Tad said.

"Sounds likely," Kayla said.

"Guesswork," Tad said. "What's left of the body could be over there behind that tree, for all I know."

"We've done all we can do tonight," Kayla said. "Let's call in the dogs."

48

Harry and Kayla sat with Tad at his house, drank diet colas and decaffeinated coffee until one in the morning, rehashing the night's events.

Harry felt as if he had been pulled through the small end of a funnel, but all this talk, even if it was about the night's events, was good. It kept him from remembering alone, kept him from thinking maybe the shadows weren't gone, that they were hanging in the belfry of his head like cobwebs.

Yeah. That was a help, having Tad and Kayla. But a drink . . . God, a drink. And then another drink. Cold beer or hot whiskey. That would be the ticket for the pleasant ride to Numb Land.

Tad showed how he could throw coins and knock knickknacks off a shelf and break them. A pile of shattered elephants and assorted ceramic animals lay Humpty-Dumptied all over the place. Scattered amongst them were winks of shiny minted silver.

"My mother-in-law gave us that shit," Tad said. "Me and the wife hated them. Been meaning to get rid of them. When I was drunk I thought about it all the time, but then I was too drunk to do anything."

"Are those quarters you're throwing?"

"Nickels. It's all in the wrist."

Finally Kayla took Harry back to her place, so he could pick up his car.

They lingered at the door, Kayla's perfume driving him crazy, but there was no kissing. Harry liked to think it was in the air, a kiss, but if it was, he didn't try to make it materialize. He wasn't exactly feeling like Don Juan, not after tonight. An event like that, it could put the shrinkage on a man's equipment.

"See you later," Kayla said.

"Sure."

"Thanks for your help."

"Not a problem."

"I like your friend."

"Tad. Yeah, he's great."

"Really, Harry. I know it must have been terrible for you."

"You're right. It was. But I hope I helped."

"You did. I'm not sure where to go with it now, but you helped. Lots."

"Yeah, well . . ." They were very near now to that kiss hanging in the air, but, alas, he hadn't the will to try it. What if she said no? He wasn't up to the disappointment right now.

"Good night, Kayla."

"Good night, Harry."

When Harry got home there was a light on the answering machine. The first message was from Tad.

"Kid. I know what you're thinking. Don't drink. I know, 'cause I'm thinking the same thing. You need me, call. I'll come get you."

Harry grinned, let the other messages come. There was one from his mother, one from Joey.

It was too late to call his mother, but he decided, what the hell, might as well get it over with, call Joey. Shit, I'm going forgive him, way I always do, and he's going piss me off again. How it works.

When Joey answered, he sounded as if he were climbing out of a hole in the ground.

"Yeah."

"It's me, Harry."

"Good. I was wondering . . . I mean, I didn't mean to hurt your feelings."

"Yes, you did. And you'll be happy to know it didn't work out, the thing with me and Talia. Oh, I was in the saddle for a while, but it's all over now."

"Well, you done pretty good then, considering who she is."

"So you're gonna sideways insult me, Joey?"

"Nope. I was wondering. Can we still be friends?"

"Sure. We're always gonna be friends, it's just I got to wonder why."

"How about I drop by tomorrow night? We can have a beer."

"I don't drink anymore. Remember?"

"Not at all?"

"We did this last time, Joey. You're already starting it again."

"Sorry, man. That not-drinking business. How's that working out for you?"

"Damn good." Then, trying to change the subject: "Know who I saw tonight?"

"Who?"

"Kayla."

"Our Kayla?"

"One and the same."

"How's she look?"

"Like a million bucks. She's a cop in town. We visited."

"She beat me up once."

"I remember. It's one of my fondest memories."

"She could hit really hard."

"I know. She beat me up too."

"She used to really smell nice."

"Still does."

"Kayla. I'll be damned."

"Well, good night, Joey."

"Good night, Harry . . . And hey . . ."

"Yeah."

"Thanks for calling. I've missed you."

"Can't say the same."

Harry showered and went to bed, tried not to think about what he'd seen there in the garage, but every time he closed his eyes, the images came back.

He was glad when the phone rang. He didn't check the caller ID. He thought it was Joey.

"Harry?"

"Kayla?"

"You know that wooden bear in my place?"

"Sure."

"It's named Harry."

"What a coincidence."

"No, it isn't."

"Oh."

"I thought you were going to kiss me."

"I started to try. Really. Just wasn't certain. Not exactly at my peak, you know."

"You should have tried. Good night, Harry."

About five A.M., Harry awoke.

He had struggled to fall asleep, and when he did it had been deep and solid, and now, suddenly, he was awake—bright eyed, bushy tailed, and nervous.

He sat up in bed and thought for a while, then got dressed, drove over to his mother's house, and sat out front. He wanted to see her, but it was too early, and he didn't want to wake her. If he did, she would know something was wrong, something was bothering him. He thought about how she would feel if she knew he was taking martial arts lessons, that he actually got hit and it hurt. She'd want him to wear a helmet, knee pads. She'd want him to quit.

He drove down where the honky-tonk had once been, now bulldozed over and growing pine trees. Somewhere in all that, the sounds of an old murder hid.

He tooled over to the entrance to the drive-in and let his high beams rest on it. The great frame for the drive-in screen still stood, as did the old ticket booth. The snack bar was collapsed and dark from having caught fire some years back. If he kicked something out there, maybe it would activate a memory. Lot of date rapes in those old cars, most likely. Some of those cars were still on the road. In junkyards, holding badness in a shadow bag.

Harry backed out, drove around trying to find the entrance to the road that led behind the McGuires'. Finally he found a way. There was a lot of garbage tossed back there, even an old armchair. Cruising to the end of the turnoff, Harry came to where he and Tad and Kayla had stood. He killed the lights and sat there. Finally he switched the beams on again, backed out, tried to decide if Tad was right about their carrying the body away.

When he was back on the main road he turned so that he was facing the way he had come, then he backed into the side road and considered.

The road T-boned, and he tried to decide which direction they might have hauled a body, if they hauled one at all.

If they went left, that led alongside the golf course and finally onto the little road that ran alongside Mr. Jones's garage. They could have gone that way, the way he had come, but it seemed pretty open and well lit, wound down between houses and dumped headlong onto the highway. No problem, but if you had a dead body with you, you might want to stay in seclusion as much as possible, just in case. Even if the corpse was coiled around a spare tire in the trunk.

T-bone to the right . . . well, he didn't know where that went. But it was darker that way, with more trees on either side, and seemed more likely if you were gonna be sneaking around.

He turned right.

In the headlights the clay road was red as blood and wound its way slightly upward. There were a number of little turnoffs along the way, and Harry thought any of them might have served as a place to bury a body. But the practical side of it was this: They didn't want to just dump the body. They needed to get rid of it. Without Vincent's body, there was no way to prove he had been there when Mr. Jones died. He could have gone home long before it happened. Something could have happened to him later. He might have cleared out. There were all kinds of explanations, but a dead body—that was an explanation that might throw off the whole program. Whatever that program was.

Harry was considering this while he drove, and as he wheeled around a curve there was a break in the trees and across the way, in the distance he could see a great and rare rise in the landscape.

He recognized it immediately, though he had not seen it from this angle before. Humper's Hill. Nothing else around was that tall. It was a good distance away, but just looking at it brought back memories of Talia's fine ass in the moonlight, of moments sublime.

And it made him think of something else.

It was a hunch, but it made a kind of sense.

He drove around the curve, and sure enough there was a road that went right. In a short time that would put him onto the highway, and then, in a matter of moments, he would be at the turnoff to Humper's Hill.

He thought: If I were going to dispose of a body, that would be the place. Up there on Humper's Hill, tossed over the edge to end up lying down there in the undergrowth, hidden from view, to rot and be eaten by wild animals and insects. Someone found the body, it could be years later, there would still be no direct connection to Jones's murder.

He felt a chill run down his spine that had nothing to do with the weather. He felt so goddamn certain of what he was thinking, his stomach churned.

"Rope?" Tad said. "For me to hang you with, I hope."

"I'm sorry, Tad. Really."

They were in Tad's living room. Harry had awakened him by leaning on the bell.

"So you had a hot flash and suddenly decided you need rope?"

"I think I know where Vincent's body is. Or might be."

"No shit?"

"No shit."

"I remember this place," Tad said.

"You've been up here?"

"Just to jack off."

While Harry was thinking on that, Tad said, "Hey, I'm fucking with you. This hill was popular in my time too. I used to bring my dates here."

"Funny thing is," Harry said, "sometimes you seem like a wise old sage. Rest of the time, you're just kind of a regular A-one asshole."

They got out of the car and Tad dragged the coil of rope out of the backseat. They walked over to the edge of the rise and looked down. It had a slight slope to it. It dropped about a hundred feet into a kind of poor-man's ravine. The brush was thick there and trees grew straight out from the slope and curved up, seeking sunlight. In the starlight they looked like alien creatures.

"You got your cell phone?" Tad asked.

"Oh, yeah. I forgot about it."

"Figured that's why you came over and sat on my doorbell. Make sure it's on, that way you can keep me posted, and what I'll do is I'll fasten one end of the rope to something under the Mercedes, and when you need me to pull you up, I can do that with the car, the phone stuck to one ear, you giving me information. You know, 'too fast, too slow, my neck's tangled up.' Shit like that."

"Great."

"What you're thinking, that the body is down there, might be right," Tad said. "But the odds are you ain't gonna find shit. It's been years now, and the meat would have long come off the bones, and the bones would have come apart and been spread all over hell and back. Some dog, coyote, some kind of critter has probably got a leg bone in his den somewhere, using it as a conversation piece."

Tad fastened the rope under the car, then Harry coiled it once around his waist and held the loose part so he could lean back and let it out, yet maintain the wrap as he went down.

"Watch for snakes."

"It's too cold for them, isn't it?"

"That's what they say, but hey, you could wake one up."

"Thanks."

Harry went to the edge, turned his back to the drop, held tight to the rope, leaned way out, leaped slightly, and went down about ten feet. When he landed, letting the rope loose as he went, he was surprised at how much the rope cut into him. It looked so much easier in the movies. The brush was also thicker than he imagined, stuck straight out of the sides of the slope as much as two to three feet.

Harry twisted and looked down. That would be some drop.

There was a tree directly below him, standing out from the drop at an angle, twisting back up toward the sun in a U shape. Harry made that his target. He thought, If they were going to dump someone over the side, they'd probably do it where the place dropped the most, and that was it. He tried to figure where a heavy body would fall, even with two guys slinging it. He thought the tree looked about right.

He roped on down, and when he got to the tree he put his back to the twisted trunk and took a rest. He pulled the rope off and rolled around so that his belly was against the trunk. He got the flashlight Tad had given him out of his coat pocket and moved the beam around.

There was so much brush you couldn't tell shit about much of anything. Tad was right. The body could be anywhere, and this was no easy place to search.

Harry decided he would work his way to the bottom, or at least until his rope played out. He had a lot of rope to work with, maybe two hundred feet, but he couldn't tell dick about how far it was to the bottom. Taking a deep breath, Harry worked the rope around his waist again, and with his back to the tree, digging his feet into the ground and leaning back out into the wind, he began to work his way down.

He had gone only a short distance when his shoes bumped something.

It wasn't a body. Of that he was certain. It was something more solid.

Harry turned for a look, saw that his feet were on something metallic. There was another tree about ten feet beyond what he was touching, and as before, he made that his target.

When he was up against it, he found the trunk took a kind of dip and that its roots were buried deeper into the slope than he had expected. When he came to rest, his back against the trunk, he saw through a burst of foliage that he was looking directly into the dark windshield of a car.

49

In a moment he realized he was actually looking at where the windshield used to be. This one was knocked out, just a few starred fragments jutting up from corners of the frame.

His feet were on the hood, and the hood was crumpled, and brush grew all around it and vines overlapped it.

Could Vincent have had a car?

If he did, they'd have to have disposed of that as well. But that didn't quite work in with his theory.

He thought about a way to find out, but thinking about it made him feel cold. He leaned back and took a breath and looked up through the branches of the tree and spotted a star and held his vision on that.

He was tired, so tired of being scared.

He had to know. And there was only one way to find out.

The phone in his coat pocket rang.

He positioned himself solidly against the trunk of the gnarled pine and took the phone from his pocket. While he spoke, he looked up to see Tad's head hanging over the ledge. He was on his belly, and his face was a faded gray mask without features.

"Barbershop," Harry answered.

"How's it look for a little off the sides?"

"Well, I should have answered Used Car Lot. I'm standing on top of a car hood, leaned up against a tree."

"I see you. . . . A car. No shit?"

"No shit."

"I don't suppose there's anyone in it?"

"I'm afraid to look. The windshield is knocked out, and I'm thinking of going inside that way."

"It could shift, kid. You and it could end up down there at the bottom of the hill, you trying to pick a transmission out of your ass."

"Only way this thing would fall is if someone went at the brush and vines with a chain saw. It's wrapped up tight, Tad. Been here a long time."

"Maybe you could get it running. It's bound to be better than that piece of shit you drive."

"Maybe some new tires . . . I'm going in, Tad."

"Hey!"

"What?"

"You seem to have sort of gotten your game on, kid."

"You think?"

"I think."

Harry put the phone away, loosed the rope, let it dangle by the tree. He crawled over the hood and went up and onto the sloping front seat through the missing windshield, managing to cut himself on its glassy remains only once. It was his knee. The shard cut right through his pants and got him.

As he crawled, the car remained solidly in place. There wasn't so much as a budge, a creak. It was held fast by the vines, years of them. He took the flashlight out of his coat and played it about. He didn't find a body or bones or much of anything in the front seat or back. The trunk, that wouldn't be something he could open.

He crawled over the front seat and lost his footing, fell onto the backseat with a thud, rolled on his back, put out his hand, and caught the back of the front seat to keep from rolling onto the floor-board—

—and there was a woman lying inside of him, and a man on top of her, holding her shoulders down, the man's face strained and twisted, his teeth and tongue showing, and Harry felt as if the very nature of fear had slipped into every cell of his body.

She was being raped. And the man doing it was the man he had seen before. The man with the hat. This time without the hat, but the same man. Had his pants pulled down and was going at it.

Harry could feel the woman's horror, and it stuffed him with nausea and revulsion. He scrambled onto the front seat and landed hard, found a man's body there, lying faceup, eyes open. A black man. A young man. Dead. Harry's knee was poking right through him. There was a bullet hole through his forehead. Small. Neat. Behind his head the car seat was dark with pooling blood.

The images began to fade, became outlines.

Harry slapped the front seat with his hand—

—he jerked his head toward the driver's window, saw that the car was on flat ground, Humper's Hill, surrounded by trees and moon-light, and his quick glimpse had given him a view of the tail end of a muzzle flash.

As the image faded, Harry slapped the seat again twice, very hard.

—sailed backward through time, and the black man was rising up and the muzzle flash was going back into the gun, and then the image hung, went forward again, instant replay off a rewind, the black man falling backward onto the seat.

In the flash Harry caught a glimpse of the executioner's face. It was a big man with even features. He looked familiar, but Harry couldn't quite place him. Behind the shooter, not far away, another man-sized shape could be seen in the flash of the muzzle fire. He seemed adrift, apart from it all. Observing.

Fading—

Slap.

—looking over the seat this time, trying to ignore the gun poking through the window, directly at his face. Harry turned his head, looked through the rear passenger window, could see a woman being shoved against the car, slapped. The back door opening—

My God. I'm moving backward and forward on this, wobbling through time. . . . This is earlier . . . maybe.

Slap.

Slap.

Slap.

—woman being shoved into the car, the man coming in on top of her. And out there in the dark, the shooter, and the other man in the darkness, the shadow guy with his back turned, his shoulders heaving. He seemed to be crying, or about to throw up. And then his face turned slightly, as if he might be looking over his shoulder to see what was gaining on him. A piece of light from the moon fell on his features and lit them up.

Kayla's dad.

Fading.

Slap.

Slap.

Images swarmed him, overlapping and horrible, and he felt the woman's terror, the quick spurt of fear the man felt when the gun poked through the open window—

—and then it all faded and Harry went limp.

There was a buzzing noise, and Harry couldn't place it.

It went on for a long time, and finally Harry realized it was coming from his pocket.

He opened his eyes. He was no longer on top of Humper's Hill. He was now back to being in the banged-up wreck of the car, angled on a brush-covered slope. He was lying up against the steering wheel, uncertain of how he'd come to be there. The sky was lightening. His head was full of confusing images.

Since there was nothing in his visions about the car going down the side of the slope, that meant to Harry that both the man and woman were dead when the car was pushed over.

Yeah. That was it. . . . Goddamn buzzing.

The buzzing continued.

Harry positioned himself so that he was stretched out on the seat, his head against the open driver's-side window, his side against the steering wheel.

The buzzing was his phone.

Harry removed it from his pocket and answered.

"Hey, goddamn it, I was about to come down for you," Tad said.

"Sorry. I sort of fainted."

"You okay, kid?"

"Not really."

"You saw something?"

"I saw a lot."

Slowly the Mercedes moved forward, and Harry went up the hill, the rope tied around him, using his legs to bounce along as he was pulled up. He tried to use the phone, but that wasn't working out so good. He could hardly hang onto it, let alone talk into it. He finally put it in his coat pocket and hoped for the best.

At the top, daylight was spilling through the trees, and the Mercedes stopped. With shaking hands, Harry removed the rope.

Tad got out of the car and walked back.

"You found Vincent?"

"Found something else."

"And?"

"I think I have more questions than answers."

PART FIVE

The Spine of the Crime

50

Harry spent the rest of the morning at Tad's place, sleeping fitfully.

All he could think about was how Kayla would feel when he told her what he had seen. Her father standing on the sidelines.

Should he tell her? Did it matter anymore? It had happened so long ago.

The car. It had to be the one he had heard about, the one he thought was most likely a legend. The car with the lovers in it. Or that was the story. The bodies had long ago been removed, or they had been removed after lying undiscovered for years. Their killers were never caught.

And the old car just left there, too much trouble to free. That's the way it would have been done in the past, a little town like this. Forensics would have been thought to be some kind of disease. And the story of the murders would go around, and in time, unless you were really willing to research, it would be thought to be no more than a legend.

It all twisted inside of Harry's head until he could take no more. He had tried hiding in sleep for a while, but the horror of it would uncoil again and noodle about at the edges of his dreams, and he would awaken.

He not only remembered what he had seen, he felt it all. It was as if he was the one who had been raped. And he had felt the man's fear just as the gun went off, a sudden sickness and a sad realization that there was no more to his life.

Harry sat up in bed, wadded a pillow behind his head, and watched the sunlight trace along the edges of the window, then flood it.

He got up to make coffee, but Tad was already there. Coffee made. Cooking eggs.

They drank coffee and ate toast and eggs, and when they were finished Tad said, "You're sure what you saw?"

Harry nodded.

"It was all kind of confusing. The whole event was jumbled."

"Gonna tell Kayla?"

"Don't know. Maybe we should just forget the whole thing."

"Maybe."

"Would you?"

"Probably not."

"Come on. Would you?"

"No."

"Even if it meant you were going to hurt someone you cared about?"

"That question has a lot of roads that can be taken. But if you're asking me specifically if I were you, and knew what you know, and I had a girlfriend like Kayla—"

"Just friends."

"Okay. A friend like Kayla. And she trusted you. And she wanted to know what happened to her father. . . . Yeah. I'd tell her."

"She'll hate me."

"She might. If she does, you won't have that between the two of you, at least."

"We won't have anything between us."

"Could be."

"But you'd do it anyway?"

"I would, Harry. But I'm not you. You got to make your own deci-sions."

"Shit," Harry said. "I hate that part. I really do."

51

She could still hit very hard.

Hard enough he was almost knocked off his feet. He fell backward against Harry the bear, making his wooden namesake wobble, but he managed to keep his feet by grabbing at the wall.

"Kayla—" he said.

She hit him again with the flat of her hand, grabbed his arm, twisted it so that it went behind his back, and he let her. Well, actually he liked to think he let her. Still, he didn't fight it. No struggle whatsoever. He wouldn't have been surprised if she pistol-whipped him.

Harry said, "Kayla, I'm sorry."

"You're a liar. You're a goddamn liar."

"I could be wrong."

"You are wrong. You and your sounds. What shit, Harry. What shit."

"I know."

She let go of him with a shove, fell on the couch, and rolled the side of her face against the back of it. She heaved and then burst out crying.

Harry stood where he was, his face red on both sides, his arm aching from being twisted. He looked at Kayla's back rising up and down, listened to her bawl. She was still wearing her uniform, fresh off the night shift, her gun was on her hip.

It didn't seem right, seeing a policewoman cry like that.

"I'm sorry—"

"Just shut up, Harry." When Kayla spoke her voice was muffled, pushed into the couch.

"Sure."

"Completely shut up."

"Okay."

"I mean not another word."

Harry caught himself in midapology, realized he was about to speak. He stood silent by Harry the bear. Without thinking about it, he patted the wooden critter on the head. After a moment he put his hands in his pockets.

Well, he thought, this has gone well.

He headed out the door.

"Harry," Kayla said.

"Yes."

"Don't you dare leave."

"Are you going to hit me any more?"

"No." Kayla rolled over and slowly sat forward on the couch. She said, "I'm sorry. I just can't believe it. I don't understand. It doesn't make sense."

"I don't know what it means, Kayla. No idea."

"Come sit beside me."

"You sure you aren't going to bitch-slap me again?"

"Positive."

"No arm-twisting either?"

"No arm-twisting."

"Could you put the pistol away?"

"Harry, come here."

He sat down beside her. She touched his face where she had struck him. "Can't believe I did that."

"It's still pretty fresh in my memory."

"Thanks for not hitting back."

"I didn't want to open that can of worms."

She kissed him on his reddened cheek. "I am sorry."

"Okay."

"I'm sorry I said what I said. But maybe it's not like it seems. Like it looked."

"I'm just reporting here. Just tell 'em like I see 'em. I may simply be crazy, you know."

"You're not. I'm the one who got you into this."

"I'm into it every day of my life."

"Did you report it to the department?"

"What's to report? I found an old car and had some dreams. I didn't find Vincent's remains. That's what I went out there for. But I think he's on that hill somewhere, covered in vines. What's left of him anyway. A few bones here and there."

She turned his face toward hers, kissed him on the lips.

"Harry?"

"Yeah."

"I just want you to know, and believe me when I say this: I'm not trying to get your gum, so don't fight me."

"I'm not chewing gum."

"Just an example of how you're acting. To kiss, you have to open your mouth a little."

"I know that."

"It's really okay to kiss back."

"I'm a little leery."

"I can understand. But it's okay."

He kissed back. It certainly was okay. He took her in his arms. They kissed deeply.

"I've thought about you ever since the day you moved away," Harry said.

"Except when you were with Talia?"

"I thought about you then too."

"Bet there were a number of moments you weren't thinking of me."

"Got a point. But I didn't know you were available."

"Good answer . . . I've thought about you too, Harry. Really. I had all this planned better. But tonight . . . I'm so sorry."

"For what?" he said, and kissed her.

They came up for air late midday and ate sandwiches in the nude. It was a short-lived break, and then they were at it again in Kayla's darkened bedroom, hammering away, making the bedsprings squeak like a wounded mouse.

Once, they looked up to see Winston with his head bent down, staring through the window, trying to figure things out. Kayla got up and closed the curtain, came back to bed.

After a while they lay in the dark, Kayla in Harry's arms. She said, "I'm getting sore."

"Me too."

"Want to quit?"

"Are you kidding?"

"Shall we proceed then?"

"Once more, into the breach."

She laughed. "That's one way to put it."

"Oh, there's lots of ways to put it."

The rest of the day went by and the dark room turned darker yet. They dozed off and on, and when they awoke they made love. Harry had never felt like this before. Kayla, though busy about it all, wasn't as savage as Talia. Talia had been good, no doubt, but it was all pretty much like a game plan brought to fruition, the storming of the beach on D-day, a job well-done. With Kayla it came about naturally. They seemed to know exactly what the other wanted, and neither seemed to be trying to prove anything.

After a time Kayla said. "That one was the best."

"Frankly, I don't know I remember it all that well. I feel sort of as if I'm slipping into a coma."

"Oh, now there's a compliment for a girl."

"It's just all been so good I can't take any more."

"That's better," Kayla said. "Was it good with Talia?"

"Oh, come on, Kayla. To men, the worst is good."

"Was she the worst?"

"Yes." He thought it was the proper lie to tell.

"I can whip her ass, you know."

"Never doubted it."

"What say we sleep a little? I have to go back to work later."

"Sure."

Kayla set the alarm. While she was stretched out, messing with the clock radio, Harry took a moment to look at her. It was dark, but not so dark he couldn't make out the long, lean shape of her body, and he enjoyed seeing it.

When the clock was set, she turned back to him and they shifted comfortably together.

"Maybe just one more time," she said. "Just so we won't forget how."

"Oh, shit," Kayla said.

The radio was playing, and had been for a while. Kayla rolled out of bed, said, "I set it for an hour ago. I'm going to have to quick-shower and go. Sorry, Harry."

Harry leaned up on one elbow while Kayla darted for the bathroom. A moment later he heard the shower running. He padded a couple of pillows together and sat up in bed with his back against them, savoring the darkness.

After a short time the bathroom door opened and gave the room some light and some steam from the shower. Kayla stood drying herself with a towel, another one turban-wrapped around her head. He watched as she finished drying and pulled on her panties. They were black, and there was very little of them.

It was like watching the Venus de Milo put on her first set of clothes. Not a bad way to spend time.

"Damn," Kayla said as she danced around the room, one leg in her uniform pants. She finally got settled, pulled the pants on, then her shirt over her bra. She sat on the bed and put on socks and shoes in the light from the bathroom. Harry kissed her neck.

"Don't do that, or I'm going to be late for work."

He pulled back.

"Well, you can do it just a little, while I tie my shoes."

He did.

"Damn, what did I do with my gun? Sorry, got to turn on the overhead."

She did. Her gun and holster were on a chair. Harry saw a photo on the night table. He had seen it in the dark, but couldn't make it out, hadn't been interested. In the overhead light he could see that it was an actual photo of the newspaper picture he had seen when Kayla became a local cop. This was a sharper, cleaner version, and more widely cropped. You could see that there were people to the left and right in the photo. Other cops watching the ceremony.

Harry rolled out of bed quickly, grabbed the photo, and looked at it closely.

"Kayla?"

Kayla looked up from fastening her gun belt.

"This man," Harry said. "At the corner of the photo here."

"What?"

"This guy. Who is he?"

Kayla looked. It was a tall, big-bodied, gray-haired man. He looked like the grandpa who would take you to your first movie, maybe buy you a snow cone and slip you dollars. He was staring at the proceedings from the wings, looking very grandfatherly and proud.

"That's the chief."

"Chief of police?" Harry said.

"Yeah . . . What's with you, Harry?"

"Shit," Harry said. "That's the guy. That's the guy in the garage with your father, and on the hill, one that raped the woman. He was with your father and the guy who fired the gun."

Kayla sat on the edge of the bed and looked at the photo.

"The chief? He and my dad, they were so close."

"It's him, Kayla."

"He helped me get in the academy."

"Maybe he felt sorry for what he did."

"If he did what you said he did, he doesn't seem like a man who feels real sorry."

"I have to agree."

"Jesus. Not the chief. Could you be wrong?"

"For all I know I got a tumor."

"You don't have a tumor."

Kayla sat for a couple of minutes in silence, and Harry didn't break it. What had been a perfect day now had shit on it.

"All right," Kayla said. "I've got an idea or two. I'm going to do a bit of investigating myself. This couple in the car, for one thing. Going to give a fresh eye to my dad's murder, knowing what I know now, what you've told me. Can you come see me when I get off tomorrow morning?"

"I got school and work. Can you call me midday?"

Kayla nodded, and then she trembled.

"Shit. The chief. He murdered my father. The lying, two-faced son of a bitch."

"You're not going to do anything stupid, are you?" Harry said. "I know how hot-tempered you are."

"I want to shoot him."

"Your first idea is the best. No one's going to believe some nut who gets images through sounds, not without evidence. You do the cop work, and I'll help you any way I can."

Kayla nodded.

"Promise?" Harry said.

Kayla reached out and took Harry's hand. "Promise."

52

When Harry got to the top of the stairs and touched his door, he discovered it was open. Had he left it open? He couldn't remember. That wasn't like him, but sometimes, things he had on his mind, the old brain went on vacation.

He entered cautiously, reached for the light, flicked it.

Nothing happened.

Joey. Goddamn it. Joey was supposed to come by, and he had forgotten. It didn't break his heart that he had, but he did sort of regret standing the dumb shit up. Though, considering what his night had been like, not much.

Then he saw a shadow dangling from the ceiling, from the light fixture. He pushed the door wider so the streetlight entered the room.

The light fixture had come loose from the ceiling, so there was raw wire hanging down about a foot before the fixture. All the bulbs were knocked out of the fixture itself, and Joey was hanging from that. His feet should have touched the ground, but they were cranked up behind him and tied. His knees were less than an inch from the floor, and his head and shoulders were covered in ceiling plaster. The room smelled of shit. Joey, in death, had let it go.

Harry moved toward him slowly, his knees feeling as if they were going to give way. He touched Joey, hoping. But the moment he touched him he knew he was dead. The wire fastened to the fixture and to Joey's neck caused the body to turn. The light fixture squeaked, and there was a flash—

—and out of the flash came a black dot, and the black dot expanded and there were shapes in the black dot, and soon the dot was gone and what he saw standing in his dark apartment was the chief and the other man, and now he knew who the other man was, because he could see the scar. The sergeant. It had been him before, but the scar had not been there then. That's why the man had been familiar in the visions out there on Humper's Hill. But Harry couldn't place him. Not without the scar. That event was yet to happen. The sergeant was the guy who had shot the black kid in the front seat, had probably taken his turn with the woman.

They were watching Joey hang. Joey was still alive. Struggling. Thrashing. The fixture was still fastened to the ceiling, but it was beginning to sag. Joey vibrated for a moment as if trying to crawl out of his skin, and his fear jumped around the room like a kangaroo. And in that flash Harry felt every nasty thing that had ever happened to Joey. That had never happened before, but this time it was every-where. Every time Joey had taken a slap, been called a name, it rushed over him in a flood of voices and images that knocked him to his knees.

The images dissolved into a black swirl, then they were gone, leaving Harry looking at the results. One very dead Joey, his tongue poking out of his mouth, his head twisted a little too far. The smell of shit was so strong it seemed to be in the walls.

Harry struggled to his feet, his face popped with sweat, his heart pounding against his chest, and looked about the room. The couch had been moved. Harry took a deep breath, kicked it so that it slid, and at the same time he spun the wire that held Joey.

Squeaks and slides became loud, and out of them fear shot in patterns of light and images formed.

—Joey wrestling against the couch, two men grappling with him. One of them, the scarred man, had his legs. They rolled him on his side. The sergeant tied Joey's legs behind him with wire, fastening his hands to his feet.

With Joey on his knees, the chief came up behind him, slipped another wire, a kind of cable, over Joey's head, pulled it taut, and choked him with it. As the chief reared back, his knee in Joey's spine, he looked up, paused, slowly lifted his head, took in the light fixture. And smiled.

His face transformed from grandfatherly to something quite different. His eyes rolled into his head like a shark about to bite. His lips went thin and the veins stood out on his neck like cables. He looked like a man about to have an ejaculation.

He removed the wire, and Joey coughed. The chief grabbed a chair, went to the center of the room. From under his coat he pulled a pistol, climbed on the chair, whacked the lights out of the overhead. They dragged Joey over. The chief climbed onto the chair, hooked the wire on the fixture, then they lifted Joey up and looped the cable around his neck, let go of him. Joey twirled and twisted, couldn't even kick his legs, not pulled up behind him like that. His feet, in the center of his back, flexed like little flippers, then the image began to fade and Joey's pain faded with it—

And now Harry realized he was sitting on the floor, right next to Joey, looking up at the body, still spinning slightly from where he had touched him.

Life had finally worked out just as shitty for Joey as he always expected.

Harry got his feet under him. His whole body was racked with Joey's fear, the anger, hatred, the repulsiveness of the chief and the sergeant—the goddamn police themselves.

Jesus. The perfect cover for a killer.

"What am I going to do?"

Harry was sitting on the bottom of the outside stairs, talking on his cell phone with Tad, who was still sleepy.

"Shit, Harry. You got to tell the police."

"The police killed him. Are you fucking crazy?"

"I know. But you can't just walk off. It could look worse, you did that."

"No shit."

"Take it easy, Harry."

"Easy? Joey is swinging from my goddamn light, and I'm supposed to take it easy? I feel naked sitting out here. They could come back. They were probably waiting for me. The sergeant, he interviewed me. He knew I was telling the truth, Tad. He knew it because he and the chief killed Vincent. The sergeant has a scar now. That's why when I saw him in the vision he looked familiar. He didn't have the scar then. But now he's got it. Him and the chief, they got to thinking, thought they might ought to get rid of a loose end. My sound business may be hard to prove. They could make me look like a nut. But dead—that works real good.

"I think they killed Joey 'cause they were waiting for me. They couldn't let him go; he'd seen their faces. So they killed him. Maybe they killed him as a warning to me. Shit . . . No. I'll tell you why they did it. Because they don't have any problem doing it. It's not like it's the first time. They like it, Tad. And now it looks like I did it."

"All right. Here's what we do. We call a cop. But we call Kayla. Can you get in touch with her?"

"She's at work. I don't know how to do that without giving something away. I make a call, that isn't going to look so good for her."

"The cell phone is registered to me, if anyone checks later. Never mind, kid. Hang on. I'm coming. We'll take care of it. Hard as it is, I suggest you go back in the apartment, close the door, and wait for me. Do you have a gun?"

"No."

"Probably best. You'd shoot your dick off. Go in and lock the door."

"I locked it when I left. It was unlocked when I got here. They can pick a lock, Tad. Besides, I don't think the lock works anymore."

"Go behind the apartment and wait. I'll come right over."

"Then what?"

"We're gonna get rid of the body."

"Oh, shit. I'm gonna be in deeper yet."

"Kid, you're already in deep. Only thing now is to get down so deep we come out on the other side."

"This puts you in too, you know?"

"What the fuck are friends for? Someday I might want you to loan me some money."

53

There were icicles under his nose. His eyes, though open, were frosted over. Where there had been snot on his upper lip was now a sheen like glazed sugar. His hands and legs were still tied up with wire, and his mouth was wide-open, and his tongue, black as coal tar, jutted out like some kind of critter poking its head from a den.

At least this way he didn't stink.

Trembling, Harry closed the freezer lid.

"Oh, shit," Kayla said.

"We get caught with him in the freezer," Harry said, "it won't look so good, will it?"

"Shit," Kayla said. "That was Joey."

"Yep."

"Shit. You know, except for the tongue, the icicles, and such, he looks just the same."

"And there's the being-dead part."

"I know you were still friends. This has got to be rough. Shit. I'm so sorry."

"The friendship was on the fringe, to tell the truth, and now we can kind of figure it isn't going to get patched up."

"Shit," Kayla said again.

"It may seem inappropriate," Tad said, coming into the laundry room where the freezer was stored, "but if you two are finished looking at the weasel, would either of you like something to drink?"

"That's not very nice," Kayla said.

"Dead or alive," Tad said, "he was a fucking weasel. Drinks?"

In the living room, drinking diet colas, and in Tad's case, coffee, Tad said, "I guess we could bury the motherfucker. Maybe take him out somewhere in the deep woods and plant his ass. That might work. You know, when the shuttle exploded over East Texas, over in Nacogdoches County, when they were looking for debris, the bodies of those poor astronauts, they found five or six bodies that weren't the astronauts'. Barring another shuttle blowup, we might could lose that little fucker out there under some dirt and leaves from about now until forever."

"Joey was a little shitty," Harry said, "and I guess I'm so upset I don't know I'm upset anymore. . . . I mean, I don't know how to feel. But maybe you might not want to call the poor murdered guy a motherfucker or a weasel with him lying in there dead, getting frozen and all."

"You say so, kid. He was your weasel, so have it your way. Besides, it isn't like it's hurting his feelings."

"That is pretty cold, Tad," Kayla said.

"Call 'em like I see 'em."

"What do I do?" Harry said. "I've sort of got it in the wringer, you know?"

"What do you and I do?" Tad said. "Way I see it, it's you and me, kid."

"What do *we* do?" Kayla said. "We're all in on it."

"This is like a goddamn musketeer meeting," Tad said.

"Thanks for coming over," Harry said to Kayla.

"Guess I should say thanks for thinking of me," Kayla said.

"We invited someone we trusted," Harry said.

"In fact," Tad said, "this exhausts the list. Us three. Problem here is that the cops, present company excluded, are in on it. They know the kid is having, like, TV spots in his head, running film on events. That puts Harry, as he said, with his tallywhacker in the wringer. This chief is a fucking murderer, and so is the scar-faced man. So what we gonna do?"

"I don't know if it would work well to tell the police," Kayla said. "Even if you got past the chief and the sergeant on the matter, there's still that pesky sound business, Harry. It's all in your head, the evidence. But the body, Tad, it's in your freezer."

"That is a drawback," Tad said.

"Thing that's confused me," Kayla said, "is why and how does it connect with my father? But now . . . well, it's not pleasant, and none of it works out real favorably, but I'm starting to put it together."

"Enlighten us, would you?" Harry said. "I'm the one seeing this stuff in my head, and I don't know any more about what's going on than I do about college algebra, which I failed, by the way."

"I snuck some research today," Kayla said. "I get caught, I'm out on my ass. Maybe worse. Thing kills me is, the chief, he complains about my perfume like it's a crime, but isn't bothered by hanging some kid, killing my father, the kids in the car out at Humper's Hill. Others."

"You could back off on the perfume some, dear," Tad said. "It's making my eyes water."

"I know. I mean to. It's a habit. Growing up, we didn't always have running water. Started using it to hide that fact. It's like a security blanket."

"And as thick as one," Tad said.

"Shit, Tad," Harry said, "lighten up."

"Sorry, sweetie," Tad said. "But to get back on the subject, think you got more to worry about than how much perfume you got on, or sneaking some shit from the cop shop. Thing that's bigger is we got that weasel-dick in the freezer, and someone finds him, we got to explain that shit. Try and do that. See how that works out. What we gonna tell them? He got sick, tied himself up, crawled in the freezer, and fucking died?"

"Freezer was your idea," Harry said.

"I take credit for it," Tad said, "but the thing to do now is figure out what to do with his dead weasel ass."

"You're going to stay on the weasel stuff, aren't you?" Harry said.

"I might as well be straight with you. I can't let it go."

"You want to hear this or not?" Kayla said.

"Lay it on us," Harry said.

"I've been copying some of the files, ones that aren't supposed to leave the office. Showed you some, Harry. Pretended to be digging in cold cases, which wasn't all pretend. I was. But I didn't want them to know which ones. I had permission to take certain ones out, but this one, I didn't want them to know I was interested. Because it has to do with my dad. And with them. I didn't know it then, but now I do. I got the stuff in the car. I'll get it."

Kayla went out and Tad said, "She's a keeper, Harry."

Harry said, "I'm fucked. I really am fucked. They don't kill me, they're gonna throw me in jail. I can't believe I helped put Joey in the freezer."

"Think it would have been better they found him at your place?"

"No. But they'll see the apartment, the light fixture, the wire."

"You had a party over there, you and me. We got drunk, you swung on the goddamn wire. Drunks will do things like that. I know. Once I tried to jump off the roof here."

"Tried?"

"Never got the chance. I fell. Just jarred myself. I was lucky. Hit a pile of leaves. Well, actually, I landed on the Mexican raking them, then the leaves. But I was lucky. The rake broke and he got his hat crushed, but he was all right too. Bottom line, Harry: This way we got some room to fuck around, figure things out, though I got to throw away some meat and plastic containers of frozen chili. Without the freezer, that shit is gonna turn fast. No matter how stuff shakes out, I lose some frozen goods. And I'm not sure I'm gonna want to put shit back in there when he's out of it. He kind of fucks it up for good, as far as storage is concerned. I'm starting to see it as a Goodwill item. Guess it's just psychological, but you know, putting what you eat in there with a dead body that's got shitty pants . . . It's the thought."

"You've put your neck on the block. I know that."

"I'm not asking for any praise. Not saying I don't like praise, just saying I'm not asking for any. It's the freezer I'm talking about. It's not even a year old."

"You getting Kayla over here and all . . . helping me get Joey . . . Shit, poor guy. He was a shit, but he didn't deserve to have his ass strung up to a goddamn light fixture."

"Not everyone votes that way," Tad said.

Kayla came back in the house, the files under her arm.

"You didn't come over here in a cruiser, did you?" Harry asked.

"Harry, I'm not dumb. I'm in my car. It's parked around back, the way Tad asked. I just haven't had time to change."

Harry shook his head. "I'm just fucked-up is all."

"I got to tell you," Kayla said, "I'm more shook than you are. Something I should have told you the other night, but I was hoping it wouldn't matter. Wasn't sure it was what it was, to tell the truth. Dad. He had been in trouble before. For rape."

"When?" Harry asked.

"Just listen," Kayla said. "Walking out to the car, I get a few more flashes, things that fit the facts I got here, things I know now. Parts are coming together better and better."

She spread the files on the table. "Harry, I didn't tell you everything. Why I was so upset when you told me what you told me yesterday."

"It was your father. How else would you react?"

"It was more than that. He always had a roving eye for the ladies. But once there was a report of rape. Person reporting it wasn't held in too high esteem. So Dad got off. Maybe he raped her, maybe he didn't. Mom was always suspicious. I don't know the truth. Thing was, it was Joey's mom."

"No shit?" Harry said. "That's why you thought Joey's dad might be one of the guys?"

"Yeah. She claimed Dad raped her, but he told Mom it was consensual, and when he wasn't interested anymore, she cried rape. Joey's father and my dad, they were gonna do a garage together, you remember that, Harry?"

"I think so."

"Well, that's what put the kibosh on that deal. I think Joey's dad figured the old lady might have been lying, as neither of them were known to be upstanding citizens, and there was my dad, on the cops, which put him on a higher playing field. I can tell you this—Barnhouse beat her ass for it."

"Joey know about this?" Harry asked.

"I don't know. Maybe. He was used to ass whippings, so it wasn't anything to him to see his mom with a black eye and a fat lip. You remember how it was. Anyway, when this happened—or didn't happen—the department closed ranks. They got Dad off. Got the whole thing dropped. Dad might have given the Barnhouses some money. I don't know. But there's this thing hanging over his head, and the guys who close ranks are the guys who are now the chief and guess who?"

"The scar-faced sergeant?" Harry said.

"Bingo. They said they were with him, playing cards, some such thing, and he gets off. That's what Mom told me anyway, and I'm thinking maybe she's just telling me that 'cause she believed he did it. Maybe she just wants to get even for what he did with Joey's mom, even if it was consensual. I don't know. She still doesn't talk about it. Anyway, he and Mom, they couldn't work it out, so they split. In the meantime there's been a rape and murder right here in our good citizen town. Not the first rapes and murders to happen here for sure, but this one is kind of strange. They don't find the bodies for a few years. Truthfully, no one knows there's been a rape, nothing left in the way of real evidence in that area, but I'm adding that in because of what you saw, Harry, in your visions. The murders, that's certain from the police end, and you've filled in the blanks. Another thing is certain, they identified the couple, white girl, black guy. You saw them, Harry, both killed, up close and personal."

Harry nodded.

Kayla opened up another file and slid it toward Harry and Tad.

"Turns out there had been other similar cases, just not as well hidden. Two others. Some of this, by the way, before the chief was the chief. He was just a cop then, on his second divorce. A scenario Sergeant Pale follows as well. But get this. Chief lived in a town called Millview before this. That's a small town, and it's had about five murders since it was founded, back in the late eighteen hundreds. And I got to thinking about how this all works, and I went to snooping there, making calls, asking about crimes in that area in the past that might fit this MO, and what I got was a very similar crime when the chief was a young man. Fact was, there were two of them. Rape and murder. Killer used a rubber, no sperm. So what are the odds, maybe five murders in their history, and two of them happen while the chief is there, before he's the chief?"

"It don't look good in the chief's favor," Tad said.

"Odd he would hire you . . . after murdering your dad," Harry said.

"Not really. A power thing. Killed my father, and now he's my boss. It fits, actually. Also, he likes to have me around to remind him about Dad. He gets off on this shit. There's sex crimes in it, but it's more than that. It's about power."

"I'm still not quite getting how this fits in with what happened to your dad and Vincent," Harry said.

"Dad, he was protected by those two. Maybe . . . maybe he gets in with what they're doing. I don't know. You know, they're riding around, bored, get to sipping. They get to talking. See a guy and a girl, and they don't like it 'cause they aren't getting any action, and Dad, he might have gone along with them, you see, just talking, 'cause he owed them, and pretty soon it isn't talk anymore. They follow a couple up to Humper's Hill. It gets out of hand. Dad doesn't know his partners are serious about this shit. He's not expecting it to go that far. I don't know the truth. Maybe he was right in the middle of it. I don't like to think that, but could be.

"However it goes down, he sees it happen. Later he doesn't want to play. Doesn't want to cover up. 'Cause maybe he thinks they'll do it again. His conscience is bothering him and he's not wanting to keep it a secret anymore—"

"So they kill him in a way to discredit him," Tad said. "The kid, Vincent, they have to kill him too. It all goes to shit."

"Then it gets forgotten pretty much, and the chief becomes the chief, and the sergeant becomes the sergeant and gets scared when you come along with the head movies. May not be the perfect scenario, but it fits pretty good. There's some truth in there somewhere. Think I've got hold of what I like to call the spine of the crime. But, figured out or not, this I'm certain of: Now they got one more on their list."

"The weasel in the freezer," Tad said.

"No. He's scratched off the list. Joey doesn't count anymore. They got Harry here on the list. And if they get it figured right, you and me, Tad. Thing is, they do it right, they can make us look like the bad guys. And they got the whole department, the goddamn justice system, on their side."

"The justice system, the police department," Tad said, "they're bigger than us."

"Way bigger," Kayla said.

"Don't suppose you have a plan?" Harry asked.

"Not yet," Kayla said.

"I got, like, a piece of one," Tad said. "You know, I think there's nothing going on up there sometimes, and then I get like a flash, and realize that, though I can hide it, I'm kind of a goddamn genius."

54

A couple days later, the chief of police came home late at night, pretty worn out from what he liked to call a function, a goddamn cop fundraiser where you had to smile, make some shitty uncomfortable speech; came home feeling stuffed and uncomfortable from a rubber-chicken dinner, some poisonous side dishes, came in the door loosening his belt, flicked on the light, and there, positioned upright on his couch like a fucking freelance contortionist or failed escape artist, legs coiled tightly under and behind him, hands tied so that the wire was cut near to the wristbones, propped there, glistening in the light, eyes milky, throat a big dark rip like an ugly second mouth in need of dentures, the first mouth sticking its tongue out at him, was this guy soaking water into the cushions, dripping more of it on the floor, stinking like an overthawed chunk of rib roast dipped in sewage.

It was the kid he and Pale had hung from the Wilkes's boy's light fixture. There was a cardboard sign around his neck. Newspaper and magazine letters had been cut and glued to the cardboard. It read: WE KNOW.

"What the fuck?"

Joey offered no response.

55

They were in bed at Tad's house. Kayla rolled over and put her arm over Harry's sweaty chest. "I give that one a nine," she said.

"What? No ten? I thought that was pretty goddamn magnificent, if I say so myself. And I do. You weren't faking, were you?"

"Now that's an ugly question. No. But, we call it a ten, what have we got to work toward?"

"Good point."

"Damn, I'd have loved to have seen the chief's face when he got home and there was Joey."

"Poor Joey," Harry said. "Thing is, Kayla, when I found him, I felt his fear. It wasn't just fear of that moment in time, when he was murdered. It was all his fear. It all came out. And he was full of it. His whole life was fear. It was horrible. I felt so sorry for him."

"Shit, Harry. Joey would have loved the joke. He would have. Think about it. After all he's been through, what happened to him. What we did with his body, he would have appreciated it."

"I reckon you're right. But it's starting to get to me now. I'm starting to feel sick about it."

"I saw the chief today, and he didn't say much of anything. Usually he's pretty jovial, see. But today he was quiet, and everyone was asking, 'What's wrong with the chief?' and I'm saying, 'I couldn't begin to guess,' but, shit, I'm not guessing. I know. He's got his own murder victim visiting on his couch, thawing out like a TV dinner. Good guys one, bad guys zero."

"It was a good idea. Funny, anyway. Now he's got the body."

"Your friend Tad, he's got a wicked mind."

"Yeah," Harry said. "He does. He's a guy you don't want for an enemy. He's got this, what do you call it . . . sense of irony."

"I'll say."

"Thing is," Harry said, pulling Kayla closer, "what's next?"

"We can try another position."

"You know what I mean."

"Do we have to think about that right now?"

"I guess not," Harry said, and kissed her. "But do you ever think maybe this isn't going to work out so well? Now that they have the body, they can maybe find some DNA on it, a smudge where I had hold of it. Seems like that shit's all over the place."

"You wore gloves. We all wore gloves. We were careful. DNA is real enough, but it isn't magic. It's not like those TV shows. Those things are science fiction."

"Consider this, however. My life, my gift, so to speak. It's pretty science fiction unto itself."

"Point taken. But it was great getting something on that bastard, Harry. You got to understand, he killed my daddy. And that little sign, that was the kicker. 'We know.'"

"You made a very good sign, no doubt. Very artsy-craftsy. But it still doesn't look good for me. I can't even go back to my apartment. I'm afraid it'll be me next time, hanging from that light fixture. They haven't stopped looking for me, to nail me semilegal or in some dark alley somewhere. In the end it's all the same. I don't get to do Christmas shopping this year."

"I'm sorry, Harry. Guess I'm gloating over my little piece of revenge. But it isn't over, baby. We got to keep thinking. Thing to do, is we got to turn it on them. Play it so smart and tight they won't know me and Tad are connected to you. They don't know you have allies. They don't even know to look here, and I'm careful when I come over. I use my car, I park in the back. I can even fuck quieter I have to."

"I wouldn't want that."

"Tad might."

"He's way down the hall. Thing is, Kayla, I've just got a feeling, you know, this sort of built-in shit detector telling me I'm fucked. And maybe you and Tad too. Like maybe we're a whole lot too damn clever for our own good."

Kayla rubbed her hand across his chest, and then lower. Her perfume filled Harry's nostrils, made them flare. God, that sweet and musky smell. Wonderful.

"Well," she said, "if it turns bad, what say let's go out happy as we can make ourselves?"

56

Two days later, midnight, Harry and Tad sat at the living room table playing chess. So far Tad had whipped Harry's ass twice and had eaten most of the taco chips, turning the bag toward himself, making Harry work for any he might want.

"You really need more practice," Tad said.

"Chess, or capturing taco chips?"

"Both."

"My mind is drifting."

"You still need more practice. The knight—the horse, as you call it—doesn't move in a fucking X pattern. I've told you that. And point his head in the direction of my men, not back toward you. It's disconcerting. It's like he's riding backward."

"Tad, there's no knight on the horse. It's just a horse's head."

"Have you no imagination?"

"Not that much."

Tad turned the knight around so that it faced the proper direction. Harry said, "Happy?"

"Fucking ecstatic. Listen here. No moment beyond the moment you're in is known to you. You plan ahead, of course. You take precautions, but all you can do in between is live as best you can."

"Is this like a lesson?"

"It is, grasshopper."

"You're saying life is preordained?"

"No. That's stupid. I hear people say that, then I say, 'Hey, you look both ways before you cross the street?' And they say: 'Sure, of course. I don't want to get killed.' And then I say, 'If it's all truly preordained? What's it gonna matter, it's all in the cards already?' So much for pre-destination. We all have a built-in survival card and we play it whenever we need it. You can fuck with the deck, Harry. Sometimes really good, sometimes not so good. In the end, the game folds for everyone, but you can sure draw in some big pots before that moment."

Before Harry could respond, his cell phone rang.

It was Kayla. Her voice was husky-sounding. "Come see me."

"Aren't you at work?"

"I'm at home."

Harry walked outside, into the backyard. It was chilly and moonless.

"I don't know I can go out," Harry said. "Not sure that's a good idea."

"I've got something I really need to show you. I can't bring it there. . . . Something's happened. It'll be easier if you come here. Walk to your place, get your car, drive it over."

"My car?"

"Yes."

"That seems risky."

"It is, a little, but I can't come there. I've found something you've got to see, and I can only show it to you here."

"Kayla, I don't know. Why there?"

"I know what I'm asking. But if you're careful, you'll be okay. Don't bring Tad. He would be in the way on this one. You have got to see this. I think it's going to fix things for you. Make it quick."

"Can't you just bring it here?"

"It's too heavy. Well, I could. But I'd be more likely to get caught than you, lugging it around."

"It? Heavy?"

"Harry. Trust me."

"Yeah . . . well . . . it's a little mysterious."

"Damned if I don't know it. I wouldn't ask it if it wasn't important, Harry. Trust me."

"All right."

"Harry?"

"Yes?"

"I know what I'm asking. Be careful. Be very careful."

Tad looked up as Harry came back in. "Kayla, of course," Tad said. The phone was in Tad's name, and only three people had the cell phone number. Kayla, Harry's mother, and himself. So it wasn't much of a guess.

"Yeah. She was just telling me things could be working out."

"Really?"

"Yeah. Nothing specific. I think she was trying to be encouraging."

"Wasn't I laying some philosophy on you when you left?"

"You were."

"Well, whatever it was, I'm all out of it. Probably full of shit anyway. I don't know about you, but I've had enough. I'm off to bed."

Harry went to his room, left the door slightly ajar so he could hear Tad down the hall, hear him doing his throat-clearing shit, the bathroom toilet being flushed, gargling, the sink water running.

Harry felt like hell not telling Tad about Kayla's call. Didn't seem right, even if Kayla was correct that Tad didn't need to know everything. He and Kayla, they had a piece of this business, but Tad, he had no reason to get in any deeper. He was already up to his neck. No use dropping him in over his head. He waited some more, then slipped out, hands in coat pockets, walking fast.

It was a longer walk than he remembered, and the cold air bit at his lungs. There was no moon, just streetlights, and he kept thinking he'd see a cop car coming around a corner, a light flashing on him, nailing him. But it didn't happen.

He got to thinking about what Kayla was asking, and he started to get mad. Started to get mad at himself for listening. There wasn't anything worth his getting out here in the dark. He should have had her come get him, let him lie down in the backseat. Should have told Tad after all. He thought about all this, but he kept walking.

He got to his place and watched from across the street, stood in the shadow of an elm.

Cops could easily post a watch at his place. He would if he were them. They could hide and wait for him to show up for his car, get something from his house. The whole damn thing made him nervous. Course, Kayla was a cop. She'd probably know if it was done through the department, any kind of watchdog business like that. But it could be the chief, the sergeant. They could be doing it on their own.

Course, that would be harder, just the two of them. How many shifts could they manage?

Maybe the thing was to turn himself in, or go to Tyler, tell the cops there the situation, get some help.

Yeah. That would be good: "I hear sounds. I found a dead body in my house. Me and some friends, one of them a cop, put the corpse in a freezer; then we decided to put it on the chief's couch with a sign around its neck, 'cause we know he and the sergeant murdered Joey because I saw it in a fucking vision."

Harry took a deep breath and let out a puff of cold white air. He was just about to step across the street when he was nabbed and spun around.

Tad said, "You don't sneak for shit, kid. What the fuck are you doing?"

"I didn't want to tell you."

"No shit. Figured that much. You got to learn to watch behind you."

"I did."

"I was in the shadows. You had your shit together better, you'd have seen me. What the fuck is wrong with you?"

"Tad, I didn't mean to sneak."

"You call that sneaking? You came in from that call, you had a look on your face like you were gonna steal the silverware. Since I use mostly plastic throwaways, I knew that was out. Just waited till you got ready to do what you were gonna do. And by the way, don't try to play poker. You can't hide shit with that face. Come on, kid. Give me the rundown."

Harry told Tad what Kayla had told him.

"Look, whatever she's got, she can tell me," Tad said. "Fact is, this hurts my goddamn sensitive feelings. I'm in on this, kid. I said that and meant it. Can't really get any fucking deeper, you understand?"

"I'm sorry. Just she's got something she wants me to see and she said not to bring you."

"Something heavy? That's what she said?"

"Yeah."

"It's heavy, how'd she get it to her house, and now how come she can't move it?"

"I don't know. . . . You're not saying—"

"That I don't trust Kayla? Course not. She wanted to nail your ass, help the cops out, get that big promotion, she could have had you nailed long ago. Your balls would be bronzed and mounted on a piece of board. She's got a stake in this herself, so I trust her. It's a screwy setup, no shit, but I've got no reason to doubt her."

"You said that twice."

"Did I?"

"You did."

"I'm just suspicious by nature. Kind of guy that's skeptical of being skeptical. So, though I trust her just fine, what say we do some insurance?"

"I feel guilty doing a thing like that."

"Me too. For about fifteen minutes."

Harry and Tad pulled over a block up from Kayla's place, next to a big sweet gum that grew out from the curb, alongside a clutch of tall, sharp-bladed bushes. The moon made the bushes throw swordlike shadows. They got out of the car, stood in those shadows. Harry unlocked the trunk.

"I don't know, man," Harry said, "the fucking trunk? It's nasty in there. You could die of carbon monoxide or something."

"Not just going a block down. Don't lock it. Just let me hold it nearly shut. After a bit, I'll get out and check around, see if things are okay."

"You could just ride in the driver's seat."

"You're expected. I don't want to embarrass you by showing up like that. Just do it my way."

"This is bullshit, Tad. Kayla wouldn't play me."

"Talia played you."

"Different."

"Do it for me. I get there, look around, take a peek inside from the outside, things seem all right, I'll walk home."

"Too far."

"I'll walk up a few blocks, go to the shopping center there, maybe catch a picture show, get a taxi home. Come on, do it. We're out here in the big middle of everyone, someone puts an eye to their window, they might see us, wonder what the fuck I'm doing getting in the trunk. They could call the cops, and, as we both know, they aren't the folks we want to see right now."

"All right."

Harry lifted the trunk and Tad climbed inside and pulled the lid down most of the way, left a crack he could see out of. "Drive slow," he said.

Harry parked out back in the alley. As he got out, he saw Winston sniffing about. The dog raised its head and looked at him, then went back to sniffing, eating something out of a bush at the corner of the house.

A gritty-kitty turd, most likely.

Harry went through an alley between houses to the front of Kayla's place and, feeling nervous, he knocked.

He was glad everything was okay and Tad was full of it, because as soon as he came in the door to Kayla's throaty, "Come in," he knew there were no problems.

Things were cool as an ice tray.

He felt the tension go out of him as he walked down the hallway, smelled her perfume on the air, looked through the gap that divided hallway and den, saw Kayla sitting in a chair in the near dark (there was a dim light from the kitchen), her uniform shirt open, her breast exposed, smiling.

And he thought: She did lie. She brought me here for another reason.

A good one.

That's why she didn't want Tad to know. But is it really worth the chance of me cruising about in my own car? Couldn't we have done this in the bedroom at Tad's place?

Then Harry realized something.

Kayla wasn't smiling.

She was showing her teeth, but it wasn't a smile. He couldn't tell that right off in little to no light, but now that his eyes had adjusted a bit more, he realized she was grimacing.

And her breasts, they were pocked with dots. He could make those out now. A cigarette smell was mixed with the perfume. He hadn't noticed that before, but now that his lust had subsided, he did.

Kayla didn't smoke.

The sergeant, who had been against the wall near Harry the bear, stepped out into the wide breach between hallway and den, said, "Howdy, dumb dick."

"I'm sorry, Harry," Kayla said. "I'm so sorry."

Harry felt someone behind him, turned. It was the chief. He looked a lot less like a grandfather now. And he had a friend with him. A black automatic.

"A gal can only take so many cigarette burns on the tits before she calls," the chief said. "And actually, that's not what did it. I promised to put a cigar in her nether regions and light it, let it burn down. She wasn't up for that. True love has its limitations. Am I right, Officer?"

Kayla's head drooped as if it might fall off her neck. "I'm so sorry, Harry. So sorry."

"You two, you thought you were so smart, but there was one problem. Kayla's perfume. She wasn't supposed to wear perfume to work, you know, but alas, just couldn't help herself. And that dead body you left on my couch, awful, but the sign—the sign Kayla made—it stunk of her perfume, and no one else has that smell but Kayla. . . . Who's Tad?"

Harry's mind raced, thought, oh, yeah, she mentioned him on the phone when she called. But, she didn't say who he was. Or did she? Does he know? Is he just jacking with me? He took a flier.

"My dog," Harry said.

"Your dog?"

"Yeah. Shepherd."

"You don't have a dog," the chief said. "We been to your place, remember? It's where the unfortunate Mr. Barnhouse, instead of you, met his fate. No dog."

"My mother has him. That's where I was when Kayla called. With her and Tad."

"It could be checked, you know."

"I'm sure."

"A dog?"

"Yep."

"You believe that, Pale?" the chief said. "We talked to his mother. Remember a dog?"

"He was with me then," Harry said.

"Sounds like some shit to me," the chief said.

"Hell, why not?" Pale said. "I'll buy it. Who the fuck names a person Tad? Hey . . . guess we don't need to call each other code names, do we? They know who we are."

"Of course not," the chief said. "Are you fucking high? Of course not." Then he turned his attention back to Harry. "Bottom line, my young man, is you aren't going to get but just a few hours older. The two of you, you're going to meet a nasty fate. Tell 'em, Sergeant, a nasty fate."

"He's right," said Sergeant Pale, coming up behind Harry, striking him hard with the side of his hand on the back of the neck, causing him to drop to his knees. "Nasty. Old Testament–style nasty."

Tad waited in the trunk awhile. It wasn't that he didn't trust Kayla, he just didn't trust circumstances. His wife, Dorothy, always said he spent so much time trying to figure what people were really thinking, instead of just going with the flow. She was probably right. But part of martial arts was going with the flow, and part of it was being prepared for what might happen inside the flow. Even smooth-looking water can have a fast-churning undercurrent. Way he saw it, way he looked at things, he was doing the Boy Scout motto: Be prepared.

He started to lift the trunk, but decided against it. Better to listen and wait. He'd give it two, maybe three more minutes. He could stand that much. Then he was going to start snooping around the house, see that things were okay. Worst that would probably happen was that he would end up seeing a movie at the dollar rerun show.

What the fuck was showing anyway?

There was a sudden rushing noise and a thump and the trunk went shut and everything was completely dark. Tad heard something walking up the trunk, and then the noise was a bit more distant, as if it were on top of the car.

Yep. That was it. The top of the car.

Then the noise returned to the trunk, and finally he could hear just outside the trunk a sniffing noise.

A goddamn dog. That fucking big idiot Winston.

"Shit," Tad said.

Winston, with cat turds on his breath, stood with his front paws on the trunk and sniffed the air, turned his head and bent his body so he could smell where trunk and car came together. Winston knew someone was inside the trunk, but it was nothing to him. They weren't going to let him ride, he could tell that.

But you never knew.

Sometimes they might.

It could happen.

The dog lifted his head, his nose pointing up. He twitched it.

More cat shit. One block down, partially buried, pretty fresh. Near that was the smell of some other dog that left urine messages.

Winston's tongue came out and rolled along his snout, then he dropped down on all fours and went off at a trot.

"What we're gonna do," the chief said, "is we're going to take a little ride, gonna go in your car, and Pale here, he's gonna follow in our car. Now, he's gonna walk down the block, get it out of the church parking lot, drive up out back, and you guys, you're gonna go out the back door and get in your car without giving me any trouble. And Mr. Wilkes, you're gonna drive. Me, I'm gonna sit in the back with a pistol to the back of her head, because she's gonna sit by you. That way you get to smell this sweet thing all the way out to the cliff. Course, all that perfume, I'd smell her too, even if I was following in the other car."

"Cliff?" Harry said.

"Humper's Hill. And we're gonna have a companion with us. Someone you know well."

All right, Tad thought. How the hell do I get out of this motherfucker? It's no use pushing at the trunk, but, what the hell, I've got to give it a try.

He did.

He was right. No use in that.

He checked to see if the trunk was connected to the backseat, to see if he could push the seat down from inside the trunk, get out that way.

He used the light on his cell phone to look. Nope. A metal wall between him and the seat.

He was fucked.

He took a deep breath, considered.

Okay, now. Don't panic.

How much air have I got?

Quite a bit. As long as I don't breathe.

Maybe I can roll on my back, put my feet against the trunk, and push until the lock breaks. And that would be a good plan if I had the legs of a goddamn bull elephant. Otherwise, not so smart.

Maybe Harry will come back and check on me, and I can feel like a big idiot, and Kayla will get mad, think I didn't trust her, and . . . well, it beats smothering.

Shit. I can call Harry on the phone. What the hell am I thinking? I can call him and he can come and get me.

I'll give it a minute, see if he shows up, then I'll call. In the meantime, I'll just lay here and feel like shit with my goddamn side lying on a tire iron and my ass pushed up against a spare tire. How the fuck old is this car anyway? Didn't they stop making these about the time of the Flintstones?

Flintstones?

How did the theme song go?

". . . huh, huh, huh, something in history."

Damn. That's some shit. Can't remember the theme song. I used to watch that when I was a kid.

I'm sure it sucked.

But I watched it.

What time is it anyway?

What the fuck does it matter? I'm not taking medicine.

I was on that Atkins diet plan, some kind of goddamn diet plan, I might not be so uncomfortable in this goddamn trunk, because there might not be so much of me. I ought to try that. Eat all the bacon and eggs and steak and fat I want. Sounds pretty good.

Except for the heart part. Bound to bad for your heart, all that grease. How can that be good for you?

Shit, I was on the Atkins plan or not, it still wouldn't be comfortable in this goddamn trunk. What the fuck am I thinking? Stay here long enough, I'll get thin, all right. From dying and rotting.

What the hell is that?

Something was prodding him in the side, and it wasn't the tire tool. It was something sharp. He shifted, put his hand in his coat pocket, got poked.

Damn. Those darts. Forgot about those dudes. They had been there since Kayla gave them him.

Tad put his hand to his mouth, sucked on the puncture.

All right, he thought. That's enough. Time to call . . .

Nah. I'll give it another minute. He might come out and check on me.

But why would he?

He's not going to do that. That wasn't the plan. Shit, I set the plan up. I ought to know that. I'm getting dingy. Wonder if that fucking Atkins diet helps with the memory?

I'll call. Now.

"He's got a phone in his pocket," Sergeant Pale said.

Harry had been pulled up from the floor and pushed against the wall, and the sergeant was giving him a search.

"Get rid of it," the chief said.

Sergeant Pale dropped it on the floor, lifted his foot up with deliberation and placed it on the phone, and put all his weight on it. It snapped.

Tad, lying in the trunk, holding his phone, got a photo sent to him—photo of a guy's big foot coming down. And he could see a face too, leaning over, looking down. Just a glimpse of it. Scarred. Photo deal must have been activated when the phone was dropped or thrown.

Who the fuck was this guy? Looked like he'd caught his fucking face in a lawn mower.

Damn. He had been right. There was some shit going down, and here he was, locked in the trunk of a car. By a dog, no less.

But he did have his phone. He could call someone.

But, shit, the police? Chief would have that all sewn up.

Let's see. Who did he know?

Not much of anybody anymore.

Harry's mother.

What the fuck was her phone number? He could call information. Her name was Wilkes, he knew that. He could figure it out, maybe she could help him. Then he'd have to explain everything going on, scare the shit out of her.

Then again, there was that limited-air thing. . . .

Sounds.

Someone was opening a door of the car.

The sergeant, after stomping Harry's phone and giving him another love tap with his gun, took Harry's keys and went out.

Harry, when he was able, moved to the couch near Kayla. He sat there rubbing the back of his head. The chief pulled a chair up close to Harry and sat down, draping his gun hand over one knee, letting the automatic dangle.

Kayla, lips trembling, looked at Harry. "I'm so sorry. I wasn't as tough as I thought."

Harry could see the spots on her breast clearly now. They were dark and raw. He reached out and touched her knee. "It's okay. Really. You couldn't have done anything else."

"You are one understanding son of a bitch," the chief said. "Me, I'd want to beat her with a goddamn chair leg. Just break it off and go to work. Want to know something? None of this had to happen, you know. What we did long ago, it was a drunk thing. Your father was with us, Kayla. He wanted to get him some too, but then he got cold feet. Chickenshitted out. Sobered up and then felt like he was better than me and Pale. Got him a conscience. Which, considering he was fucking around with every stray piece of tail he could find, wives, daughters of people he knew, was kind of a hoot. And we'd backed him up on that rape thing. Shit, he didn't rape that woman. She was willing. Your dad, he was a cocksman. I'll give him that. He could talk one of God's own female angels out of a piece of ass, get her to suck and swallow. He was that kind of guy. Smooth as a Slurpee."

"He didn't murder anyone," Kayla said. "He didn't rape that woman. He wasn't like you. And I don't believe that was the only time with you."

"You want to know something?" the chief said. "You might be right. I've done some bad things."

"You're doing a bad thing now," Harry said.

"This is about survival." The chief leaned back in the chair and studied Harry for a long moment, said, "What I want to know is this: How'd you know what happened in that shelter? Out there on Humper's Hill. . . . Yeah, Kayla told me all about it. Between cigarette burns. She tells me it's visions. But that's bullshit, isn't it? You know some other kind of way, don't you? Some witness told you, didn't they?"

"It's just like she said," Harry said.

"No, it isn't. I don't buy that for a minute."

"That's all I can tell you, because it's the truth."

"There's someone else saw us, isn't there? Some witness."

Harry shook his head.

The chief leaned forward and struck Harry a sharp blow across the jaw with the back of his hand. Then he put the automatic against Harry's forehead. "You ought to just go on and tell us. No use being brave now. What's gonna happen is gonna happen, but it could happen quicker. You know, you pull a fish out of the water, you can let it die gasping for air on the bank, or you can get it over quick with a sharp blow, a cut. You want to be that gasping fish?"

"I'm telling you the truth."

"I could make it tough on the girl instead of you. Would that help you talk?"

"If I knew anything, believe me, I'm not that brave, I would have talked already. You think someone was hiding inside that little shelter watching? You really think that?"

The chief pulled the gun back and let it rest across his knee again. Harry thought about jumping him. It might be the thing to do, take his chances here.

The chief got up and walked across the room, leaned against the wall, the automatic hanging by his side. Harry realized his chance was over.

"Sounds, huh?"

Harry nodded.

"That's some wacky crap. Makes my goddamn skin crawl thinking about that kind of woo-woo shit . . . Whatever. We're gonna have to get it over with. There's a late movie I want to record. Got it all set up, but forgot to turn it on. You know something? It's a musical. Wouldn't think I'm a musical kind of guy, but I am. *Seven Brides for Seven Brothers*, that's the one. *Sound of Music*. Seen it ten times. *West Side Story*, maybe the same."

He looked at his watch. "I got enough time to do what we got to do and get back, push the button, so let's get this show on the road. Sounds? The past hidden in sounds. That's your story and you're sticking to it?"

"It's the truth."

"Well, even if it isn't, I'll deal with any witnesses when they show. There's a time when you got to cut your losses and just take it as it comes. Something I've learned about life. You should have had that lesson, just let all this shit go. Done that, you'd be banging tail tonight, having eggs and coffee tomorrow."

The chief raised his pistol, waved it at Harry. "Untie her, help her button up there, then let's go out the back way. Come on. Make it pronto. You got to twist the wire apart on her wrists; it's kind of wound together there. You'll see where it's gathered."

When Tad heard the car door open, he started to call out, but then he heard a voice he didn't know say, "Goddamn, that stinks," so he remained silent.

Pale parked his car next to Harry's, and when he got out he looked around carefully before opening his trunk pulling out a heavy package wrapped in thick plastic.

He laid the package near the back left side of Harry's car, opened the left rear door with Harry's key. He looked down at the heavy plastic package, at the dark shape inside of it. He looked around the dark alley again, quickly unwrapped the package. A stink came out of the opening and nearly knocked him down.

Turning away, he took in a deep breath, then, using gloves he pulled from his coat pocket, he returned to his work, lifted Joey's ripe body out of the wrappings and placed it on the backseat behind the driver's spot.

"Goddamn, that stinks," he said.

He quickly folded up the plastic, returned it to the trunk of his car, removed his gloves, dropped them inside as well, and closed the trunk lid.

Tad could hear the plastic unwrapping, feel the car shake as the door was opened and something was put on the backseat. He had an uncomfortable feeling it might be Harry's body.

Damn. He had been right. This had been some kind of trap, and now here he was, Mr. Helpful, locked in the trunk trying to remember the goddamn *Flintstones* theme song.

Even with what was going on outside, he kept trying to remember the damn thing. Wasn't there something about Bedrock in it, that being Fred Flintstone's hometown?

Goddamn. Forget the fucking Flintstones.

Now he heard another voice.

"Get in behind the wheel. Give him the key, he's driving."

Tad felt the sensation of the car door opening, heard it slam. Then the doors on the other side of the car, front and back, slamming not quite in unison.

Okay. That meant at least three or four. Someone was behind the wheel, someone beside the driver, and one or two in the back. All four doors had slammed, and the car had moved in such a way to indicate that.

And, oh, let's not forget another rider.

A big dumb-ass in the trunk.

The car started up. Tad heard another car engine turn over nearby. Okay. That means there may be five. Or more. Someone has got to drive the other car, and there could be someone with him. And if I weren't inside the trunk I could probably count them and be sure.

The car began to move.

"You know where Humper's Hill is, boy?" the chief asked. The chief was sitting in the backseat, the automatic close to Kayla's head. Harry was at the wheel. Joey's body was propped on the backseat across from the chief. Sergeant Pale was in his car, following.

"Never heard of it," Harry said. No use making it easy.

"Sure you know. It was part of one of those sound things. . . . All right, you listen to me. We'll do it your way. I'll give directions. Get cute, and your girl gets one in the back of the head. . . . Goddamn, your friend here stinks."

"Being dead will do that," Harry said.

"You'll be stinking soon enough," the chief said. "You thought that body on my couch was some funny shit, didn't you? Well, when they find your bodies, and who knows when that'll be, you'll have this guy with you, all trussed up. And the way I'll see it, if I'm still chief, it'll be read like this: You killed him. You and your girlfriend. For what, who knows? But you trussed him up, killed him for whatever reason. . . . Fun, maybe. Just to see if you could. And you took him out to Humper's Hill to dump him, but, goddamn if you didn't fuck up, and the car gear slipped, and in a moment of panic or excitement you put your foot on the gas thinking it was the brake, and damned if the whole kit and fucking caboodle of you didn't go over the side.

"Out there, there's a pretty good drop, youngsters, and it's my feeling it'll kill you. And if it doesn't, well, there's always me climbing down there and giving you a tire iron to the head. No one will be the wiser to what happened. No connection to me. And, hey, they may never find you. Considering most people go there to get laid, you're just gonna be something for the kudzu to crawl over.

"Another way you can look at it to make you feel a little less blue is, you'll be part of the cycle of life. You know, the worms, the soil, all that shit. I think about death, I think about that, and it gives me some comfort. How about you? Cheered up?"

"Fuck you," Harry said.

The chief leaned over and clipped Harry's ear with the automatic. Harry swerved.

"Pay attention to the goddamn road. You've turned over your boy back here."

Joey, legs still bound behind him with his hands, lay on his side on the seat now. He looked like an old man from the decay. His face hung loose, and parts of it were coming off on the seat covers.

"Goddamn," the chief said, and rolled down his window.

Tad caught bits and pieces of the conversation. He could also smell Joey. The trunk was filling with an odor like a slaughterhouse.

He pulled the tire iron out from under him, then removed his belt, took out his Swiss army knife, and carefully began cutting from the belt a long strip of leather. He found a loop in the trunk lock and ran the strip through it. He pulled the loose end of the strip back and looped it around his left wrist so when he popped the trunk he could keep it from swinging open. He took the tire iron and put it in under the lock and applied pressure. It was like trying to lever the world with a toothpick.

Following the chief's direction, Harry went the route he already knew but didn't admit to. He thought about Tad. If he looked around, he was bound to have figured out something was wrong. Surely he didn't just get out of the trunk and go to the movies. That didn't make sense.

But where was he?

He looked out of the corner of his eye at Kayla. She was steaming, he could see that. She was past being scared. She was starting to get mad. He had seen that look before, when she punched his ass long ago, and the other day when she slapped him, pushed his arm behind his back.

She was pissed.

Pissed she had been found out so easy.

Pissed she had been surprised and tied to a chair.

Pissed she had been burned with cigarettes, threatened with a lit cigar to her nether regions.

Pissed she had betrayed him.

He wished he could tell her it was okay. He understood. Pain is pain is pain, and no one is that tough.

Well, maybe Tad. He had a feeling Tad might be as tough as they came.

Tad put the tire tool down and took a deep breath.

This sucked. He was going to go over a cliff in a car trunk. He had thought of a lot of different ways he might die, but that wasn't one of them. Novel, he had to admit, but not his choice. Probably, if he were ever found, he would have a spare tire up his ass, maybe a taillight in his teeth.

The situation was, as the philosophers said, not good.

He held his phone light close to the lock. So far he had managed to put some scratches on it, but when it came to scoring: lock, one. Tad, the big old fucking shit-covered goose egg.

He studied the lock for a time, then took out his pocketknife again.

He opened the pick blade, stuck it in the lock, went to work, hoping he'd hit a combination.

He hadn't been at it thirty seconds before he broke the pick off in the lock with an unpleasant snapping sound.

Tad folded up what was left of the pick, put the knife in his pocket, and shifted so that he was on his side, his head supported by his arm.

He said to himself: Shit. Fuck. Shit. Fuck. Shit. Fuck.

After a few seconds of continued communion with the universe, he returned to the tire tool, went back to trying to quietly lever the trunk lid open.

57

When they started up the road toward Humper's Hill, the chief said, "Stop."

Harry stopped.

"Put it in gear, slide over next to her."

Harry did as instructed.

The chief quickly came over the seat, fell in behind the wheel. He stretched his right arm out behind Harry and Kayla and put the gun to Kayla's temple, rested his left hand on the steering wheel.

"Anyone gets squirrelly, I'll blow your gal's head all over the inside of this wreck. Got me?"

"Yeah," Harry said.

"Figured I'd drive the rest of the way, case you wanted to take me over the cliff with you. You thought about it, didn't you?"

Harry didn't answer.

When the car stopped, Tad, having finally broken the lock, and having mashed the back of his knuckles, lifted up the trunk just enough for him to slide out, pulled the lid closed with the strap of his belt, and tied it off where the trunk lid snapped closed.

Then he rolled off the road like a tumblebug, out into the darkness and behind a clutch of trees. The car went on up the hill, and then a second car came up the road, lights bright.

Okay, Tad thought. I'm loose. I'm angry as a hive of hornets. And Harry is in trouble.

He put his hands in his coat pockets, found the darts again by being poked.

"Ouch," he said, watching the second car climb up the hill.

Tad moved through the darkness, climbing alongside the road as fast as he could go. He couldn't remember how far it was to the top of the hill, but he thought it wasn't far. He certainly hoped so. His legs were getting tired, and he felt a little winded, and the limbs and brush were tearing at his body, and he needed to pee. These days he always needed to pee.

He took a deep breath, put everything out of his mind, continued to climb. A wind was moving gently through the trees, and he imagined it at his back, lifting him up the hill.

The chief parked the car at the edge of the cliff, put it in gear, got out, and poked the automatic through the open window. "What I'd like you to do, Mr. Sound Man, is slide back behind the wheel, and then put it in gear and put your foot on the gas."

"You're out of your fucking mind," Harry said. "Just shoot us. I'm not driving this thing over the cliff."

"I will shoot you, you know?"

"Do it. Make some bullet holes. I don't think you're as certain of this shit as you act. You want us over that cliff, you'll have to drive us."

The chief looked at his watch.

"Like I care about your movie," Harry said. "I get one thing out of this, make you miss your recording, that's better than nothing. Learn to set the timer, you dumb son of a bitch."

"All right," the chief said. He reached through the window, got hold of the gearshift, put it in neutral. "Me and Pale, we thought about this. We didn't expect it to be easy. Would have been nice, but . . ."

Pale's car lights came up behind them and the car bumped up against Harry's car, started it rolling.

As the chief pulled his hand back, Harry leaped for the gun. He grabbed it, turning it up to the ceiling. A shot went off, knocked a hole in the roof, made Harry's head ring. The car picked up speed. The chief lost his footing, but Harry hung onto his hand. The car got bumped again and charged over the edge, dragging the chief with it, but at the last moment he twisted free and fell for about ten feet. He landed on a rise of dirt and stopped, the gun tumbled from his hand. He grabbed at a clutch of roots. They held him.

The car went sailing through the air, ducked over the edge, and disappeared from the chief's view. He heard it hit. Several times. Bouncing.

He started working his way back up, hanging onto old roots and vines, thinking once he got up there, he'd have to go back down. Get another gun, climb down there and make sure they were finished, or at least hurt so bad they weren't going to recover. Maybe he could beat them to death with something. That would be satisfying. That would be good. He hung from a vine and looked at the glow of his watch.

He still had time to set the recording, if everything went smooth from here on. Shit, worst-case scenario, he could buy the DVD.

Tad saw the car go over just as he came to a line of trees on the top of the hill, saw the headlights of the other car shining on the burnt ground. His heart went over with Harry's car. His stomach twisted; it was like that day he heard about his wife and son.

Maybe, just maybe, Harry and Kayla were alive and the car was on top of that sonofabitch Chief Asshole.

Christ, don't let it happen twice. Don't let me lose my boy again.

Tad watched as Pale got out of his car quickly and ran over to the edge. Tad took that moment to move into the opening, his hand dipping into his coat pocket, bringing out the six darts. He shifted all but one to his left hand.

As he trotted toward Pale, Pale turned, saw him, reached inside his coat.

Tad couldn't really see the guy's face, but he could see his shape, knew where his target was by reflex. He flicked the dart.

Sergeant Pale saw what looked like a black spot jump up in front of his eye, and then he was hit, thinking at first a bug had flown into his face, into his eye, but when the pain started he knew better.

He screamed and grabbed at the dart, twisted his body, dropped to one knee, pulled the dart free, and most of his eye came with it.

"You bastard!"

Tad kept coming at a kind of slow trot.

Pale tried to get his gun out from under his coat, but another dart hit him in the hand. He jerked it back, saw the dart standing up on the back of his palm, saw with his good eye a big man running toward him like a locomotive.

He tried for the gun again, but now the guy was on him, and—

Tad kicked, caught Pale solidly under the chin, sent him spinning to the edge of the drop. But Pale scuttled around on his hands and knees, and even with one eye gone, a dart stuck in his hand, he made it to his feet, jogged for his car.

Tad tried to cut him off, but he faked right, went left. Some football maneuver. Tad hated football. Run, bump, and mill, that was all that shit was, bunch of goobers in pads and helmets running together, and here was this motherfucker, blind in one eye, outmaneuvering him with some football move, and now he was drawing a gun from under his coat.

Tad flicked a dart from his left hand to his right, twisted his wrist. The dart made a humming sound, went right into the guy's throat. Pale gagged, fell to the ground, crawled behind his car.

Tad jumped on the hood and took a leap, and there was Pale on his back, looking up, gun in hand, and as Tad came down on him like a big panther, the goddamn *Flintstones* song jumping into his head, the whole fucking thing in a wink of the eye, the gun fired.

The chief worked his way steadily to the top of the hill. As he pulled himself over, he looked about cautiously, having heard a gunshot.

Tad was amazed.

The guy missed. Here he was, the biggest goddamn target in creation, and the guy missed.

He thought: One eye will throw you off, won't it, motherfucker?

Tad had dropped his two remaining darts, was on top of the guy now, and the man was strong. Tad didn't fight the strength. He snatched at the man's wrist, flexed it where the nerves gathered, made the man's wrist go weak. The gun dropped. Tad brought his fist down with all his weight behind it, hit Pale in his wounded throat, hit the dart there, drove it in deeper. Pale raised his shoulders and head, let out with a sound somewhere between a burp and a gurgle. Tad reached behind the man's ear, brought his hand back sharply, as if he might thump his own chest, and caught him on the rear point of the jaw, knocking him out.

Tad stood up, said, "Love tap, cocksucker."

As he put a hand on the hood of the car, he realized he had allowed himself to be distracted.

He heard movement, turned, thinking: I'm getting old.

He started to duck.

But he was a heartbeat too slow.

The chief swung a large limb and it caught Tad on the forehead, knocked him to the ground. Tad tried to get up, but the chief hit him again, this time behind the neck. Tad hit the dirt like he lived there.

The chief hit him another time, in the head.

Another time.

He tossed the limb aside and leaned against the car, took in some deep breaths.

"Pale," he said.

Pale didn't answer.

The chief bent over him, saw the dart in his throat. He pulled it out, flicked it away. He lifted Pale's head. "Sergeant, you with me, man?"

Pale blinked his eyes. Blood ran out of the ruined one, blossomed like a ripe strawberry on his neck.

"I said, you with me?"

Pale said, "He put my goddamn eye out!"

The chief could see that now. There was blood all over the place. "Yeah, man. He did. Can you get up?"

The chief helped him. Pale pulled the dart out of the back of his hand, tossed it aside, put that hand over his eye.

"Sit in the car," the chief said. "You got some first-aid shit, right?"

"Glove box. But there ain't no eye in there. Man, God, fuck, it hurts."

"All right. Come on."

The chief walked him around to the driver's side, helped him in. "My gun. It's on the ground," Pale said.

"Sit there a minute," the chief said. "I'll get the gun, the first aid." The chief closed the door, hurried to the other side of the car, stopped to kick Tad in the head, looked around until he saw the automatic. He picked it up, opened the door on the passenger's side, climbed in.

"God," said Pale, his hand over his ruined eye. "I hurt bad. I'm fucking blind. My eye. It's gone, man. Gone."

"You go home, gonna be hard to explain."

"Oh, God. I don't know what to do. That fucker. I hope he's dead."

"I believe he's dead and then some. Pale, look at me."

Pale looked.

The chief lifted the automatic quickly, put the gun to Pale's blind eye, and pulled the trigger.

58

When the car went over, Harry thought, this is some shit, and he thought maybe if they hit certain spots, he was going to get a flashback replay of what had happened to the other couple. It was a thought that ran through his mind, then he remembered they had been dead when they went over, or so it had seemed in his previous visions. And besides, the gunfire at close range had kicked his eardrum wicked hard, made it difficult for him to hear himself yell. Which he was doing.

He and Kayla banged together, flew against the glass and all about the car like Ping-Pong balls. The car hit on its front bumper, did a headstand, and went completely over, partially crushing the roof in, knocked the flapping trunk lid off, finished a complete flip, and came to rest with the nose of Harry's car smashed up against a tree.

There was a flutter of images, weak, like a dying bird trying to lift its wings a last time, and then there was the darkness.

Harry lay there blinking, turned his head to the left. He was lying partially on the dash, partially draped over the steering wheel.

He hurt, and though he wasn't hearing all that well, something inside of him had come undone and all the sounds of horror and misery and destruction were moving about in his head, bumping together, and he felt all of them, and they made him sick. He lay there not moving, feeling all the terrible things there were to feel until they slowly began to subside.

He was so tired of being afraid.

"I'm sick of it," he said aloud, "and I'm not going to take it any-more."

He was staring out of the windshield of his car. The glass was spiderwebbed. There was a tree in his view. He had seen the tree before, a few days back. He realized he was on top of the car where he had had the visions.

Thank goodness for this big-ass tree, he thought.

Cautiously Harry rolled off the dash, tried to get some kind of balance, but the angle made it difficult. At first he thought Kayla had been thrown from the car, because the back right door was open, almost knocked off, and he didn't see her. He did see Joey through the open door, though. He was positioned with his head against the ground, his neck bent like a wire hanger. He was supported on his knees, his legs still bound up behind him.

Harry leaned over the front seat and saw Kayla on the floorboard of the backseat, lying facedown. Not moving.

Harry coughed, spit up some blood. He hoped it was from some-thing banged inside his mouth, not inside his gut. He leaned over and touched her. The car shifted to the left.

"Shit." With the ringing in his ear, he couldn't even hear himself speak. He called Kayla's name a few times, but she didn't move. Again, he could hardly hear the sound of his own voice. Had no idea if he was yelling or whispering.

Carefully he climbed over and fell against the backseat. The car creaked, shifted more to the left. Harry pushed his weight slowly to the right, lay on the seat, put his hand on Kayla's back. He could feel her breathing.

He tried the door on his left. It opened. He got hold of Kayla and pulled her out of the car, onto the slope. It was a little precarious, but the slope wasn't too radical there, had some shape to it. He could keep his footing, could lay Kayla out fairly straight, her feet drifting a bit toward the bottom of the hill.

Lying there on his back in the dark, Kayla beside him, looking up the hill, he could see the shape of tree limbs overhanging the slope, and he could see spotted between them ragged rips of night sky; stars, like the silver tips of straight pins, poked out suddenly as his eyes become accustomed to the night.

His thoughts were rattled. He wondered about the chief. He had had hold of him as they went over, but he didn't see him lying about. Had the bastard gone all the way to the bottom?

He thought he heard a kind of snapping sound up the hill, but his hearing was still messed up. He felt as if his balance was off as well; the hill seemed to tilt precariously. He turned and looked at Kayla, lying in the vines and leaves. She was breathing heavily now, one arm was twisted funny, and he could see something poking up under her cop shirt. Her eyes fluttered but didn't open.

Harry leaned over her. "Can you hear me?"

He couldn't hear himself, but he hoped she could.

Her eyes came open and she moved her mouth. Harry thought the word was *yes*.

"I can't hear well, but I want you to listen. I'm going up the hill. See what's going on. I think you're going to need a doctor."

Harry unbuttoned her shirt, moved it aside carefully. There was a rip in her side, and a rib was poking up through the wound.

"All right. It's not bad." He tried not to lie too obviously, tried to look certain, like someone who knew. He wasn't sure how she was doing or even how he was doing. "I don't want you to move. I've got to go up, see how things are. Got to get you a doctor. Don't know if I should move you again."

He didn't say what he was thinking: They may come down to finish you and me.

He couldn't just sit and wait. He had to go up and see how things were, on the sneak. Had to get Kayla a doctor. And if there was a chance, any kind of chance at all, he had to kill both of those sons of bitches. An unlikely event, but it was all he had; it was the thing that gave him juice.

He was lucky, the hill might have taken care of the chief and he was lying at the bottom of it all, wadded up like a ball of aluminum foil.

That still left the other guy.

Kayla grabbed his arm. He looked at her lips, tried to understand what she was saying. He got it. It was easy.

"Sorry," she said.

He patted her shoulder, said, "They wouldn't have had to burn me with a cigarette. They just showed me one and a match, a lighter, I'd have sung like a goddamn canary."

She tried to smile, but the smile crawled away, became a tight line.

He gave her one more pat on the shoulder, and steeled himself, started up the hill.

So, I'm kind of fucked here, the chief thought. Or I could be fucked, if I'm not fucked now. Got to put it together. They find this business, it's gonna look weird, but way I see it, I push this car over the hill too, it comes out like this: Guy comes up here to push an unsuspecting couple over the lip of the hill, a renegade cop.

Yeah. That's good.

Then he shoots himself in the eye, and drives himself over.

Now that sucks.

Let me see. Okay. I leave the car at the top of the hill. I wipe the gun clean. I put it in Pale's hand. He committed suicide. Shot himself up here on the hill. Maybe he gets found, and no one will find the car down the hill. Least not right away, therefore no connection.

All right. That sucks too. But it's a little better.

And what if I sit here long enough someone wants to neck comes up the hill, and I have to kill them too. Then I got a pile of bodies.

Shit. I got a pile now. I got these two, the trussed-up guy, and Harry and Kayla.

I'm getting quite a congregation.

And I don't even know if they're all dead. Got to finish the job. Shit. Got to go down there and do that. Make sure they're in the deceased column.

What a mess.

Think, man, think.

It's a problem. Could be a bigger problem I fuck around here long enough. Thing is, I make sure those two are finished, then I just leave, walk off, work my way to town, it'll take me . . . Good grief, three hours, maybe more. It's a good walk. I might be seen.

I could stick to the woods. There's just that highway problem, and if I wait until there's no traffic, I can run across, and then there's woods bordering the road there, and I can work my way back toward town. Then there's that space of houses and the like before I get to my place.

Not easy, but shit, it's what I got.

It beats sitting here watching Pale's brains drip off the upholstery.

The chief got out of the car, looked at Tad's body.

Who is this guy? What's his story? What's with the darts? What is he, a freelance dart master hiding in the woods, ready to try out victims?

What do I do with him?

Okay. I can put him in the car with Pale. That would work. I could put his fingers on the gun, make it look like he shot Pale. Yeah, that would work.

When everyone gets a look at this, it'll be a big mystery. But there's nothing to connect me. Just some cop gone bad had a deal of some kind going down, and it didn't work out. Maybe it'll look like he picked this guy up for a blow job, and the guy turned on him, shot him.

Oh, wait. How did this guy die? He'll have marks on him from the limb. So that won't work. Not unless they want to believe he beat himself with a stick.

Okay. I could fire a round into his head, and it could look like they had a fight maybe, and the guy on the ground, he got in the car as Pale was trying to get away, shot him, then for some godforsaken reason, shot himself.

Not so good.

The chief's head was starting to hurt.

Okay, let's go at it again. . . .

Fuck it.

I'll make sure those kids are done for, leave everything as it is. No way anyone is going to figure out this goddamn mess. I made the mess, and I'm not sure what's going on, so how's anyone else gonna figure it?

Come to think of it, this is good. It's like the Gordian knot of crime, so interwoven and messed-up it's impossible to figure out.

Now, if a UFO would just crash into the side of the hill, it would be a perfect night.

The chief checked his watch.

Okay. I buy the DVD.

The chief felt pressure on his ankle.

He looked down, tried to move his foot, couldn't.

It was the guy on the ground, the one he had batted with the stick like a tetherball.

He had grabbed his ankle, and now the man's other hand shot out, his forearm striking the inside of his leg, working a nerve there, knocking him backward and down.

The chief had stuck the gun in his belt, and he pulled it out, tried to shoot the bastard. A hand slapped up, got hold of the chief's wrist. It hurt. He dropped the gun. He kicked with his other foot, knocking the guy off of him, scrambled to his feet.

But now the man was up, on his feet, wobbling from all those blows from the limb, but, goddamn it, he was standing.

They both looked at the gun lying on the ground, wet-black in the starlight.

Harry came over the lip of the overhang and looked up to see Tad and the chief struggling on the ground. A moment later the chief rose up with something in his hand.

A gun.

Tad, like some kind of jet-propelled shadow, shot across the ground, extended a palm, hit the chief in the chest, knocked him up and onto the car hood, and caused him to do a flip and go over to the other side.

Tad limped around the front of the car, trying to get to him.

The chief, looking as if he might need a winch to get him up, grabbed hold of the car's tire, made it to his knees. He still had the gun. Tad came around the front of the car and Harry yelled, "Look out, Tad. He's still got the gun."

Tad shifted as the chief fired. The shot hit Tad high in the left shoulder and spun him around and knocked him on the ground.

Harry was on his feet now, on the cliff's edge, seemed to have some of his balance back. He ran toward the chief screaming.

The chief took careful aim at Harry.

Fired.

Harry, when he saw the gun point in his direction, held it a beat, the way he thought Tad would, then dropped so low he was running on hands as well as feet, like a big ape—a spotted-ass ape. There was a burst of light from the automatic and the bullet sang by his head, and now he was almost on the chief, and there was no way the bastard was gonna miss from there, but he couldn't stop, couldn't do it, was mad as a pig that had just found out sausage was his cousin, was through being afraid. He kept coming and the chief, still on his knees, rose up so that one knee was lifted, took careful aim, and then—

Just before he fired, Tad, lying on the ground, seeing almost double, the night spinning black and star-pricked in his head, managed to grab a handful of dirt and throw it, hitting the chief in the face. The chief, jerked, fired—

—and it was a miss, and Harry was on him.

Tad lay down on the cold ground and rolled onto his back and looked up at the night and all the stars, and they did a milky spin up there, around and around, and he found that he could not feel the ground anymore. All he felt was cold, and as if he were falling, one moment down a bottomless pit, the next, upward into the star-specked eternity of space. Then he didn't feel anything.

Harry and the chief rolled over and over, and when the roll ended, the chief's gun was gone. The chief wobbled to his feet. The chief threw a right as Harry came into range, and Harry remembered what Tad had once told him. What they do doesn't matter. Be like the monkey. Be selfish. Don't care. Do your thing.

And he relaxed, not worrying about the punch. He did his thing. The punch hit him and knocked him on his ass.

Goddamn, Harry thought. That hurt. Maybe what they do does matter. He rolled to his hands and knees and the chief kicked at him. Harry took the kick, grunted, rolled into the chief's leg, pushing at it with his body, dropping him to the ground.

Harry scurried on top of him. The chief tried to put his thumbs in Harry's eyes, but Harry twisted away and dropped between the chief's arms, letting his elbow fall into the chief's face.

The chief barked like a dog, was suddenly possessed of tremendous strength, tossed Harry off of him. He got to his feet. Harry could see he was looking for the gun.

Harry rolled up and started to lunge, hit the chief with a tackle, knocked him to the ground. As he got up, the chief got up. Harry spotted the gun, and so did the chief.

And the chief was closer.

Harry ran full-out. He and the chief collided, knocked each other down. Harry was up first, and he kicked at the gun with all his might. It went skidding along the ground to the cliff's edge, stopped there.

Damn it.

The chief was running for it.

Harry darted toward the ledge as the chief neared it, and then he put on another burst of speed as he felt the wind whistling around him, the dry leaves spinning, and he was one with them, moving fast, not worried, no, sir, he was the monkey, and he was selfish, and he was coming, baby. Batten down the hatches, motherfucker, or hide in the barn, or mix any goddamn metaphor you want, because I *am* coming.

But it was all a little too late. The chief took hold of the automatic.

Harry leaped. Just threw his body sideways, hit the chief as he lifted the automatic, and it went off right by Harry's ear, the evil ear, the one that had already been numbed, and over went the chief with a groan.

And Harry went too.

But this time it was Harry who grabbed a root, hung onto it, looked down quickly, saw the chief sail way out, hit a high point, bounce.

Harry took a deep breath. He could feel something warm running out of his injured ear.

Blood.

And there was a kind of hollow buzzing sound inside, as if a magnificent seashell had been plastered over his ear and what he was hearing was not the sea, but all the roars of all the waters that existed, oceans, rivers, creeks, and runny taps.

It hurt.

Kayla, now awake and in pain, heard something tumbling. She tried to twist a bit to see, but it hurt too much.

A body bounced over her, landed just below her feet, then whirled with a twist off the slope and was sucked into the darkness by gravity. Leaves and dust that had enveloped him spun in the night air and drifted down on her like dirty snow.

She smiled. She had recognized that flying gentleman.

"Good riddance, asshole," she said aloud.

59

And so I lay me down to sleep at night, and the bad ear, the gun-banged ear, lies dead, and the other, it does not pick up sound. No, sir.

I hear. But I do not hear what I used to hear. I do not hear behind the sounds. The images rest. No flashes at the edge of the eye, no wiggles of light, and no sensations of terror.

It's just me now. No time-traveling souls.

And I realize something that I should have realized all along. I wasn't just afraid of what was in those sounds. I was just afraid. Afraid of life. Afraid of failure. But I had a moment. I was brave. I actually fought well. Even if I won through luck. Had the chief not been standing on that ledge, had his arm lifted a bit more quickly, he might be writing in his journal, telling it what a fine shot he was.

Yeah. I was brave. Or crazy. Angry. And, for one fleeting second, I was one with the universe.

Good for me!

I did what I did, scared or not.

And you want to know something, my journal friend?

Come on. I know you're curious.

Here it is. I'm still scared.

Scared my hearing in my right ear will come back, and with it will come again my special gift. My fucking curse.

Seems likely. It was just a sudden explosion. Temporary, the doctor says.

I'm scared of that, the sounds returning. Scared I might like a drink someday. Scared of lots of things.

But maybe not so much as before.

60

A week after it all happened, Harry and Kayla met at the hospital, in Tad's room.

"I to'ed when I should have fro'ed," Tad said.

Harry reached down and took Tad's hand, lying limp on the hospital bed, and squeezed it.

Kayla, sharp in uniform, with a cast on her arm, sat stiffly in a chair on the other side of the bed. Tad turned his head to look at her. "You make me feel better than he does. He's got bruises."

"I've got rib wrappings and some cement," Kayla said.

"You still look better than he does."

"We were worried," Harry said. "Doctor said it was a concussion, and a pretty bad bullet wound, and you were in a delirium for some time, kept asking the same question over and over."

"What was it?"

" 'Why is he hitting me with that stick?' "

"Oh. Well, yeah. I wondered about that at the time. The chief? What happened to him?"

"He bounced real hard," Harry said. "Over the side of the cliff. I think when they found him they had to pick his teeth out of his ass.

But here's the thing. He lived. He does any kind of activity from here on out, it'll be like, you know, the Special Olympics. Maybe they got something there like the Jell-O roll."

"Figures he would live."

"It's best," Kayla said. "We can prove what he did much more easily. Even if he lies, he can't say he wasn't there, and his fingerprints are on the gun that killed Sergeant Pale, and there's my word on things. And the files I used to put it together. I doubt Harry's sound stuff is something we want to mention too much, if at all. But it won't be too hard to prove the chief's a killer. We also got you, and your testimony, and Harry's. Joey, he's in the morgue."

"Poor guy," Harry said, "he just can't get buried."

"Weasels are not one with the universe," Tad said. "Even the ground doesn't want to accept him." Tad turned his head to look at Harry. "You did it. You actually fought a real bad guy and won."

Harry shook his head. "After you softened him up. Anyway, looks as if it might all be over with."

"Yeah," Tad said. "Just might work out. You two do me a favor?"

"Name it," Harry said.

"Leave me alone so I can rest. Go somewhere and commune with the universe. Or the bed linens."

"Tad," Kayla said.

"Or whatever, and later, maybe you can see if you can sneak me in a bag of taco chips. The hot kind. Maybe some kind of cheese dip."